I0788204

Judge's Waltz

KATHERINE BURNETTE

ISBNs
Hardcover: 978-1-951503-47-5
Paperback: 978-1-951503-48-2
Ebook: 978-1-951503-49-9

Authorsunite.com

For my husband

PROLOGUE

Barely audible above the hum of the ancient air conditioner came the creak, creak, creak of the thick rope affixed to the brass chandelier. Swaying ten feet above the intricately carved, pre-Civil War bench, the Honorable Patrick Ryan O'Shea had adjourned to a higher court.

Twenty years ago, when he was just plain Patrick, the soon-to-be-jurist was barely making it through law school, scrabbling at outlines and notes prepared by brighter students. The murky depths of Torts, Real Property, Civil Procedure, and Evidence were never plumbed by the young O'Shea. His final year galvanized him into short bursts of panicky perambulations through the law library, alternating with all-night study fests.

"I was a late bloomer," O'Shea boasted of his surprisingly impressive third year in law school at the University of North Carolina at Chapel Hill. This line frequently was used as the judge's opening line to spew forth on a myriad of subjects to anyone who cared to listen and to many who did not. The latter were compelled to don a deferential mask of acute attention or rapture according to the seriousness of the reason they were in the august presence of his honor.

"Yes, I was a late bloomer, really put my nose to the old grindstone my last year," he would pontificate. The ill-guarded truth was that the only thing O'Shea ever put his nose to his third year, and in all succeeding years, was the ass of a certain professor and the collective asses of well-placed politicians. Ass-kissing was a hell of a lot easier if you already had your nose in the vicinity.

Now O'Shea would kiss no more asses—or anything else for that matter. The only thing O'Shea could do—was doing—was a slow, discordant waltz at the end of a long rope.

Chapter One

Buck hunched over his third cup of coffee. He stirred in his second pack of sugar and looked around the drug store for the day's Assistant District Attorney for traffic court. He had arrived later than usual after spending thirty wasted minutes chasing after Charles, his big Labrador retriever, in the dew-soaked grass. He'd had to change his khaki pants, spending another thirty minutes trying to find his dry cleaning. Charles kept trying to roll his slobbery tennis ball onto the knees of Buck's newly pressed pants.

The drug store crowd was thinning. Picking up the office coffee and the gossip for the day, the administrative assistants, tellers, and working crews rustled off to start the morning. Court staff sat at the counter, talking for a few more minutes before heading to the Granville County courthouse next door.

Today's courtroom deals were made in the few minutes it took to eat a sausage biscuit. Buck could see Judge Jones and the court bailiffs laughing over at their section of the counter. Several attorneys hung on the periphery, like carrion birds, trying to squeeze in a word with Judge Jones, but the visiting judge was preoccupied with catching the eye of the new court reporter whose skirt was short enough to make the old jurist reach for his heart medicine.

The drugstore had three official sections. One end of the counter belonged to the town's retired men. Like old cart horses, they blew into their coffee and shook their gray heads over some town trivia. Or maybe the price of tomatoes. At the other end of the counter, where Buck sat, businessmen, bankers, and elected officials put together their lists of things to do and people to meet for the day. The ice cream parlor tables in the back, next to the suppositories, were reserved for dowagers, matrons with their brood, and giggling, dewy-eyed teenaged girls, in that order of importance. Blue rinse out-ranked blue jeans.

Oxford was home to the Perry drugstore, Buck Davis, and eight thousand other folks, give or take a few hundred seasonal tobacco workers. Located forty miles north of Raleigh, the capital of North Carolina, what once had been a moderately successful tobacco town was now the whore of fickle indus-try. The textiles had pulled out long ago and left nothing behind but husks of buildings in their wake. The uneducated, untrained workforce left stranded either turned to working tobacco or selling illegal drugs.

Gulping down the hot brew liberally called coffee, Buck studied the legal pad before him. He was a lists man. If it didn't go down on his legal pad, he was apt to forget it until 2:00 a.m. the next morning when he would sit bolt upright in bed, sweating and swearing.

Traffic court and domestic court. Great way to start the week. He wiped the biscuit crumbs off his lips as he rose from the bar stool and strode toward the cash register, calling out greetings to the other bar stool occupants.

Doris rang him up on the museum piece that served as a cash register. Old man Perry did not keep up with the times—except for his prices. Most swore that Perry still had his first dollar tacked up on a cork board grubby with old newspaper clippings. The only two things anyone could bring up to old man Perry that ever riled him was what he called the "War,

Roman Numeral Two" and his five daughters. Otherwise, Perry was like an old tabby cat, easing around his bottles of elixirs, eau de toilet, and Di-Gel.

"How's ya mama, Buck?" Doris asked.

"As well as can be expected, Doris, thanks for asking. She's at my sister's house. Been there almost two weeks. Mom says she's thinking about moving down there, where it's civilized," he replied. Down there was Atlanta. A place Buck's mom hated when she was there and loved when she got back to Oxford.

"Well, it might not be such a bad thing for ya. That woman clucks after you like you're still a baby chick. I know she's your mama and all, but goodness, a man's gotta breathe!" Doris sputtered.

"Mom's alright. She just needs more projects—like organizing someone else's life," he grinned. He grabbed a toothpick and left his change on the counter. The drugstore door jangled shut behind him.

Traffic court looked like the city of lost souls. Attorneys shouted up and down the courtroom for their clients. The accused and their extended families slumped on the benches, leaned against the walls, and clogged up the hallways. One small boy stood peeing against the hall water fountain until a beefy sheriff's deputy swatted him away.

In the back room behind the judge's bench, court was being held. The prosecutor assigned to traffic court that day, Sally Winton, had the traffic citation shucks spread out before her like a game of double solitaire. Depending on the lawyers' whines, yarns, and profanity, Sally reduced, dismissed, or set aside the traffic charge for disposal.

Fresh out of law school, Sally was bright and always eager to begin her day in court. Her black linen dress and blazer were pure camouflage for the barracuda beneath. Although usually laid back in traffic court, she was relentlessly brutal at felony trials.

Buck walked into the room full of lawyers and lawmen and sat at the opposite end of the long table. A bored highway patrolman sat on his left, cleaning his nails with a credit card. Smoke swirled through the air, partially hiding Judge Jones. No one was going to tell the presiding judge smoking had been banned from the courthouse ten years ago.

As one rumpled old lawyer moved, swearing from her side, Sally saw Buck shuffling files, and said, "Whatcha have, Buck? Please tell me you have nothing to try with Trooper Graham."

"Two speeding tickets, a seventy-five in a fifty-five and a forty-five in a business zone. First-time ticket on the first one and third ticket this year on the second. It's Mavis Williams and Bobby Currin," Buck drawled.

Sally searched for the corresponding shucks in her heap on the table. She pulled the envelope-styled file out for Mavis Williams and opened it. She raised her eyebrows at Buck. "Trooper clocked Mavis going eighty but cut it down to seventy-five. Mavis in some kind of a hurry?"

"Mavis was on her way to Lynette's beauty parlor. She has a standing appointment, and she was late. C'mon Sally. When the trooper pulled her over, she almost had a stroke. She doesn't need a ticket. Besides, what'll all the girls at Antioch Baptist Church say when it hits the local?" Buck cajoled.

The "local" was a weekly ten-page rag that managed to print or hint at all the dirt in town. Wedding or engagement announcements may be run at the wrong time or be grossly misspelled, but the arrests and convictions columns were printed without a flaw.

"Alright on Mavis. If Trooper Sturges has no objection, I'll agree to a PJC on a sixty-five in a fifty-five." The PJC, or prayer for judgment continued, meant the judgment would not be entered against Mavis unless she received another ticket. At eighty years of age and given the pristine condition of her '97 baby blue Buick LeSabre, such an event was unlikely.

"Hell, Sally. Can't you just dismiss it? Mavis needs to be able to hold her head up high at the bridge club."

Sally looked at him sharply. "Now about Bobby Currin's ticket…"

Buck held his hands palms up and in front of him.

"I know he has a piss poor record. I'll take anything that will keep his license."

Sally opened the shuck and sighed.

"Bobby's record stretches back to the courthouse doors. He doesn't deserve a break."

"Come on, you know Bobby, Sally. He just had his mind on other things. Completely forgot where he was when he blew through downtown. Look, it was one o'clock in the morning. It wasn't like he was gonna knock off schoolchildren in the crosswalks."

"All I can do for you is talk to Trooper Graham. If he agrees, I'll drop it to something you can live with. If not…" she shrugged.

"Thank you. Bobby has called me every day about his ticket. Having to beg mercy from Graham is a painful proposition. Is he due in court before nine?"

She glanced over at Trooper Roberts seated at Buck's left. Roberts stopped grooming his fingernails and responded to Buck. "Well, yeah he is—if he hasn't stopped to spit-shine his shoes. His shoes get mighty dirty kicking the asses of your sorry clients," Roberts grinned.

Buck put away his iPad and headed toward the door back to the courtroom. "Yeah, more likely he's picking up coffee and donuts. Trooper brain food. Tell him I'm looking for him; he should take a break from writing up his use of excessive force reports and get to court on time." He closed the door against the sound of laughter and pushed his way into the courtroom to take Mavis and Bobby to the attorney conference rooms.

Shortly thereafter, Buck realized he'd made a bad mistake by cutting through the district courtroom on his way back to the office. Before he'd gone halfway down the aisle between the crowd, a deep voice bellowed:

"Mr. Davis, Mr. Davis!"

Turning, he saw Judge Jones gesture him up to the bench.

"May I approach your Honor?"

"Yes, yes. Hurry up now. See those men seated over by the sheriff's deputies? I want you to represent them. The state defense attorney didn't show up today to take in appointed cases so I'm appointing you."

"I appreciate it, sir, but I'm not on the indigent appointment list."

"Listen here. You're on it if I say you're on it. Now get over there and talk to those defendants so the jailers can take them on back to jail after you interview them."

The judge dismissed him and told the clerk to put Buck's name on all of the appointments' sheets. She glanced at Buck in sympathy after Judge Jones started court back up.

Buck approached the first inmate in leg shackles and walked him back to the tiny interview room.

"Okay. I'm your attorney at least for today. What's your name and your charge?"

The small wiry guy with prison tattoos in blue ink on his knuckles, spelling out "Tanisha," smirked at Buck.

"Yeah, right. You're gonna walk as soon as that visiting judge takes off. Why should I tell you a damn thing?"

"Because dim wit, if you want me to make a bond motion for you, I have to have something to work with."

Nodding towards the tatts, Buck said, "Looks like you grew up in prison."

The guy slid further down in his seat but kept a steady eye on Buck.

"Yeah, what the fuck of it? I got railroaded for a B and E I didn't do. Spent a few years in. Now I got drug charges. Bringing drugs into the jail. What can you do for me?"

"Let me pull your record first. Was it weed or something else?"

"Nah man. It was Suboxone. I had a friend in there who was hurting so I mailed him some strips."

"Tell me the cops got someone else on camera at the post office."

He straightened up. "They got fucking cameras at the post office? Well, shit. I didn't know. No, my girlfriend mailed it, but she put our goddamn return address on it."

"Okay. You're pretty young. Hope the judge will reduce it some. Let me talk to the rest of these guys then I'll talk to the ADA first, see where we are."

"Yeah man. You're alright. How about sticking on the case?"

"I'll see what I can do. Not sure the indigent defense fund is going to be happy about me staying on though. What's your name so I can run your record?"

"Jimmy Royster. Later."

The inmate shuffled out the door and back into the courtroom. He sent the next guy on the bench out to see Buck.

The new guy sat down and cranked back the chair onto two legs. Heavily built, he had a tight afro and narrow hazel eyes. He eyed Buck suspiciously.

Buck said, "Hey, I know you, don't I?"

"Yeah. My daddy used to be Cal's client. I'm Little Curtis, Curtis Hockaday."

"Your daddy went federal, didn't he?"

"Yeah, some drug bullshit."

"What are your charges, um, Little Curtis?"

Little Curtis looked away. "They said I had drugs and a gun in the car. But it weren't my car and it weren't my drugs. I can't have no gun. I'm a felon. I ain't no drug dealer. 'Sides, it was only weed."

"How much weed? Where was it?"

"Aw, about this much," he said, opening his hands about a foot wide and then two feet tall. "Man, them deodorizers don't do from shit. That guy had a bunch of them in the garbage bag, but them cops didn't even need a dog—it smelled to high heaven in that car."

"Why did they stop you? Do you know?"

"Some bullshit about dark window tint and the tag."

"You're in deep trouble. You got any money if I can get the bond lowered?"

"I got a little, but, about a week ago on my last court date, I heard that ADA bitch talking about sending me federal this time."

"Okay, let me finish up with the row and I'll talk to the state about a bond motion. Not sure I can get it reduced though."

Little Curtis stood up. "Just do what you can, man. The jail sucks. Too many of us in one cell and I'm sleeping on a mattress on the floor 'bout the width of a nickel. You wouldn't put your dog on it. Just see if you can get me out."

Buck talked to the last men seated on the wooden pew behind plastic sheets to keep them separated from the courtroom onlookers. It didn't stop them from waving to their babies or shouting to their moms to put some money on their canteen.

The last two were being held for a misdemeanor, resisting a public officer, and an extradition warrant. Buck got the bond unsecured for the man that resisted an officer, when he'd been too drunk to know where he was at the time, and the guy wanted by Virginia for car theft waived his extradition.

Buck talked quietly to the young ADA, Grady Capps, about reduced bonds for Jimmy Royster and Little Curtis. The ADA laughed in his face about Little Curtis's bond request.

"Bullshit, Buck. I'm not agreeing to cut his bond. He had a carload of marijuana all prepacked for sale and a Glock with an extended magazine in the console. You can ask the judge if you want to, but I'm not agreeing to it."

"How about the young skinny guy? He doesn't have much on his sheet."

"That's 'cause his longest sheet is in juvenile court where he racked up an armed robbery conviction and a couple of burglaries. No way. Ask the judge; I'm not doing squat."

"You can't bring up his juvenile history."

"I won't, but I can't in good conscience agree to a reduction either."

Judge Jones returned refreshed from his smoke break and Buck stood asking to be heard on bond for two of his appointed clients.

"I'll hear you."

"Your honor, Little, um, Mr. Hockaday, denies that the car, the drugs, and the gun were his. He has been enrolled in the local community college and has a job at Walmart distribution center. Plus, he has two small children to support which he can't do when he's being held in the local jail."

The ADA stood up, slowly shaking his head.

"Your honor, this man has one felony and a long list of misdemeanor drug convictions, and most were pled down from felonies."

"Which plea agreements your office approved, right?" said Judge Jones.

"That's right, your honor, but now he's been caught with drugs and a gun and he's a danger to the public."

Judge Jones looked down at the ADA for a minute.

"I'm cutting his bond from $50,00 to $10,000. The charges are getting old, and you haven't been to grand jury. Next case?"

Buck said, "Your honor, the next is a young man who has been charged for something that someone else did. His record is not unblemished, but he's taken classes in prison and has several job interviews lined up if he can get released pending trial."

The ADA shuffled some papers.

"Ah, your honor, well then, I think this defendant may be a flight risk. He has no real ties to the community."

Judge Jones frowned. "This man said, earlier this morning, that his mama and his grandmother live here."

"Oh. Well. He has a serious charge pending and I think the bond is appropriate."

"Humpf. I'm reducing the bond from $20,000, to $5,000. Next case."

"That's all for this morning your honor," mumbled the ADA.

Judge Jones rose. "Mr. Sheriff, put us in recess until the afternoon."

CHAPTER TWO

A couple of hours later, Buck opened the heavy mahogany law office door to the gentle ping, ping, ping of beads rolling on a hard surface. His secretary, or "legal assistant," Emma Jean, looked stricken.

"I just busted these pearls," she wailed. "First the coffee, now this."

As he looked closer, he could see the tell-tale stains of coffee along the top left half of her blouse. He scrubbed his hand over his face, picked up his messages from the front desk, and turned to head back to his office.

Emma Jean catapulted klutziness to a science. No one and no thing was safe while she was in the office. Buck was certain his fire insurance premiums would double if his carrier ever met Emma Jean.

"Damn," Emma Jean softly swore, reaching for an errant bead. "You've had several calls," she said from half under the front office desk. "Um, Trooper Graham, that attorney from over in Waynesville, and uh, oh yeah," she huffed as she pulled herself up off the floor, "your ma." Sweat was pouring down her face and dust clung to her hair. There was a small rip in the shoulder seam of her blouse where it had snagged on a nail.

Buck always felt just a little overwhelmed in his assistant's catastrophic presence. She was a wizard on the word processor and a pinnacle of client small talk, but every day by lunch time, some small disaster manifested itself on her person. Without a doubt, Emma Jean was the most likely woman he knew to have a safe dropped on her, to be flattened by a runaway horse, or to step through a plate glass window—all within the space of a morning.

The office of Hobgood and Davis was ideally located across from the county courthouse in a restored Victorian house. The outside was painted light blue with white shutters. The house's wraparound porch looked cool and inviting on hot summer days. Huge magnolias and splendid dogwoods graced the side lawn. Old man Royster, who lived in the fine home to the left, planted his tomatoes up to and on the property line so, as he said often to Emma Jean, "to show those lawyers what fer."

Absentmindedly, Buck pulled up on the window in this office. It stuck fast. Forgetting the lick and a promise outdoor paint job one of his clients had supplied last fall in return for Buck's services in a paternity dispute, Buck began to tug on the window in earnest.

Emma Jean came hobbling down the hall and opened Buck's door a crack. "Oh, um, Buck," she whispered. She repeated this when he took a break from swearing.

"Yeah? What?" He turned in exasperation away from the stubborn window and toward her. Wiping away the sweat streaming in his eyes, he saw that Emma Jean held a pink message slip.

She cleared her throat. 'I completely forgot to tell you. This morning, Judge Foster called. He said he needs you to call him. He wouldn't leave a message."

"Okay, Emma Jean, but I've told you before, this is the type of phone message I need to get first."

She looked down at her chipped nails and whispered, "Sorry."

"It's okay," he replied. 'I'll call Judge Foster back now. Just take messages from anybody else who calls—especially if it's Trooper Graham."

Buck would have to dodge the irate trooper for a few weeks to let him cool down. Graham had been after Bobby Currin for six months ever since Bobby took a swing at the burly officer. This morning, Graham failed to show in time for court, and the judge dismissed Currin's speeding ticket.

Emma Jean pulled the door closed. As it clicked shut, he heard a wrenching sound. He closed his eyes. If he was not mistaken, she was on the other side, holding the loose door-knob in her hand.

Chapter Three

Buck clutched the steering wheel of his old gray Lexus so hard his palms ached. He forced himself to relax. As he drove, he kept running through his telephone conversation with Judge Foster over and over. Foster himself had answered the phone. A subdued Foster told Buck of O'Shea's death.

Apparently, no one had missed O'Shea over the weekend. So, first thing Monday morning, when the security guard unlocked the federal courtroom, he was greeted by the gruesome figure of Patrick Ryan O'Shea dangling from the ceiling, fluttering like a large black bird. O'Shea was wearing his robe—and nothing else.

Buck had difficulty reconciling the pompous judge he had known with this tragic suicide. When clerking for Judge Foster about fifteen years ago, he had peripheral dealings with Judge O'Shea and O'Shea's two law clerks. Judge O'Shea always paraded through the hallways, expecting all gathered to part like the waters in his wake. An entourage of law clerks, clerical staff, and courtroom deputies typically followed O'Shea.

Although Foster was chief judge of the District Court for the Eastern District of North Carolina, O'Shea coveted the role for himself. He postured and fawned over every politician drifting within his sphere. Within two years of his appointment to the federal district court bench, he'd gathered an impressive bevy of opportunists and political hacks. No charity dinner or benefit went unattended; no chance at capturing the limelight escaped.

Recently, it was rumored O'Shea was a serious candidate for the upcoming vacancy at the appellate court, the Fourth Circuit Court of Appeals. One of the respected jurists on the Court had announced his retirement due to poor health. A seat on the appellate court in Richmond would command respect and confer prestige. O'Shea craved both.

Not noted for weighty opinions from the bench, O'Shea had come to be noted for the weighty politicians who stood behind him and his bid for a higher court. Apparently, these politicians had garnered their strength and their favors to foist O'Shea upon the unsuspecting Fourth Circuit court.

Now, Judge O'Shea, in all his judicial glory, was stretched out on a cold mortician's table. His expectations and thirst for elevation extinguished.

Buck hit his brake pedal hard as he noticed the truck in front of him turning left into a large tobacco field. Bumping along in the truck bed, the migrant workers waved their arms and shouted at him in Spanish. A few herds of cattle, a couple of ponds, and Falls Lake broke up the rural roadside. Houses with wells and buried tires for fences dotted the landscape.

Buck had agreed to meet Judge Foster in his chambers as soon as he could get to Raleigh. The judge had made the meeting sound urgent. He thought of the chief judge as the country miles clicked by on the two-lane highway to Raleigh.

Judge Foster was an ethical and intellectual jurist. By pure luck, right after law school, Buck had learned of a clerkship vacancy in Foster's office right before he took the bar exam. Desperately needing a job, Buck hand-delivered his resume to the courthouse.

He'd arrived early for his interview, close to the court's scheduled lunch break. After one trip to the men's room and three trips to the water fountain, Buck decided to sit in on the end of the judge's calendar.

The courtroom was legendary. The tiled ceiling and beautifully carved cherry bench dominated the room. Dark paneling and deep blue carpet completed the picture of cool austerity. Attorneys spoke in hushed tones. Dressed in various shades of gray, their obvious respect for Judge Foster further formalized the setting.

While Buck watched from the gallery, attorneys presented their cases in subdued voices. No postulating, no posturing, no theatrics. The difference between the federal courtroom and the county courtroom was startling. The federal proceedings ran as smoothly as a symphonic *pas de deux*. The state court proceedings ran as erratically as a cacophonic jitterbug.

He looked at the petitioning party. He'd focused on the blonde ringlets cascading down the back of the lady's bent head, imagining what she must look like from the front. From her alluring profile, she appeared to be petite and slim.

Imperceptibly, the atmosphere in the courtroom changed. The quiet murmurings of the lawyers uninvolved in the present case stopped. Buck pulled his gaze from the blond and looked at Judge Foster.

Judge Foster's jaw clenched. A deadly glint sparked in his brown eyes. Tersely he addressed the lawyer representing the blonde petitioner: "Your prior pleadings in this matter reflect the opposite of what you are stating today, Mr. Rohn. You signed those pleadings and the other pleadings currently before the court. Which set contains the true facts, Mr. Rohn?"

The lawyers sitting directly behind the hapless Rohn shifted slightly away from him. They flinched in unison as if they might receive blows from the scatter shot of the Judge's words.

Mr. Rohn's flushed face deepened in hue. His client looked up at Rohn and said in a harsh whisper, "Sam, what's happening?"

Rohn cleared his throat and made a show of straightening the papers in front of him. "I can explain, Your Honor," he stammered. "An associate of mine prepared the initial pleadings without access to the full facts. Um, it's most unfortunate…" His voice trailed off in a barely audible whisper.

If the judge had clenched his jaw any harder, it would have cracked. "Are you not responsible for those working for you, Mr. Rohn? Are you not ultimately responsible for those documents which you personally have signed?"

Mr. Rohn's shoulders sagged. His client started tugging at Rohn's sleeve.

The courtroom was perfectly silent. All assembled could hear Rohn's breath coming in near gasps. Buck tried to make himself smaller. As still as a statue, he was afraid any movement might draw the judge's baleful stare.

Rohn's suit was noticeably darker under the armpits. His client now was frantically tugging at his jacket. Rohn flipped through his file as if he was looking for an answer to the judge's question.

Judge Foster glared at counsel. "I will see you and opposing counsel in chambers. Now." Foster rose from the bench and exited the courtroom. Rohn moved as if he had received an electric shock. He and opposing counsel nearly tripped over each other scrambling to follow the judge.

After twenty minutes or so, all counsel reappeared in the courtroom. Rohn's hair on the left side of his head stood straight out. The rest was plastered down with sweat. He hurriedly stuffed files into his briefcase and headed for the exit. His whining client clattered behind him.

As the parties disappeared from view, someone tapped Buck on the shoulder. His heart slammed up into his throat.

"Judge Foster will see you now," the young, dark-haired woman working as the senior law clerk told him. "Please follow me." Buck trod obediently behind her, afraid to utter a word.

More elegant than the institutional reception area, the court's chambers reflected a quiet, classic taste. Burgundy leather chairs and a leather sofa were complemented by the warm cherry hues of a small round conference table and the judge's walnut desk. Prints of George Washington and Alexander Hamilton dominated the room. The only acknowledgment of the twenty-first century was a laptop computer sitting on the judge's credenza.

In his shirtsleeves, Foster rose from behind the desk and shook Buck's hand. Buck hoped his blue blazer was not as wet in appearance as the suit jacket of the newly departed Mr. Rohn and that his Pontiac Catalina had not shed the foam rubber from its split seats onto his backside. Within the first five minutes of the interview, Buck discovered he and Judge Foster shared a mutual love of tennis and had attended the same law school. Reminiscing over some of the older and more eccentric professors, Buck had a hard time reconciling this genial man with the one he'd just watched on the bench.

Tentatively, he said, "That was an interesting matter before your honor. Was the case with Mr. Rohn resolved?"

Foster stared into space for a moment before he spoke. "Yes, it was resolved. He will not be practicing before me for at least six months for his, ah, indiscretion." The judge paused. "If you learn nothing else in the practice of law, learn this: Never lie. Mr. Rohn's misrepresentations could have cost him his license. More importantly, it's cost him my good opinion of him and the good opinion of his fellow lawyers. He'll have difficulty getting other attorneys or clients to trust him after today. Lies will buy you more trouble than you can imagine. If you tell enough, pretty soon even you won't be able to distinguish a lie from the truth."

From that moment until the end of his clerkship with Judge Foster two years later, he had lived an almost lie-free existence. Lies to his matchmaking mother did not count.

Chapter Four

Buck unfolded his lanky frame from his old Lexus. At six-foot-five, he looked a lot like the forward he'd been for Wake Forest's basketball team years ago. His early ability to hit three-pointers and provide some defense in high school had earned him a college scholarship, enabling him to save money for law school.

After law school and his federal clerkship, he'd taken a couple years off to play ball in Italy. Unfortunately, his knee didn't hold up, so he ended up traveling from country to country. He lucked into an associate's position with a medium-sized D.C. firm. The competition for billable hours and solvent clients between the young lawyers in his firm was fierce. Competition between his firm and other lawyers was all but lethal. Cal called him one day asking if he was interested in a partnership and without a backwards glance, Buck left for North Carolina.

His dark features set off his vivid blue eyes. The only clues of his real age were in the tiny lines around those eyes and a little extra weight at the waistline. He was still "available" as his mother would say, which she said plenty of times.

He flashed his bar card and license to the court security officers in the main lobby of the federal courthouse and walked through the metal detector. Surrounded by dilapidated homes, soup kitchens, and shelters, the government building was a tiny oasis of order in a sea of human misery. He punched the elevator button for the seventh floor.

The judge was waiting for him and thanked him for coming over on such short notice. He seemed smaller than Buck remembered.

"I'll get right to the point of this visit," the judge began. "O'Shea's office is total chaos. His clerks are too inexperienced to deal with the pandemonium of his death. The phone's ringing off the hook with lawyers and judges calling to see if it's true he's dead. It'll be an administrative nightmare trying to get a handle on his caseload. I'm in charge of helping the clerk's office determine the status of each of his cases and of informing the public and interested parties of his unfortunate death.

"My own docket's a nightmare. I cannot assign my more complex cases to other judges in this district. Right now, I'm in the middle of a jury trial that has been ongoing for three months.

"The point is I need someone I can depend on in O'Shea's office. I need the status of matters summarized and categorized. His two law clerks and the clerk's office will help you in any way they can. You and I'll meet every third day or so to discuss progress. If you need me urgently, let my law clerk, Lisa, know. This is highly sensitive. I wouldn't ask you to do this, but I'm in a real bind. I hope in a couple of weeks things will be on a more even keel."

Buck ran his hand through his hair. Mentally, he reviewed his own caseload. "I'd like to help you out, Judge. If I can move a couple of cases that're set for criminal superior court next week, I think I can do it. I'll also need to get my partner's okay. Cal's in a deposition in Surrey County but will be back in the office tonight. Can I call you tomorrow morning?"

Foster looked relieved. "I really appreciate this. As a former clerk, you know how things run here, and you'll be able to do case reports quickly. If you know something about your schedule this evening, don't hesitate to call me at home—and listen, O'Shea was in the middle of a Section 1983 civil rights violation action, but basically still at the motions stage. I'll need that case update first."

Buck stood up and extended his hand. "I'll help in any way I can. I know how much losing a judge can affect the rest of the court."

After leaving chambers, Buck took the interior marble steps down to the small parking lot out back. As he eased himself into the old Lexus, he was making a list of cases to continue, clients to call, and tennis matches to reschedule. He was pretty certain his partner, Calvin Coolidge Hobgood, would agree to cover matters he could not continue. Hopefully, none involved Trooper Graham. As a seasoned legal veteran of thirty years, Cal should have no problem filling in for him. Cal, named for a short-time Republican president, was easygoing. A former North Carolina State college football star, Cal took most all life had to offer in stride.

If Cal doesn't kill Emma Jean in the two weeks I'm gone, everything will work out. Turning up the radio and rolling down the windows, he headed back to the office. It was late enough that the sun glinted off the lake and small bass boats near the shore.

Cal and Emma Jean's feud was legendary. The town craved weekly updates on the latest slur or trick played. Local score-keepers had Emma Jean ahead by a point this week. She'd bribed her brother, Roy, to call Cal. Roy, acting as if he was phoning for Letty's Dry Cleaning, told Cal he refused to clean Cal's shirts because they had lipstick on the collar that did not match Mrs. Hobgood's. Roy said he knew this because Mrs. Hobgood was standing right there and was hysterical. Roy's wife, Dawn, let go with appropriate background screams and sobs. Roy demanded Cal come over to Letty's and pick up his shirts and Mrs. Hobgood. Cal had slammed down the phone and headed over to Letty's in the pouring rain. Emma Jean laughed herself sick. In her exuberance, she knocked over a vase of flowers and soaked both shoes. She spent the rest of the day drying out several estate files with a hair dryer, and hiding from Cal.

Cal refused to fire Emma Jean, and Emma Jean refused to resign because they were cousins on their fathers' side. And family was family. It had been like this between Cal and Emma Jean since Buck had added his name to the practice.

He sighed. Without him to act as referee for the hard-headed cousins, he hoped there would be a law office to come back to after helping out Judge Foster.

Buck pulled in the small gravel drive next to the office, parked his car beside Cal's cherry red Cadillac, and mounted the steps. It was dusk and the hum of bees in the wisteria made him feel a little drowsy. Shaking his head, he put his hand on the old crystal doorknob and stepped into the reception area.

Emma Jean was just putting the phone into its cradle. She picked it back up when she saw Buck open the firm's door. "Oh, Mrs. Davis, here's your son now. He's just come back in." She plucked off a piece of tape that had stuck to her fingers and told Buck this was his mother's third call that afternoon. He sighed. As he walked toward his office, out of the corner of his eye, he saw Emma Jean's feet pitch above her head as her chair tilted and then scooted out from under her.

"I won't miss this," he muttered as he reached for the phone. He put his right ear on autopilot as his mother extolled the successes of his sister and her family in Atlanta, her visit to the Peachtree Driving Club, shopping at the Lenox Mall, and on and on. His mind was already organizing his departure and lining up possible dog care for Charles.

A few minutes later, he was saved from the further raptures of Atlanta by Cal's arrival and hastily hung up. Cal's solid frame dominated his office, making his client chairs look like spindly Victorian pieces. Buck explained Judge Foster's request to Cal, who wished him well, clapped him on the back, and told him to go on to Raleigh tomorrow and not worry. Buck was already down the front steps when Cal opened the door and called him back.

"Hey, Buck, should I give Emma Jean some time off? It's just, well, she's a walking disaster, and she gets ten times worse when you're out of the office. She almost burnt the damn place down when you were trying that case over in Henderson last year."

Buck laughed, remembering. Every volunteer fireman within ten miles raced over in their pickup trucks to put out Emma Jean's smoldering coffee pot. The brand-new coffee pot caught fire when she had left it plugged in, filled with coffee but no water. Two Dalmatians, dripping wet, marveled at the explosion of foam and charred coffee pot.

"Good luck to you, Cal. Oh, and Cal?" Buck called back over his shoulder.

"Yeah?"

"Don't forget. Next week is Administrative Professionals Day. Take Emma Jean someplace special. And don't forget the flowers."

He pulled out of the driveway as Cal shouted at him. Next door, Buck could see old man Royster rock back on his heels with a trowel in one hand and a tomato plant in the other, shaking his grizzled head. Buck could almost hear the old man say what he'd said twenty times before: "Them lawyer boys are at it again."

Chapter Five

Early the next morning, Buck sped into the parking lot of the federal courthouse. He'd gotten stuck behind every school bus, combine, and horse trailer on Highway 15. He had two minutes before he was late to get to Judge Foster's office. He slammed his car door and sprinted for the entrance to the courthouse.

Buck's chest and shoulder hit something solid, and he went down hard. He heard a deep moan coming from his left. Buck lifted his aching head and saw the biggest guy he'd ever seen off the basketball court—Detective Walter A. Johnson—struggle to his knees. Johnson's Styrofoam coffee cup had disintegrated, and coffee dripped down his light-colored slacks. The detective's tie was cock-eyed, and an ugly welt was protruding from just over his eyebrow.

Buck offered a hand to him and a hurried apology. The angry man held up his hand, which looked like a baseball glove. "Look, asshole, you'd better be a judge, be on the way to deliver a baby, or be running to stay some other asshole's execution," the detective growled without looking up. "Otherwise, you're going to spend a day in jail for assaulting an officer!"

By this point, the court security officers, post office employees, and court personnel about to enter the building had stopped to stare at the two disheveled big men. Other uniformed officers, who appeared to be with the detective, stood a respectful distance away.

"Look, man, I'm sorry about the crash, but I'm late getting to Judge Foster's office. I really need to get going," Buck started again. But the bump on Detective Johnson's head and his mood were getting uglier.

"Look, dickweed…" the detective sputtered.

Buck neatly sidestepped the detective's hand holding the crushed fried pie and walked through security. He thought the guy looked familiar but couldn't place him. He ran up the three flights of stairs instead of waiting for the elevator.

Foster was agitated and pacing when Buck arrived and made his second set of apologizes for the morning. Foster waved them aside.

"Sit down," he said. Foster took a deep breath. "The medical examiner thinks O'Shea was murdered."

Buck's mouth gaped. "Why, when…"

"It's incredible. We're all in total shock. It's too horrible. For the court…" Foster collected himself. "Well, I'll need your help now more than ever. Detective Johnson has agreed to release Judge O'Shea's office early this morning after he and his men go through it. Johnson should be here any minute. His team arrived early and should soon be about through interviewing O'Shea's clerks."

Buck winced thinking of the detective he'd left flailing near the courthouse boxwoods.

"Judge O'Shea's widow already arrived in town to start making the funeral arrangements. The funeral's going to have to be delayed based on this new information, and the delay will not sit well with the almost ex-Mrs. O'Shea. She will be livid."

He rubbed his eyes and sighed. "Mary Frances has called twice this morning. Maybe I'll give her the medical examiner's direct number so she can worry him for a while."

Buck spent the remainder of the morning talking to O'Shea's courtroom deputy and trying to keep himself out of law enforcement's way. After five cups of coffee, he could no longer delay a trip to the men's room. Peering out into the hall, he made sure the coast was clear. As he stood in front of the urinal, he heard the outer door open and the sound of heavy footsteps. He zipped up, hunched down, grabbed a newspaper off a chair in the far corner, and tried to pass the detective with the newspaper open, hiding his face.

Detective Johnson grabbed the paper out of Buck's hand with a snap. "Idiot," the detective spit, jamming his finger in Buck's face. "I'm sending you my dry-cleaning bill. You've ruined this jacket and my pants." He turned so Buck could see a big rent in the shoulder of the navy polyester blazer.

Buck put his hands up. "Look, I'll get the bill. Take them down to Ace Cleaners. They have a tailor and do everything by hand. Sorry, I was in a big a hurry this morning for my meeting with the judge. Wait a minute. Johnson, are you from Oxford?"

The detective squinted up at him. "Yeah, so what?"

"You played football at Webb. You were a damn fine linebacker. We beat South Granville four years in a row when you were playing."

Johnson's shoulders relaxed as they walked out of the men's room.

"Yeah, man, those were some good years. I miss being on the field not worrying about anything but the game. You go to Webb too?"

"Yeah. I played basketball. A sport that requires finesse and skill. A lot of intellect and speed."

Johnson snorted. "Man, I gotta get some glasses. I didn't recognize your skinny white ass. I remember your lame reverse layup though. Got us a few points a game. Ain't you Jeb's brother? Him and I were in a lot of classes together."

Rehashing their high school years, the two headed to the conference room. Johnson reached for his water bottle on top of a stack of files. "O'Shea's murder investigation is top priority. The feds are all out at the Raleigh-Durham airport 'cause some idiot left what may be a bomb under the wheel of the Vice President's plane. The VP was going home after he and his wife had picked up their daughter at Duke and headed to Figure Eight for a week of vacation. That's why we got called in, me and Lt. O'Connor. The Lieutenant's been a task force officer for the FBI for a couple of years. She's worked on a bunch of violent crimes' cases for them. Most of 'em have been here in Raleigh and Durham. The resident agent in charge deputized a few of us guys over the phone last night and told us to get up here."

"Look, Johnson, just get your guys out of the office quick, so I can get to the files. Judge Foster wants a status report on O'Shea's cases." Buck opened the office door then looked at his blackened hand. "There's fingerprint powder all over the damn place."

"I don't give a rat's ass about that. I am trying to investigate the murder of a federal judge here, and I don't need some point guard getting in my way."

"Throwing powder around instead of looking for the man's killer seems like a waste of time to me."

"Stick to your files and let the trained investigators do their job. We'll be interviewing court staff downstairs in the break room. Can you send O'Shea's law clerks down again in about an hour?"

"Yeah, okay. See you around."

"Yeah. Just watch where the hell you're going next time."

* * *

A few minutes later, Mary Frances Margaret O'Shea presented herself at Judge O'Shea's chambers. In a raw silk blue suit and with makeup applied with a lavish hand, the new widow looked Buck up and down.

"You're a bit old to be a law clerk, aren't you?" she sneered.

"I'm afraid so. I'm Buck Davis," he said, extending his hand. "I'm truly sorry about Judge O'Shea."

She turned her head and pointedly ignored his outstretched hand. "Well, I'm here to retrieve my husband's personal papers. Then I'm going to the funeral home and to St. Michael's to organize the mass."

"Mrs. O'Shea, I'm sorry, but the police haven't released Judge O'Shea's personal office yet. I'm sure Detective Johnson would be happy to discuss the matter with you. The detective has set up a room in the clerk's office. He's down there now."

She fixed Buck with an icy stare. "This is most inconvenient. Highly irregular." She crossed her arms and glared at him.

He nodded. "I completely agree with you. I would make a point of telling the detective how irregular and inconvenient this is to you."

Without another word, Mary Frances O'Shea turned on her heel and headed toward the clerk's office. Her back was rigid and her carmine mouth was set. He almost felt sorry for Detective Johnson.

This was the first time Buck had met Mrs. O'Shea. He tried to remember what he'd heard about her. Mary Frances, or "Binky" to her friends, had always been described as attractive, but in a hard way. She had attended St. Mary's, then Bryn Mawr, meeting new lawyer Patrick O'Shea during her college days at someone's house in the Hamptons. O'Shea left his New York law firm to follow Binky to North Carolina in an effort to court the Southern beauty and her father's money. The New York law firm expressed little regret on O'Shea's premature departure.

Buck also remembered she was at least five years younger than her husband and obsessive about her youth and looks. The couple had never had any children. For the past year, it'd been rumored the couple was estranged. Mary Frances either lived or travelled overseas while the judge remained in the palatial family home on Glenwood Avenue in Raleigh. The breath of scandal was there, but it was extinguished before it gained credence.

After meeting her today, he could not imagine her as the grieving widow. The fact that Judge O'Shea was dead, possibly murdered, seemed merely inconvenient to her and her itinerary, a personal affront not to be tolerated. He wondered if Detective Johnson was down in the clerk's office calling her an asshole. He'd put his money on Mary Frances in that battle of wills.

CHAPTER SIX

In O'Shea's chambers, Buck met with the two law clerks who both looked as if they had not slept. Stale sweat permeated the air.

"Judge Foster's asked me to summarize the cases on Judge O'Shea's current docket and to flag any matters that are urgent. You need to pull all files from your office that have any outstanding orders you're waiting on from attorneys. Also, he said Judge O'Shea was working on a controversial Section 1983 violation of civil rights case. I need to discuss the case status with you first thing tomorrow. Which one of you was helping Judge O'Shea on that one?"

Jennifer lifted her hand and said, "I was assigned to be the primary clerk on that case. Phillip and I both worked on the case preliminaries, but Judge O'Shea took Phillip off the case so he could work on other things."

Phillip nodded. He was a slender young man, only slightly taller than the petite Jennifer. Almost inaudibly, he agreed: "I was helping with the more routine matters, so Judge O'Shea could focus on the 1983 case. He wanted to be kept up to date on case status. I briefed him on new cases that had been filed, along with new filings in the 1983 case before Jennifer took over on that one."

Each clerk headed back to their small individual offices to get the judge's files for Buck.

Between the time Mrs. O'Shea had stomped out of the entrance to O'Shea's office on her expensive kitten heels and the time the deputies had finished talking to O'Shea's two clerks, Buck searched for and found the judge's file of notes on the civil rights case, *United States v. Wilkerson, et. al.* He opened up the court's file and began reading.

One of the defendants was a small-town farm implement business and convenience store owner who had gone after his three teenaged assailants with his dogs and his rifle. Wilkerson had been deputized earlier in the year as one of the sheriff's deputies. The sheriff's office was operating two men down due to retirement, budget cuts, and fewer graduates than normal from the local Basic Law Enforcement Training classes. The three Black youths had jumped the businessman at his two-pump convenience store while he was closing up one night. Badly beaten, Wilkerson had crawled to his truck and driven home. Wilkerson picked up his son, Earl Junior, his bird dogs, and his guns, and with the interior blue lights on his dashboard flashing, headed across town. Spotting two white men with a pack of dogs and guns, a Black woman sitting on the sofa on her porch had yelled out a warning, and all hell broke loose. Wilkerson had yelled out his sheriff's truck window he was a "lawman" and held up his shield before firing. A small Black child was killed by a ricocheting bullet. The teenagers disappeared after one was grazed by a bullet. The child's parents and the community demanded justice or promised vengeance.

Buck could not understand why one of New York's most prestigious firms, Coughlin and Robertson, would represent these small-town defendants, much less be involved in a civil rights trial. More troubling, he could not imagine why O'Shea had not recused himself. He thought the judge should have considered withdrawing when he'd learned his old New York firm would continue to represent the defendants. He hoped to get an explanation of this irregularity for Judge Foster from the courtroom clerk assigned to the case.

Stepping out into the small reception area where the clerks were organizing files several hours later, Buck said, "I appreciate y'all working with me during this difficult time. Judge Foster asked me to let you know your jobs are secure, at least until the end of the summer, or until another judge is selected. You'll report directly to him and work for him after we get these files organized."

Feeling sorry for the two exhausted attorneys, he added, "Why don't y'all go home early? You both look worn out, and I know this is a sad time for you."

Jennifer and Phillip smiled their thanks and picked up their briefcases. Each said good night. In the quiet of the evening Buck headed back to a chair in the entryway of O'Shea's chambers to continue reading through the case files and the judge's personal notes.

CHAPTER SEVEN

Across the courthouse, Judge Evans unzipped her black robe, lost in thought. She slowly shrugged off the comforting folds. She shook out the wrinkles, put it on a wire hanger, and placed it on the brass hook on the back of her door.

I can't believe that bastard's really dead. Probably another publicity play or a way to raise money. She moved over to her inlaid walnut desk and sat down. Trying to ease her tension, she clasped her hands in front of her and straightened out her arms. She tried the stretch again from behind her back, raised each shoulder, and then rolled her head from side to side.

As the strain of holding four straight hours of court eased from her body, the Honorable Loretta A. Evans sat sipping hot tea and wondering if her sister Angela had heard the news of O'Shea's death. No telling what Angela would do, or how she would react when she heard.

Loretta slipped out of her leather heels and flexed her toes. She had not heard from Angela in two months, and it worried her. Angela usually called one of her sisters, and especially Loretta, every other week.

Loretta pushed back from the desk and headed to the mini-fridge in the corner of her large office. She paused in front of the gilt mirror to wipe the mascara smudges from under her eyes. A tall, striking woman looked back at her. The first Black woman ever appointed to the federal bench in Raleigh, her resilient mahogany skin and amber-almond shaped eyes belied her thirty-nine years. She opened up a yogurt container and began spooning the blueberry mass into her mouth absentmindedly.

Sometimes like now, it was hard thinking about Angela without thinking about O'Shea. Loretta let her mind drift back to her girlhood.

Days of hot, dusty summers. Snappy, crackling autumn days of football, excitement over being a cheerleader. Her father's constant urging, pleading, wheedling, and sometimes shouts that his girls "make something of themselves." Her mother always supporting their father, quietly demanding that the girls study, always be home early, go to church as a family. Her parents worked so hard to give their girls a future.

One moonless night as Angela shut her book when the county library was closing, someone had been watching. He did not know Angela was studying to be something. He did not know Angela usually obeyed her parents and always attended church "as a family." He followed Angela from the library, out the door, down the stairs, and to the bicycle rack. The librarian was turning off the lights in the back and never heard Angela's muffled shout of surprise when he grabbed her from behind. When her father found Angela, nude from the waist down and semi-conscious, the girl inside Angela had died.

O'Shea had been assigned to prosecute Angela's attacker. O'Shea, newly transplanted from New York, had been in the ninth district's district attorney's office for several months and was earning a reputation. "Wet behind the ears" was the nicest thing the local bar would say in public about him. The local attorneys did not know how long they would have to deal with O'Shea and did not want to alienate him before finding out whether the DA's office was O'Shea's last stop or a career steppingstone.

But Loretta knew about O'Shea. During the weeks preceding Angela's attacker's trial, Loretta attended every session of criminal district and superior court. She quickly discovered O'Shea was by far the weakest prosecutor in the office, despite his short stint at a big New York law firm. Worse, juries hated him. She'd watched the burgeoning disgust on the faces of each juror as O'Shea sauntered around the courtroom, unprepared and disheveled. His trumpeting, braying voice jarred, and after a while, was only a cacophony of sound.

Loretta was petrified for Angela when the time came for her attacker's trial. The son of a prosperous farmer, the defendant had the outward appearance of a slow, overgrown child. Angela had to be sedated to sit in the same room with him even after months of intense counseling and medication.

Loretta tried talking to the elected DA about assigning another prosecutor. She returned time and time again, but the DA would not budge. At the trial, she held Angela's hand as they watched Angela's attacker walk out of the courtroom a free man. O'Shea lost the case on a technicality on motions heard before the jury ever got to decide the case. Angela's attacker got probation on a minor charge instead of life for his violent assault. What Loretta saw in her sister's eyes that day has haunted her ever since.

The judge picked up the office phone to call Angela. She slowly replaced it as she realized that she did not have her sister's number.

* * *

Buck fed Charles his favorite meal of wet and dry dog food with bacon on top before they walked downtown to the Oak Room in Oxford. Named after the original bar in the New York Plaza by an overconfident owner, the Oak Room looked more like the Veneer Room. The smell of the grease from the cookers hung in the air, layered over the smell of spilled draft beer and oily wings. Buck sat in the back booth with Charles at his feet. A water for Charles and a Heineken for Buck was served with the usual grunt from the waitress.

Shielding his eyes from the fake gas lights after entering, Detective Johnson spotted Buck and slapped him hard on his back before sliding into the red faux leather booth. Charles wagged his tail as Johnson reached down to scratch his ears. Buck juggled his beer mug after the impact while Johnson stared at him.

"What're you up to? Why'd you want to meet?" Johnson asked.

Buck wiped the spilled beer off his shirt. "Look, Johnson. I couldn't figure out how to get a message to you without other people overhearing. I think I found something you'll want to see."

Johnson waved over the waitress. "Usual." The waitress humped off then returned with a white wine for Johnson and a rib bone for Charles. Only Charles looked back at her in adoration. Johnson wiped off a lipstick smudge on the glass before downing half his wine.

Johnson changed the subject. "Before you give it to me, let's wait for some of these people clear out of here first so no one overhears you. What was your take on Mrs. O'Shea?"

Buck thought a minute.

"She didn't seem too broken up about O'Shea. You figure her for it? She ain't big as a minute. How'd she get O'Shea up there in the chandelier?"

"I don't know who to figure for it. The FBI will be coming in if we don't close it up pretty soon. The Vice President wants every flight manifest checked before he'll feel safe to fly again. Seems that the mysterious bag held some ammo but no bomb. He finally agreed to ride in an armored car back to D.C. The Secret Service deputized us to work O'Shea's murder until the feds wrap up the airport case. Hope I'll get a paycheck from them *and* the FBI, being double deputized."

"Mary Frances seems to be a determined person. Maybe she wanted to get rid of O'Shea faster than the divorce was proceeding. She'd have to have help to get him swinging up there though." Buck said.

Johnson looked at his empty wine glass. Something floated in the last drop in the hollow above the stem. "The captain asked Lt. O'Connor to interview Mrs. O'Shea tomorrow. She refused to talk to me. Katie will see how cold that woman really is."

"Nice footwork outside the courthouse. Couldn't hurdle a two-foot-high boxwood? Pretty hard to imagine you were once a star linebacker at Wake Forest," Buck laughed. "You ever hear from any of your teammates?" Buck asked.

"Not from too many these days. I did catch up with a few during the Orange Bowl a while back." Both men paused in reverence, dwelling on the same thought: Wake Forest in a big football game in Florida. Wake Forest made it into few bowl games, so alumni from fifty years back showed up with their canes and scooters.

"Looks like the restaurant's clearing out. What'd you want to show me?" Johnson asked.

Buck handed him a large envelope. "There are a few letters in here addressed to Judge O'Shea threatening him. I found them when I was moving some files around his office. These fell out of his travel vouchers file. I didn't touch them but got a legal pad and slid them into the envelope. Every judge, even Judge Foster, gets these types of letters. But, you never know who might follow through on their threats. I didn't want to tell anyone else about them. If O'Shea thought the letters were serious, then the court security officers may have been made aware."

"Thanks. I'll take these over to forensics in the morning just in case they can find any latents. Any envelopes with them?" Johnson asked.

"I didn't see any. I'll give you the travel vouchers file tomorrow. Are you heading back over there tonight?" Buck asked.

"No, I'm headed home. I've been on thirty-six hours straight, and the captain said to go home tonight. Lt. O'Connor will be in first thing, and I'll get there around noon. You remember Katie, right?"

"Tall, brown hair? Yeah, I hear she's wrapped pretty tight, but also that she's a good officer. She solved that Kerr Lake case a few months back, right? She'll be good to have as the lead detective."

Johnson nodded. "Weren't you going to stay over in Raleigh?" he asked.

"Yeah, I was, but Mom called," Buck replied. "She thinks my brother's back in town. So, I wanted to stay close in case."

Johnson stood up to leave. "I hear ya. Families, huh? Can't leave 'em, and sure as hell can't live with 'em. Jeb's a good guy. Better do what your Ma says." He bent down to give Charles one last pat and left. The dog settled his head back on his front paws.

Buck raised his empty glass in a silent toast to Johnson's departing back. He thought about his younger brother, Jeb, his on-again-off-again basement tenant. James Ewell Brown Stuart Davis, or Jeb, had been gone a few weeks this time, presumably helping out on farms further south. Or living on the streets, depending on his access to and appetite for pills. He nudged Charles, "Come on boy. Let's check on Jeb." The dog lumbered to his feet. At over one hundred pounds, the big Lab faintly resembled his athletic namesake, Charles Barkley, but lacked his coordination. Buck stopped him from crashing into the waitress as he paid the bill—his *and* Johnson's.

CHAPTER EIGHT

Buck's house was two blocks from his law office in downtown Oxford and three blocks from the Oak Room. The house was a two-story, federal style brick facing Main Street. His favorite aunt, Tilley, had willed it to him and Jeb. Buck became full owner after he became legal guardian to Jeb so he could manage Jeb's finances. Jeb had had to leave school for rehab in Wilmington after stealing a car at Auburn and joyriding it into the dark Chattahoochee River. Leaving his basement apartment without telling Buck was Jeb's way of maintaining some control.

Jeb was not home. Charles moped around, then curled up in his bed and went to sleep. Several years ago, after his first year at Auburn, Jeb had brought the puppy home. Buck patted Charles on the head. "I miss him too, Charles."

Buck's cell phone rang, piercing the silence. "Hello?"

"Buck, this is Lt. Kate O'Connor. How are you?"

"Fine, fine. How are you, Kate?"

"I am okay. I appreciate the letters you gave Johnson, but don't go handling the crime scene. You don't want to become a witness."

"Right, of course."

"Anyway, I'll be down tomorrow to look at where you found them and to interview Mrs. O'Shea. Also, to go to the morgue. Can you meet me at O'Shea's office?"

"Sure, Kate."

"Let's make it eight then."

"Okay, see you there."

Buck released a breath he'd been unaware he'd been holding when he put down his cell. Katie O'Connor had been a beautiful teenager in high school. A few years behind him, he and the rest of the guys in his class loved to watch her walk down the hall in her mini skirt. Whistling at her and her long shapely legs, the guys would yell, "forty foot of leg, forty foot of leg…" He found himself looking forward to tomorrow morning.

* * *

O'Shea's former clerk, Phillip, looked terrified when Buck pushed open the door to O'Shea's reception area the next day.

"There's this detective wants to see you," Phillip whispered to Buck. Sweat stained the clerk's collar, and his hands were grubby.

"Okay, thanks. I'll go find her."

Phillip pointed a shaking finger towards O'Shea's office. "She's in there."

Buck held out his hand towards the detective. "Hey, Katie, I mean L.T."

Katie O'Connor raised one eyebrow and looked at her watch. "Bit of a late night for you at the Oak Room?"

"No, it was early. Traffic here was awful. I got behind a combine in Sandy Plains. Nobody would pass it."

"Show me where you found the letters."

"Over here at the credenza." Pulling the drawer open, he pointed, "They were in the travel voucher file. The file spilled out while I was trying to get the file with O'Shea's notes on the 1983 case."

"You been through the rest of the files?"

"No, I stopped once I found those letters."

"Good, I'm going to go through each file, and if I need help, I'll get Johnson's crew in here. Did you know that one threat letter is from the 1983 case?"

"Yeah, I saw that. The guy basically threatened to kill O'Shea if he did not recuse himself from the case."

Katie, wearing latex gloves, paused in sifting through the files. "We'll get someone down to talk to the guy who signed the threat, or I may go myself after the morgue. The medical examiner just called. He's got the preliminaries for us now."

"I hope the ME can give you some idea of what happened."

"Grab your coat. You can ID O'Shea, so Mary Frances won't have to, and you can hear all about it yourself. Then maybe you won't touch anything else in this office. We better get this solved quickly, or the FBI will waltz in and take over."

She stood with her hand on her service weapon. "Feds… good to work with but some agents are prima donnas. I don't need more headaches or paperwork."

She stripped off the gloves and put them into the brass trash can near the office door.

Buck struggled to put on his jacket, but was just able to catch a glimpse of Katie walking down the hall.

* * *

The antiseptic, green-hued waiting room of the medical examiner's office's displayed magazines issued during Bush I's administration. Putting one down in disgust, Lt. O'Connor paced in the small area while Buck took a seat in a gray metal folding chair. The ticking of the oddly cat-shaped waiting room clock kept time with O'Connor.

"Morning. I'm Donahue, the ME's investigator," bellowed a large man coming through the back door. Appraising an outstretched hand filled with a blueberry muffin, O'Connor stuck her own hand in her pocket and nodded at him.

"Lt. Kate O'Connor. This is Buck Davis here to identify the judge. Thanks for meeting with us."

"Where's Johnson?" Donahue asked, striding to the back of the building.

"He's on his way but wanted us to go ahead if he wasn't here on time."

Donahue nodded and then stepped aside to usher them into the ME's small exam room. A white-sheeted figure lay on the gurney. The air conditioning vent ruffled the ends, which billowed up and then down.

Donahue gestured with the muffin. Crumbs flew, but mercifully none hit the prone figure laid out on the dented metal gurney. "The ME's been over the judge twice. Definitely a homicide." Turning to Buck while he lifted the sheet with his empty hand, Donahue revealed the judge with a flourish.

"It's Judge O'Shea," Buck said.

Buck felt the nauseous heat coming up his legs and pooling in his stomach. O'Shea looked slightly green, reflecting the industrial paint on the cinderblock walls. Buck blindly reached for the room's only chair.

Donahue was talking, "…time of death between midnight and four a.m. Body discovered at eight a.m. Death by asphyxiation. But the ME believes Judge O'Shea was strangled prior to being hung up. The ME combed his body for fibers, hair, etc., and it was clean."

"DNA?" Katie asked.

Donahue cleared his throat, struggling to get the last of the muffin down while O'Shea kept his silent vigil and Buck struggled to keep down his morning coffee.

"The report on whether the judge had intercourse or sexual congress prior to being hung was inconclusive," Donahue said.

Katie looked incredulous. "What does 'inconclusive' mean?"

"It means he doesn't know for sure."

"Terrific. So, could any man or woman have done this? How much did the judge weigh?"

"I think so. Once he'd been strangled though, it would take some strength and ingenuity to get him hung up in the chandelier. Hold on. I have his file here. He weighed about 175."

Feeling a little better, Buck asked, "Could one person do this?"

Donahue shrugged. "I think one very determined person who was not worried about being interrupted could do it. It would take a certain amount of strength too. Moving a dead body is challenging. Were there any drag marks or body debris left on the floor? Blood, urine?"

Buck sank back down in his chair.

O'Connor responded, "No. Nothing we could find."

"We're releasing the body for burial later today. The ME didn't see any reason to keep it," Donahue said. "Also, the widow has been…persistent. I think her last call was to the Governor. Any reason you know of not to send him on his way?"

Katie shook her head, lost in thought.

"Thanks for meeting us," Buck said.

"Have you emailed the report, or can I get a paper copy of the ME's full report?" asked Katie.

Donahue handed her a copy while he walked them back to the cheerless waiting room. "It's marked draft, but it should be finalized later this week."

Nodding her thanks, Katie led the way out into the cloudless day.

*　*　*

A short time later, Katie stopped walking in front of the courthouse. "You going to O'Shea's funeral?" she asked.

"Yes, Judge Foster asked me to help get his law clerks there, and I just feel like I should," Buck said.

"Okay. I guess the widow outmaneuvered me. I'm going to have to reschedule her interview. Johnson texted he will go to the funeral, so I'm going to check with Latents and see if they've turned up anything.

"Thanks for identifying the body. I appreciate it." She turned and strode down the street to where her patrol car was parked. Buck absentmindedly watched her go.

"Hey, Buck!" Johnson appeared over his shoulder from the direction of the parking deck at the back of the courthouse.

"Hey, Johnson. What time did they set for the funeral this afternoon?"

He looked at his cell phone. "It's at five. I'm going to go into the courthouse to brief the Marshal on when the other judges are coming and where they need to sit. Security at the church is going to be a nightmare."

"I can imagine. I'm going in to tell O'Shea's clerks. Have you been able to let the whole court staff know, or just the judiciary?"

"The clerk's office was to send out an email earlier to all the staff."

"See you at the funeral." Buck walked up the three floors to O'Shea's reception area. Both law clerks were surrounded by files and busily typing on their laptops.

"Hey, Phillip and Jennifer. Did you get the email about the funeral?"

The two looked up at him and nodded in unison.

"Let's plan to leave early, and I'll take you over to the church. The court staff has a section cordoned off where we will sit," he said.

"I really wanted to finish up this project," Phillip said. "I have an interview tomorrow morning with a law firm."

"I think we need to go to the funeral. Work on your project after the interview.

Good luck with it. I hope you're interviewing for something you want to do."

"It's a small firm. Mostly civil work, which I like. I hope I get the job."

Jennifer smiled at him.

"I hope so, too. I'll meet you downstairs in the lobby at 3:30 to head over."

* * *

St. Michael's stone church was packed almost to overflowing when the three arrived. Judges from the other federal district courts and a few from the state's appellate courts were seated in the right front pews. O'Shea's sparse family, except for Mrs. O'Shea, were seated on the left. Flowers spilled down the aisles from the altar. Looking toward the back of the massive church, Buck saw a sea of dark suits white-capped by stiffly starched shirts.

The service was long. All of O'Shea's political cronies relished a chance to stand before a microphone. Most speeches celebrated the speaker and included O'Shea as an afterthought. Mrs. O'Shea sat ramrod straight throughout the ceremony. Her hair, at least from the back, was perfectly coiffed.

Following the graveside service, the reception was held at the federal courthouse. The federal courthouse architecture had all the allure a 1970s government architect could imagine—none. A big rectangle of eight stories of concrete and glass, the building was barely functional. Most federal agencies previously housed in the building had moved out to buildings with working heating and air systems. Fortunately, after the Reagan administration, someone had garnered enough federal funds to beautify the courtrooms. Most featured wainscoting and large brass chandeliers.

Buck and the law clerks squeezed into the courtroom with the other mourners. Spotting Mrs. O'Shea toward the back, he went over and stood in line to give his condolences. After several minutes, he reached the widow.

"Mrs. O'Shea, I'm truly sorry for your loss."

Mrs. O'Shea turned from her whispered conversation with a distinguished looking gentleman. She raised one eyebrow. "Thank you, Mister…"

"Buck, Buck Davis. I met you in Judge O'Shea's office earlier this week."

"Oh. Well, thank you for coming." She turned back to the gentleman, and they glided away in tandem.

"Buck, thank you for getting Judge O'Shea's law clerks to the service. How is the file review going?" Judge Foster asked.

"We're making progress. I want to talk to you sometime about the 1983 case. I know you've been in trial this week, so I didn't want to bother you with it until you'd finished."

Before Judge Foster could reply, an attractive woman approached. Foster turned to her and then to Buck, "Buck, I'd like you to meet Judge Loretta Evans, our newest member of the judiciary. Judge Evans, this is Buck Davis, my old law clerk and an attorney from Oxford."

Buck shook her hand and said, "So nice to meet you, Judge Evans."

She looked at Buck without saying anything at first. "Nice to meet you as well," she managed while looking past him. After an awkward moment of silence, she turned to him and scrutinized his face.

"Oxford? My folks, well, my mom and dad still live up there near Wilton."

"That's not too far down the road. Did you grow up in Granville County?" Buck asked.

She nodded. "I did. My sisters and I ended up at J.F. Webb instead of South Granville for high school. You?"

"J.F. Webb, class of a long time ago."

She gave a hint of a smile. "I don't get back too often. Mom likes to come over and shop in the 'big city.' I don't get to see my sisters as much as I'd like. They're scattered now."

"I understand. My mom loves to visit my sister in Atlanta for the same reason." Changing the subject, he said,

"Congratulations on your appointment. I hope you have been enjoying your new position."

"I really have." Turning to Judge Foster, she said, "I would not have survived those first weeks without Judge Foster. He's been a wonderful mentor."

Judge Foster smiled. "We're so fortunate to have you here at the court, Loretta. You've taken on a lion's share of the case load. I'm going to have to lean on you more now that Judge O'Shea's gone."

She turned somber. "Absolutely. Anything you need, please let me know." With a nod to both men, she walked over to stand in the line forming again in front of Mrs. O'Shea.

Buck said, "Loretta Evans…I think she earned some great scholarship to Harvard. Only student from J.F. Webb to go there. I didn't know her in high school since she was about five grades behind me. But I seem to remember something about her family. A tragedy…"

"She's extremely bright and a very capable jurist," Judge Foster said. "Something happened to one of her sisters, I think. Judge Evans has been very active in the domestic violence victims' shelter here in Raleigh." He paused in thought. "She and Judge O'Shea never seemed to get along. I don't know why, but it was just one of those things. I thought if he was nominated for the Fourth Circuit, the atmosphere would improve."

"I understood Judge O'Shea all but had the appellate nomination. Interviews were rumored to be held next week, but just as a courtesy to the other candidates. O'Shea would've loved presiding up there in Richmond," Buck said.

Buck put down his mostly filled glass of punch on a card table set up as an impromptu serving area. "See you tomorrow, Judge. I'm going to head back to Oxford. I need to get Charles. He can handle only so much of Emma Jean."

Judge Foster laughed. "We'll meet just as soon as I can get through this trial. Drive safely."

Buck headed back to O'Shea's office to pick up some files and call Emma Jean where he could hear over the noise of the reception which had spilled out into the hall.

"Hey, Emma Jean. Is Charles okay with you for the hour it takes me to get back? You can take him to Mom's if you have plans." He heard a metallic crash then silence. "Emma Jean?"

"It's okay, Buck. I just knocked over Charles's water bowl. We're fine. Take your time," Emma Jean said.

Buck paused while closing the door to O'Shea's office. He thought that he heard something inside. He went back in and through each office. Nothing.

With his briefcase, he walked down the hall and into the small elevator. It opened in the lobby, and he walked halfway around the courthouse to his car. Fortunately, it was intact. No beer cans under the tires or Jesus pamphlets on the windshield. He'd surprised more than one person enjoying the warmth of the day sleeping on the hood of his car. It was not as bad as in his clerkship days when the local mental health agency used to bus the patients into downtown for the day.

He heard a rustling sound in the twilight. From near the bushes separating the courthouse from the sidewalk, he watched a woman appear. She was disheveled and walked slowly toward him. At the last minute, she veered off, heading for the courthouse steps around the corner of the building.

He followed her to make sure court security saw her coming. He paused when he saw Judge Evans talking to her a few feet outside the entrance. He could not help but overhear them.

"I asked you, Angela, where have you been? I've been worried sick about you," Judge Evans said reaching for the woman's hand.

The woman did not answer, just shrugged and stared at Judge Evans.

"Angela," she said more calmly. "Have you had any dinner?" When Angela did not respond, she said, "Why don't you come home with me, and I'll fix something, or we can get takeout. We can get that pizza you love from the little Italian place near my townhouse."

Angela looked at Judge Evans and said, "I just want to know. I just want to know."

"What, Angela?"

"Is O'Shea really dead? Because I saw he was dead. On the news. I saw it on the news."

"Yes, Angela," Judge Evans said, putting her arm around her and turning her toward the courthouse. "Yes, honey, he's dead."

"Good."

"I know, honey. Now, come on, let's go get something to eat."

The court security staff, standing a respectful distance away, opened the door for them. The women disappeared into the dimly lit lobby.

CHAPTER NINE

In O'Shea's office early the next day, Buck was in a foul mood. That morning, Charles had knocked over his coffee into his open briefcase and then tracked it all over the living room rug. He thought Buck jumping up and down was a new fun game. Buck felt bad he'd yelled at the big Lab— and he'd still seen no sign of Jeb. Both he and Charles were a miserable pair when they parted at the office. Fortunately, Emma Jean had a new duck chew toy for Charles, so at least he saw the dog's tail wag before he left, if but faintly.

Files cascaded in a waterfall from the credenza in O'Shea's office. He'd been given the all-clear by Detective Johnson earlier to go back in, but the place was a mess. Trying not to crunch the papers underfoot, Buck headed for the reception area to get his soggy brief case, but when he heard a noise from the law clerks' office, he stopped.

Jennifer sat at a desk, head in hands, sobbing. Tears ran down her cheeks onto her neck, which was red and splotchy.

"Jennifer," he said. "Hey, what's wrong?"

She kept crying, her breath coming in gulps.

Buck stood there helplessly, his big hands by his side. The law clerks' office looked as bad as O'Shea's. Books and files were strewn everywhere.

He waited a few minutes and then tried again, "Jennifer, I know it must be difficult to lose a friend and mentor like Judge O'Shea in such a tragic way."

She looked at him. "You don't understand," she wailed. "They're going to charge me with Judge O'Shea's murder."

Buck was stunned speechless. He started running his hands through his hair. After a couple of minutes, he said, "I'm calling Detective Johnson. That can't be right. What are you talking about? You have to be mistaken."

She blew her nose. "No, I'm not. I'm going to be charged with his murder. It's just a matter of time before Detective Johnson arrests me. I just want to be ready when he does."

"Look, I have no idea what you're talking about, but if you are right, you need a lawyer. I will be happy to recommend one here in Raleigh. There are a lot of good ones near the courthouse who practice criminal law."

Jennifer shook her head emphatically. "You're a lawyer. Judge Foster thinks you're special. If he respects you, then you are who I want to hire. I want to talk to you about this. I haven't saved a lot, but I can retain you for a thousand dollars and then pay your hourly fee. Please."

Buck was torn. He wanted to help Jennifer, especially as he was having trouble believing she could have harmed anyone, but he had a duty to Judge Foster to help straighten out O'Shea's files and case notes so the wheels of justice could creak on turning.

"Jennifer, I can't do it, but I'm going to call a friend of mine who mainly handles criminal cases and ask him if he can meet with you. He'll work with you on the fee."

"Okay, but I want you to hear what I have to say. I want your opinion. Will you sit with me and your friend, just for the first meeting?"

"If my friend okays it, then I will. I don't want to do anything to harm your…situation."

"I don't think anyone can help me, but I'm willing to listen."

"I'll call him now and see if he can meet with you today. Give me a few minutes and I'll let you know."

"Thanks," she said. "I appreciate you doing this for me."

CHAPTER TEN

Buck lay back in his conference table chair with his feet on the chair next to him, exhausted from the two-hour meeting with Jennifer and her new attorney. He rubbed his eyes, thinking back over the conversation. Jennifer's thin shoulders shook violently throughout the telling. Her platinum blonde hair fell over her heart-shaped face during most of it.

Jennifer told the two men how several months ago she and Judge O'Shea had been working late on the 1983 case, reviewing the parties' briefs filed at the last minute. At about eight o'clock that night, O'Shea asked her to go with him to dinner so they could discuss the new filings. Because the hearing was the next afternoon, she grabbed her notes and laptop. O'Shea drove them to the Sir Raleigh Tavern, a new restaurant housed in a large Georgian style building on Hillsborough Street and only a few blocks from the district courthouse. The Sir Raleigh Tavern has fine dining on the first floor and a tavern in the basement. O'Shea and Jennifer were seated at a table on the first floor away from the front door. She was intimidated by its elegance. Their table was covered with a white tablecloth and had a small vase with a single pink rose. O'Shea touched the flower and told Jennifer he'd ordered it for her. She started to feel uncomfortable, but O'Shea started talking about his court cases.

After discussing the merits of the new briefs, O'Shea ordered a glass of wine for her and one for himself. Shortly after, she excused herself to go to the restroom. The shrimp appetizer followed by the small filet mignon were delicious. While leaving the restaurant, Jennifer had felt slightly nauseous. When the valet brought around O'Shea's sleek dark Mercedes, she had stumbled getting into the car, barely hanging onto her laptop. Her notes slipped from her hands and began blowing down the street. The valet ran after them as the bulk settled beside the wrought iron fencing around the trees lining the street.

O'Shea, concerned, asked her whether she was feeling well enough to drive home. That was the last thing she remembered until she woke up the next morning in a strange bedroom with walls covered in white and yellow wallpaper. O'Shea was naked standing at the bedroom window gazing out while holding open the sheer lace curtains. When he heard her moan, O'Shea turned and smirked. Terrified, she focused on his graying chest hairs.

Here, Jennifer stopped her story. Tears coursed down her face. Buck and her attorney looked around helplessly for tissues. It was several minutes before she could begin again. O'Shea had mockingly bowed and thanked her. He told her she had been quite energetic last night. When she began asking him what happened, his voice hardened. He said her sexual prowess was recorded in a video and he had photographs as insurance against any regret she might have this morning. Sick, horrified, and humiliated, she begged him to destroy the video and photos and to take her back to the courthouse. He silently dressed and drove her to the courthouse. When he let her out in the back parking lot where her Honda was parked, all he said to her was she had better not tell anyone what had happened.

Jennifer stopped again suffused in tears. She had looked at Buck with red eyes, twisting a Kleenex in her small hands.

"I didn't know what to do, and I didn't remember what happened. I felt so ashamed. I'd looked up to him. He told me he'd fire me if I so much as said another word about it. And I have huge student loans I'm just starting to pay back. I couldn't afford to lose my job."

She'd tried to act normally, returning to the courthouse after a shower and attending the afternoon's hearings as if everything was fine. She tried not to meet with O'Shea by herself, communicating by email when she could and leaving the office every afternoon when her co-worker Phillip did. Several days later, O'Shea's courtroom clerk asked her kindly if she was feeling well, but otherwise it seemed no one had noticed her distress. She'd almost broken down then, but she couldn't face telling the motherly clerk of O'Shea's attack.

Her retired parents would have supported her if she had told them because they were kind and decent people, but they would not have understood. In their well-ordered lives, people adhered to the rules of polite society. The quiet couple was so proud of their daughter graduating law school and working for such an important person. All her milestones were framed in silver on the family piano. She could not bear to see first their confusion and then their pity.

Jennifer's feet barely touched the ground as she shifted in the conference room chair. She said she knew Detective Johnson would be coming to arrest her soon. In a desperate effort to restore some normalcy to her shattered life, she had rifled through O'Shea's papers while he attended a daytime continuing legal education seminar as the keynote speaker to try to find the photographs of their night together, but she'd heard a noise in the hall outside of his office a few minutes after starting her search. Fearing he was returning, she had spilled both the threatening letters and travel voucher files onto the plush carpet. Scurrying to put things to rights, she had grabbed the papers and must have mixed the two. Her fingerprints would be on the papers. If Detective Johnson had succeeded in finding the photographs, she knew she'd be arrested.

When Jennifer finished speaking, Buck and her attorney remained silent. The ticking of the small brass clock on the credenza was the only sound. Buck spoke first, his voice shaking with emotion, "Jennifer, you absolutely did nothing wrong. What O'Shea did to you was horrible. You're not at fault. He took advantage of you in the worst way.

"Even if a video or pictures exist, which I doubt, I don't think Detective Johnson will arrest you."

He gestured to his colleague. "I'll defer to Bob here as your attorney. You should listen carefully to his advice. You're a victim." He stood up and started to hug Jennifer but then hesitated. Awkwardly, he straightened and turned to leave.

"Y'all take the time you need to talk. I'll be back in later to turn the lights off and lock up the office when you're done."

* * *

Buck got home late. Charles neatly tackled him as he opened the door. "Whoa, Charles!" he laughed. "I'm glad to see you too." The big Lab's tail waved back and forth.

"Hey, Buck," Jeb said coming in from the living room. Buck stood up. "Oh, my God, Jeb. It's great to have you back." Buck hugged his brother hard. He could feel Jeb's thin shoulder blades through his flannel shirt. He held him at arm's length. "You're looking good, man. How're you feeling?"

Jeb was only slightly too thin for his frame. His hair shot out in curly spirals, but his beard was matted.

"Pretty good, I guess. Thanks for taking care of Charles for me while I was gone."

Buck went to the refrigerator and handed Jeb a bottle of water.

"You told Mom you're in town?"

"Naw, not yet. I just got here this afternoon. I went to a meeting at the Episcopal church. It was a good crowd. Where've you been? I walked over to your office after the meeting, and Emma Jean acted all secret squirrel. Big case?"

"No big case. I'm helping out Judge Foster over in Raleigh on a couple of things since Judge O'Shea died. I don't mind a few days, but I really need to get back into my office. Hey, you remember Loretta Evans? Was she in your class at Webb? She's a judge now."

Jeb thought a minute. "Tall, pretty Black girl? I think I remember her from basketball. If it's the same girl, she was really smart and really sweet. Mean hook shot. Something bad happened to one of her sisters."

"Was it Angela?"

"Yeah, that's right. It was Angela. You know, Angela and I were in rehab together once. Down in Wilmington. You know, near the beach. It was a few years ago. I really liked Angela. She had a good soul. But, she was dealing with some serious shit."

Jeb tossed the bottle into the garbage with a perfect overhand throw. At six-foot-four, he had been an awesome freshman guard at Auburn—before the drugs; before the rehab; before the darkness claimed him and took him under.

Each time he allowed himself to think about those tumultuous years, his stomach clenched as if he'd been punched. Each release from rehab started out so hopeful. Jeb would climb out of the abyss only to slide back in after a few months of being sober. The slide was always gradual. Buck began keeping his phone by his nightstand every time Jeb came out just in case his brother called for help or, more likely, an officer called for him to pick Jeb up off of some highway or neighbor's lawn.

Charles circled the two, smiling his doggy smile. His tail beat a tattoo on the brothers' legs.

They sat down on opposite sofas in the living room. The room still had that "old lady" smell of stale cigarettes and White Linen Buck could not vanquish even with all the windows open or any amount of Febreeze. Each man dwarfed his matching floral sofa. Charles turned around, sighed, and plopped down between them on the red and blue oriental rug.

"Hey, Buck, I was thinking about getting my own place," Jeb said.

Here we go again. "Look, Jeb, as much as you travel, don't you think the basement is a good deal? You don't have to keep track of utilities that might get cut off if you had your own place. If you need me to clear out when you have company, I don't mind. I can bunk over in Raleigh or go over to Mom's. Whatever you want."

Jeb stood up, agitated.

"Buck, I just want my own space. I'm not a child, I don't need you managing my things. It's time I took care of myself."

"How many days sober, Jeb?"

Jeb turned away.

"What the fuck you care? I'm going downstairs. Come on, Charles." Charles looked mournfully between the two and followed Jeb's retreating figure down the old wooden steps.

Buck's eyes filled with angry tears. He thought, *How many times are we doing this same conversation? How many times do I have to be the parent? I'm tired of being the fucking parent.*

Buck was the one who had to get Jeb to his first rehab. Then his second. And third.

The trip to the first one was the worst. Nothing had prepared him for the physical and mental changes to his brother in his few months away at school after the Christmas break. Jeb was asleep and drooling on soiled sheets in his dorm room when Buck got there eight hours after the call from his Resident Assistant. Jeb had been given a choice by the coach: rehab or expulsion. Jeb's duffel bag was half packed. Pizza boxes littered his desk. Garbage spilled onto the floor from the oversized can.

The car trip was excruciating. When Jeb wasn't sleeping, he was crying. Jeb begged him to just take him home. Then he threatened to jump out of the car. His easy-going muscular brother was gone. This thin angry stranger was a shadow of Jeb.

The first time he caught Jeb with pills on the trip, he'd nearly killed him. Buck had pulled over in a rest area to stretch his legs and get a Coke. When he got back to the car, it was in time to see Jeb shovel pills into his mouth. Jerking him out of the car by his sweatshirt, Buck twisted the neck up under Jeb's chin, choking him. Moving his hands to each of Jeb's arms, he shook him until most of the pills spilled onto the ground. He grabbed the brown pill bottle and heaved it into the woods nearby. Buck ground the pills into the pavement. Jeb screamed words he couldn't understand. Jeb swung at him but was so zoned out he could barely stand. Buck grabbed him by his stick-like arm and threw him up against the car. Staring into his unfocused eyes, Buck yelled, "Fucking stop it. Stop it. Quit fighting me." Only Charles's terrified puppy barking penetrated the red mist. Jeb kicked out, and Buck fell hard. Using the back of the car, Buck painfully hauled himself to his feet ignoring the bleeding cuts on his hands. He launched himself onto Jeb's back rolling in the wet grass until he was on top of him. Not one word was said, but he could hear his brother's muffled sobs. Chest heaving, Buck got up off the ground and pulled up Jeb with him. Other people in the rest area just stared. Jeb refused to speak to Buck until they got to the reception area of the rehabilitation center.

After he was released from rehab several months later for just a weekend to attend his aunt's funeral, Jeb was crushed when he'd found out his aunt's will stipulated Buck had to remain Jeb's guardian for her bequest. Jeb, infuriated, confronted Buck outside the funeral home, pushing him in the chest as he ground out his disgust at what he'd believed was Buck's betrayal. Buck was embarrassed and angry, but the will stopped Jeb from selling the old federal style house for drugs. Small antiques disappeared from time to time, but Buck didn't have the energy to keep confronting his brother.

He and Jeb had been so close once. Allies from a young age against their sweet but strict mother, they'd played quietly together with trains or plastic army men, creating whole worlds. Every team sport they could, they played together. Buck remembered cheering Jeb on during a million city league basketball games. During the humid summers, he'd played basketball late into the night in the backyard with his little brother.

All he could hope for now was that Jeb was sober and thinking straight. Getting up off the sofa, Buck grabbed two waters from the fridge and headed to the basement door.

"Jeb, can I come down?" he hollered from the top of the stairs.

The musty smell of old books and clothes wafted up. "Yeah, c'mon."

Buck bent his head and walked down the steps. The walls in the basement were knotty pine; the floor was covered in colorful rugs knitted by Aunt Tilley. Her Regency romance book collection dominated the far wall. Heaving busts and dashing long-haired heroes winked out from the covers at him. The fragrance of damp book, dog, and the violets his aunt favored in her array of crystal candlesticks mingled and met him as he climbed down the stairs.

The living area was neat and filled with many of Aunt Tilley's favorite Victorian ladies' chairs and settees upholstered in rose-colored velvet. A barrel back chair in rose and mint stripes with a matching foot stool was a nod to Jeb's comfort. Scattered in between her treasured romances was her paperweight collection. Colorful prisms danced on the walls when the setting sun peeked in the transom windows at the top of the space. The multifaceted blue ones vied with the round red ones for primacy on the walnut shelf.

At the end of the basement, behind a louvered screen, Jeb was lying on the four-poster queen bed pushed against the far wall, his arm over his eyes. His feet were hanging over. Charles was lying next to him with eyes partially closed.

"Jeb, I don't know what to say, so I end up saying something wrong. I feel like you stay mad at me. I don't know what's best, but I want to make sure you have somewhere to come back to when you want. Can you give it a few months, and then let's talk about you getting your own place?"

Buck put his hand on his brother's arm. "I love you, and I'm proud of you for trying so damn hard to keep a handle on your illness. I want to fight the battle with you. Please tell me how."

Jeb moved his arm. His eyes still were closed. A tear trickled down from one eye into his wild curly hair. "Man, I don't want to be your burden. I don't want you to be my dad. It's just that it's awkward coming home where everybody knows me. People look at me like I'm about to trip out walking down the street. Just quit asking me about my sobriety every time I see you. Can't we have a normal conversation, just once?"

Buck stood and then popped his brother in the leg giving Jeb a charley horse. "You're on, dumbass. Game of HORSE? Or are you too scared to lose to me?"

Jeb leaned on his elbows and grinned. "Not a chance. Come on, Charles, let's go hand Buck his ass."

Jeb and Charles chased Buck upstairs and outside to the basketball hoop. The thump of the basketball on the concrete drive was a soothing sound in the moonless night. Their laughter, reverberating among the backyard magnolias, was punctuated by the sounds of good-natured taunting.

* * *

Early the next morning, Buck spoke briefly to Jennifer by phone, then went to find Judge Foster in the courthouse. Jennifer told Buck she was going with her attorney to talk to Lt. O'Connor this morning because she would feel more comfortable talking with her than with Johnson. She hesitated but agreed when Buck asked permission to let Judge Foster know what had been done to her. As Chief Judge, Buck explained,

Judge Foster handled the court's administrative duties and would be questioned by law enforcement.

Before Buck could talk to him, the judge's administrative assistant called and set up an appointment with him, Judge Foster, Judge Evans, and the two detectives.

That afternoon, Lt. O'Connor nodded to Buck when he arrived in the judge's conference room. Everyone else was seated. O'Connor said, "Buck, Jennifer and her attorney met with us earlier, but could not get through the details. She got so sick she had to leave. Her attorney called later and said she is under a doctor's care for PTSD. He also said you have her permission to give us the story. So, if you don't mind, can you summarize what she told you?"

Buck stood up, wanting movement to distract him from his emotions. He began to tell the others what O'Shea had done to Jennifer.

Judge Foster turned gray, his shoulders sagging as Buck curtly and concisely repeated the story of O'Shea's atrocities against Jennifer.

"I can't believe it. There must have been something terribly wrong with him to do such a thing. He abused her and abused her trust. Any chance you misunderstood her or what happened?"

"No, and it was one of the hardest things I've ever had to sit through. So awful for her. To start off your career so eagerly, fresh out of law school, and then to have your body violated, your self-esteem shattered like that…One of the detectives will send off O'Shea's computer for a forensic evaluation. God knows what the forensic examiner will find on it. I guess they'll get a search warrant for his other electronic devices, cell phone, personal computer."

Buck looked at Katie. She agreed and said, "The search warrants are being prepared now. I'm going to pick them up after our meeting. I will serve the ones on his personal property, and Johnson will serve the one on his courtroom laptop.

I first have to call and deliver the news to Mrs. O'Shea at her home, then arrange to transport everything to the lab. The lab will accept the devices and examine them as a rush. Hopefully, we'll have some extraction reports within a few days."

Detective Johnson said, "The FBI has agreed to help by getting the courtroom laptop to their lab at Quantico today for a rush review. We have the latent prints report and will be contacting anyone that left identifiable prints. If there's anyone at the courthouse we need to interview, we will let you know."

Judge Evans wiped tears from her eyes and said, "I just feel so helpless. What can we do for Jennifer?"

"I am going to call her and tell her she has a job here with the court for as long as she needs it," Judge Foster said. "I will check in with the Administrative Office of the Courts to see whether we can offer to pay counseling or some supportive services to her. We need to be here for her however we can. This is just awful."

Buck looked at his old mentor. "Jennifer definitely will need help, and if the photos or pictures are located on any device, she's going to be re-victimized. Also, after knowing this, what else will the officers find on his computer?"

"This is a travesty for Jennifer first, and for the judges, attorneys, clerks—everyone who works here and tries to see justice done. I'll call a meeting of the other district judges to tell them to expect the detectives to talk with them too," Foster said.

"Maybe if you called Jennifer it would help her feel her place is here with the court family. Or, just telling her she can take some time off and come back when she is ready may help her feel supported. I don't want to inflict any of Judge O'Shea's files on her," Buck said as he gestured to the double stack of file boxes.

Judge Foster turned to Katie.

"Will you be able to share with me what is found in the contents of the electronic devices?" he asked.

She glanced at Detective Johnson. "We'll share what we can, but the investigation will require some discretion. We still have a murder to solve. It looks like we're going to have to bring in the FBI after all to assist us given these newest developments."

The detectives stood to go. "Thank you for your time," she said. "I'll let you know what we seize as that will be public record. I imagine you'll hear from Mrs. O'Shea too. She strikes me as a woman who won't let go of anything too easily."

Judge Foster shook their hands. Judge Evans followed them out after telling Judge Foster that she was going to step out to talk to his administrative assistant about court for next week.

Buck went with Judge Foster to his office and updated him on his progress with the O'Shea files. He left him sitting still by his office window staring at the photographs on his desk. Judge Foster's three daughters smiled back at him, blonde hair floating on the breeze by the tennis courts.

* * *

Buck caught up with Judge Evans as she was pressing the button for the elevator. "Judge, my brother was telling me at the house last night how he remembers you from high school."

"Really? What's your brother's name?"

"Jeb. He played basketball for Webb and remembered you as a basketball star."

"Hardly that," she laughed. "If I'd gotten a scholarship anywhere to play college ball, I wouldn't be here. I'd be on television playing with the WNBA, doing commercials for my big sponsors, and driving a fancy car on my way to the next big nightclub. I think things usually work out the way they should most of the times, though. Was your brother a tall skinny guard with wild curly hair?"

"That's him. He's gained a little weight, but he hasn't changed a whole lot. I hate to admit it, but he was always the better ball player. He had a natural talent. He'd just get a rhythm going, and that would be that. I loved watching him play. They all really jelled as a team during Jeb's senior year and won the state championship."

"That team was gifted. Most of the guys went on to play college ball, and a couple of them went on to a year in the NBA. Did your brother get to go on or play in Europe?"

"He did. He played for a while at Auburn. He named his dog after Charles Barkley. A big ol' Lab that thinks the sun rises and sets on Jeb."

"That's a great name to live up to for any dog. I have two myself that I named Nelson and Wellington. Nelson's an Irish Wolfhound and Wellington's a Great Dane. When I adopted them I was doing a master's in History," she said laughing.

"That's impressive—the dogs and the degree," said Buck.

"I got caught up in the British military heroes, so the dogs got the fallout. I get some pretty odd looks when people hear me call them. Their only bad habit is how much they adore my sister Angela and have trouble calming down when she comes to visit. They slobber all over her and pile onto the bed—where they know they're not allowed, but she doesn't visit that often so they're entitled to some snuggling."

The elevator doors slowly opened and she stepped in.

"Well, I'm headed back up to my office. Good talking to you."

Buck stood in the long marble hallway deep in thought until someone tapped him on the shoulder. Over one shoulder Katie balanced a laptop bag with the court seal, her handbag, and a tote.

"Hey, you know where this thing is headed don't you?"

"Yeah. To the FBI. I figure the phone or the laptop or both will have revolting photos and maybe disgusting personal photos of the late Judge. On a more positive note, I just hope there are some emails to point y'all to whoever murdered the judge."

"You know we'll try to keep this part from the press, but that's almost impossible. Someone else that's been mistreated may come forward now that O'Shea isn't a threat anymore. If someone else does come forward, it could open the floodgates depending on what he was doing. You ever get an inkling about O'Shea while you worked here?"

"No," Buck said. "I was on my way out to Italy when he was coming into the court. I really didn't know him. Are you going back over to Oxford tonight or tomorrow?"

"Going back tonight. I've got to get the items we picked up from O'Shea's residence logged into evidence and finish up the paperwork. I wanted to send the team over to pick them up. I figured if I went she'd just hunker down and call that stiff-necked attorney of hers, but the guys just called and she's asking for me. Why do you ask?"

"I wondered if you'd like to meet for dinner tonight or for a cup of coffee tomorrow morning."

"You think I've ruled you out as a suspect?"

"I hope so. If you have, I'd like to get together. If you haven't, we can still get together, and you can interrogate me. The bad coffee at the drugstore or the marginal dinner at the Oak Room should get me talking."

"I'd like that. I'll meet you tomorrow morning at the drug-store if your reputation can withstand sitting next to a cop. You'll have to sit in the officers' section and not in your usual attorney part of the drug store. It'll be a privilege, but you'll upset the natural order of things there. Tongues will wag."

"I'm willing to risk it," he laughed. "Text me before you head up, and I'll meet you there. But, if Trooper Graham's in there, we may need to head over to Dora's Donuts. He's still mad at me, and I'm trying to avoid him."

"Graham's a great guy. What'd you do to him?"

"How can you just assume it was me? You'll have to be an impartial listener if you want me to tell you the story tomor-row. Let's just say I'm traveling the speed limit and obeying all traffic laws for the foreseeable future."

"Okay then. I'm off to Mrs. O'Shea's to read the search warrant. Want to tag along?"

"No way. I'd rather read law review articles on the new tax laws or the bankruptcy code than confront her. Hope you make it safely in and out of there."

O'Connor threw a little wave his way and hefted up the laptop. She headed for the stairs leading down to the parking lot behind the building. Buck watched her go and felt a surge of hope. They'd have to sit far away from the normal drugstore crowd to have a chance to say anything without some well-meaning deputy or attorney sitting down with them, but it'd be worth the jokes and innuendos later to spend some time with Katie.

Chapter Eleven

Early the next morning, Buck arrived at the drug store in Oxford ahead of Katie and grabbed a table by the toilet seat risers display. He texted her he was there and got her order for breakfast. He wiped his sweaty palms on his khaki pants then tried to scrub away the moisture from his pants with a napkin from the plastic dispenser. Doris ambled over, yellow pencil behind her ear.

"Hey, Buck. Ain't seen you here lately." She started flipping through the pad in her hand.

"I've been in Raleigh the last few days. What's good this morning?"

The cracked and peeling sign behind the counter was hidden by parallel towers of Styrofoam cups the owner had just stacked there. Still flipping pages, Doris paused. "I don't rightly know. I'll be right back." She shuffled away on down the aisle wearing scuffed pink bedroom slippers with their heels mashed down.

Buck had just looked back down at his paper when someone's meaty hand clapped him on his shoulder.

"Great to see you, Buck," Trooper Graham grinned easing into the small ice cream parlor chair across from him.

"Wish I could say the same. Whose license have you targeted now?" he snorted.

Graham, immaculate in his gray pressed uniform, leaned forward. "Look, jerk. You know your rotten client took a swing at me, and you got Sally to give you a deal. Your guy should be in jail."

Doris slowly came back into view. "I have the blueberry and the strawberry donuts and the bacon egg samich." On the board behind the counter to his right, now visible after the cups were moved, "egg samich" was prominently displayed for $3.99.

Buck turned to Doris. "Two bacon egg sandwiches and two coffees. And whatever the trooper here will have."

Graham smiled. "I'll also have two bacon egg sandwiches and two coffees. Thanks, counselor."

Doris, finding a blank page, painstakingly wrote down the order with the pencil she retrieved from behind her ear. She went back to the grill and handed the page to the cook.

"Coming to court? Sally's not the DA today, so your clients should get a little justice."

"No. I'm going over to Raleigh this morning. Do you have a lot of cases on the docket? Stop any poor little old ladies lately?"

Graham shook his head. "No, just a couple of old DWI charges pending. No one wants to do anything with them. The defendants show up about half the time. The defense attorneys don't want to try them, and the ADA wants to dispose of the speeding tickets first, then the assaults, then everything else. Trying the cases gets the judge irritable and sets everything back. It's especially bad when two officers are involved in a DWI—where one made the stop and the other took the driver for a breath test in the Intoxilyzer room at the sheriff's."

"You're right about that. Nobody wants to eat up court time when the judge is anxious to leave. Got some age on your cases?"

"Yep. Two years on most of 'em."

Buck handed the paper over to Graham to make room for Katie. Graham whistled. "Katie, girl, you slumming it now?"

She laughed and gave Buck a half hug with her free arm. Her big black Kate Spade purse almost hit Graham in the head when she bent down. "Whoa, that was close," she said, tossing back her auburn curls. "No, Graham, just having breakfast with my old fellow Webb Warrior. I thought you had court this morning."

Graham rubbed his hands together as their order arrived. "Yeah, I'm about to waste three hours sitting in there. See you two around. I'm going to take mine and sit over in the corner with the deputies. Thanks for the breakfast, Buck."

"You're welcome. Enjoy having your DWI cases continued."

Buck looked at Katie. She looked younger in the morning light coming in through the glass windows facing Main Street as she sipped her coffee. She smiled at him, but then turned serious.

"The latent analysis is due back today. Also, the forensics team has worked around the clock on the electronic devices. I should get that report soon." She bit into the breakfast sandwich with relish.

"Getting the electronics from Mrs. O'Shea should have been a blast. Did she say much about the search warrant?"

"She was pretty rude the first few minutes. She was 'outraged,' 'insulted,' and 'targeted by the police.' Fortunately for us, she managed to get her attorney on the line and things got better after that. We picked up a couple of phones, computers, and one camera, all listed on the search warrant return we filed with the clerk. Her attorney called us a couple of times trying to get her computer back, but I think he's just going through the motions for her."

"Can you call me or Judge Foster if you find anything about Jennifer? She'll feel less shame if you can confirm there's nothing on there about her."

Katie looked at her coffee for a minute. "Yeah, I can do that, but look, based on my experience, she really needs some mental health support. It must've been really hard for her to hold all this in while she had to see O'Shea day in and day out. Most adult rapes are not reported. I've met with a lot of victims, and many say when they do report it, they feel they are the ones under the microscope. Their lives and their choices are scrutinized."

"Thanks, she'll appreciate whatever you can tell her. I'll call her attorney and mention the counseling suggestion," Buck said. "Where's Johnson been?"

Katie laughed. "He caught a case down in the south end of the county. A huge marijuana grow on the Bumpass farm, not too far from 85. He came into the office last night reeking of the stuff. He hates strong smells of any kind: perfume, smoke, air freshener. He was gagging behind his makeshift mask. To make it worse, Johnson had to fight off three mean pit bulls who chased the guys around until somebody got smart and got their taser out. He looked like he'd gotten caught in a thresher. It was a last-minute tip, so he only had on his Gucci loafers and sports jacket with a sheriff's vest over it. He was so mad. Said he was putting in a claim for his clothes."

"I bet he was pissed. He loves those Italian loafers."

They both looked up as the store's bell, strung on some old Christmas garland, tinkled. Sally came in with her briefcase and legal pad. She looked around the drugstore and then waved to Buck and Katie. Picking up her coffee, she came over and slid into the empty chair.

"Hey, guys, how's it going today? You solve the O'Shea murder yet, lieutenant?" Sally asked.

"No. We're still working on it, but we should get some FBI agents assigned to help us out today. I'm going to meet with them over in Raleigh this afternoon," Katie replied. "How's your court looking today? Oh wait, didn't Graham say you weren't assigned to it?"

"Not too bad. Yeah, he'll be surprised to find out I switched with another ADA so I didn't have to do juvenile court, which I hate. I hope to try Trooper Graham's DWI cases, but we'll see what the judge will let me do. No luck the last two times they were set. Hey, Katie, I plan to calendar the Williamson murder case and the Hancock murder case for superior court soon but wanted to make sure you were free to testify. When should I set those two?"

"Let me look at my calendar and I'll give you a call. Is the autopsy report and the ballistics report back in those yet?"

"I got those early in the week and turned them over to the other side." Sally got up and grabbed her coffee. "Just call or text me what month we can schedule Williamson for trial first. His lawyer calls or emails me once a week." She did a little finger wave on her way out.

Buck turned to Katie and said, "You've got a full plate with all of the state stuff and the murder cases. You've got to love your job to keep up this grueling pace. I don't think I heard. How'd you get started in law enforcement? I thought that you were headed to law school?"

"I was headed to law school but took a couple of basic law enforcement classes the summer of my junior year at Vance-Granville Community College and wanted to take more. So, I applied with the sheriff when I graduated. After I got through the first few months of 'girl jokes,' the guys I worked with treated me just like one of them. I made lieutenant a couple of years ago. I'm not ready for desk duty yet, and I like working all sorts of cases, especially murder cases. I worked primarily robberies and shootings for the FBI for a couple years. When the US Marshal decided to deputize me and Johnson for this case, I was thrilled. I really hope the reports are back today so we can move ahead."

"I know everyone at the court wants closure quickly. I'll try to tell them methodical police work takes time but gets the results—as well my criminal clients know," Buck said.

Katie laughed.

He stood and took her purse from her chair, then gave her a hand to rise.

"I really enjoyed this morning. I hope you'll let me take you out to the Oak Room one night soon, or maybe somewhere over in Raleigh?" Buck asked.

"I'd love to go out to dinner. I'll call you this afternoon with any forensic results I can share, and we can talk about it. Is that okay?"

Buck watched her walk out through the drug store's dust-streaked door. The little bell tinkled merrily.

* * *

Buck went by the house to pick up some of O'Shea's files he had forgotten to return to the court. Jeb appeared in the kitchen.

"Heard you had a date with Katie this morning. I think Mom's reserving the Episcopal church for this summer. She said something about color schemes and registering for china at Ace Hardware."

"Where the hell did you hear that? For God's sake, it was not a date, date. We're seeing each other on O'Shea's murder case, and I enjoy her company. How can you know I met her? I left her two minutes ago!"

"I have my ways," smiled Jeb. "And you better watch yours, or Mom will have you measured for a tux before you know it. I like a blue tie, to go with my eyes, when you start looking. Oh, and I know a fierce wedding planner."

"Right, you idiot. That's at the top of my list, accenting your baby blues. This is ridiculous. A man can't have a civilized conversation with a female without someone playing wedding bells. I'm getting out of here."

He slammed the door to Jeb's laughter and Charles's excited barking at this new game.

By the time Buck arrived at the federal courthouse, his mood was restored listening to classic Stones, featuring Chuck

Leavell's keyboards. Relishing the spring air with his windows rolled down, he hadn't stressed at the tractor blocking part of the road near Creedmoor.

His cell phone rang, playing the "Free Bird" guitar riff. Telling Judge Foster he was on his way, he cut off a couple of cars and slid into the small court parking lot barely waiting for the electronic arm to go up. Fast food wrappers drifted by like tumbleweeds as he picked up his briefcase from the passenger's side of the car. When he arrived in the conference room to meet with the judge, Judge Evans and two others were already seated. Judge Evans stood by the window. No one was talking.

"Buck, I'd like you to meet Agents David and Thompson with the FBI. These agents have been assigned to investigate Judge O'Shea's case and will be heading it up with Lt. O'Connor. Do I have that right, gentlemen?" Judge Foster asked.

Buck reached over the table to shake each man's hand. Both appeared young, with Agent David being slightly taller, thinner, and blonder than Thompson.

"Actually, Your Honor, O'Conner and Johnson will be reporting to us, now that we've been called in on it," Agent David said. "We just wanted to meet you both and to let you know we'd be in the courthouse for the next several days reinterviewing court staff. We'll need a place to work. This conference room is perfect, assuming it is wired for internet."

"Yes, it's wired, but don't you think the FBI office nearby in Cary would be more convenient for you?" Judge Foster inquired. "Our law clerks tend to use the room during the day to pull various law review articles and organize their larger case projects. Also, Judge Evans and I both hold scheduling conferences in here with attorneys instead of in my office or in hers because it has recording equipment."

Agent David stared at him with light blue eyes. "We'll only be here a couple of days. The director wants us on site." He shot his cuffs, then inspected a microscopic piece of lint on his blue blazer. "Do I need to have the director call you, sir?"

Judge Evans interrupted. "I think what Judge Foster is trying to say to you is that it is disruptive to court business to have law enforcement in the judicial quarters. Regardless of what happened to Judge O'Shea, we have an obligation to the litigants and to their attorneys to dispense justice in a timely manner. We need to use the conference room. You'll have to find somewhere else to work. I think there's an empty office in the building on the second floor near the snack bar. Maybe GSA can show you the space, and you can determine if it will meet your needs."

"I'll take you down to GSA," Buck said, standing up. "Their employees run the federal buildings—maintenance, air, heat, all of that. Be glad to give you a hand with your bags there."

"Thanks, I appreciate it," Agent Thompson said.

Agent David took his time getting to his feet. Ignoring Judge Evans, he turned to Judge Foster. "I'll need to reinterview everyone. Give me a directory and I will arrange the times myself."

"Buck, can you grab the staff directory off my credenza on the way down? Agent David, I appreciate the FBI's involvement. Let me know if you have trouble reaching anyone. Oh, I almost forgot. Judge O'Shea's law clerk, Jennifer, is still under doctor's care, so she is not available for an interview just yet," Judge Foster said.

"That's nonnegotiable. I have to talk to her. But I'll save her interview for last.

We'll run through the courthouse list first. Come on, Thompson, let's move."

Buck and the agents, laden with multiple black bags emblazoned with the FBI logo, headed out the conference room door and straight into Detective Johnson.

"Did I miss the party? Where you guys headed?" Johnson asked.

Looking at Agent David's set grimace, Johnson said, "I told you the judge wouldn't want you two in his chambers. That's his space."

Agent David said, "No, Johnson, he didn't. Why don't you give us a hand here?"

Johnson took a couple of the black bags, shouldering them like they were empty. "Okay, gentlemen. Where are we headed? The basement or the storage room on two?"

Agent David stared stonily ahead. Agent Thompson said, "We're headed to two."

Clem, from GSA, met the unlikely entourage at the second-floor elevators. Original to the Lyndon Baines Johnson style federal building, Clem was perennially "near" retirement. Stricken with osteoporosis during Bush I's administration, he refused to slow down. He reported every weekday morning at 6:30 a.m. without fail. Over the years, he'd kept the ugly, eight-floor box-like building from total collapse.

Clem turned sideways to look up at Buck. "How you boys doing today, Buck? Detective Johnson? Shame about y'all losing Wake's football coach, isn't it?" He raised white shaggy eyebrows at the FBI agents to see if they were listening.

Before Buck could respond, Agent David bristled and cleared his throat. His outstretched hand was ignored by Clem who said, "Yep, Wake needs to get on their recruiting if they ever hope to have a chance at beating Carolina in football."

"You're right. I hear we're getting a couple of big guys from down east. They're from Wilson and Rocky Mount and should give us some size. Our line's too small now," said Buck.

Trying to keep up with Clem's deceptively quick strides down the long hall, Agent David said, "Hem, well then, I'm Agent David, and this is Agent Thompson. We're with the FBI." Thompson gave Clem a weak smile.

Clem silently scrutinized the two, moving his chewing tobacco to the other side of his mouth. He hoiked part of it into the trash can beside the elevator.

"Well, that's alright then. It's time the FBI returned to this building. All of you skedaddled in, oh let's see, was that during Mr. Clinton's time? It was, wasn't it, Buck?"

"You're absolutely right Mr. Clem. You've got a great memory."

Clem smiled with an almost full set of teeth. "Thanks Buck. I try to keep sharp with those number and word games, Soodykoo or something like that."

Turning to the agents, Clem said, "Now then, boys, don't treat this space like the old FBI did when they moved out. Keep it clean and put the trash outside in the hall each day. One of my crew will come by to pick it up."

Clem opened the door. As it creaked back on its hinges, Agent David made a strangled sound. The space had a couple of tables and chairs and two grimy windows facing New Bern Avenue that let in weak light. Dust motes danced in the air.

Agent David drew himself up to his full height and said, "You can't be serious. This is a pigsty. We're going to need this cleaned up before we even can set up our computers."

Clem spit into the old Dixie cup he kept handy and mopped his face with a white rag. He turned to peer up at Agent David.

"Okay, boy," he said. Crumpling up the rag, he handed it over to David.

"You've got to be joking, old man," David backed away with his hands up. "Can't you get some of the staff in here to do the cleaning? How in the hell can we work in these primitive conditions? We'll never get a damn thing done at this rate. This is a shithole."

Buck thought David sounded like a spoiled kid, not a seasoned FBI field agent. His disgust would have been funny if he wasn't hurting Clem's feelings.

Clem put the rag back into his pocket. He stared at the agent. Slowly, Clem straightened up as much as his twisted back allowed and put his finger in the middle of David's chest.

"Let me tell you something. If you want to use the space, I'll bring you some cleaning supplies, but you do not bother my staff. They're here to clean up for the tenants in this courthouse, especially for the judges' and clerk of court's staff. As long as we understand one another, I'll fetch some things for you."

Clem patted Buck on the arm as he walked slowly back down the hall to the janitorial closet. Detective Johnson put down the two black FBI bags. He said to David, "I've known drill sergeants with better manners. You really showed your ass. I wouldn't want to be you two right now."

"What the hell does that mean, Johnson?" David barked as he put his bags on the nearest chair after wiping it off with a paper towel roll abandoned on the nearest table.

"Do you have keys to this space? Did you ask Clem about the internet?" asked Johnson.

"No, I don't have any keys. Crap. I'll just go find the old guy and apologize for any misunderstanding. We've wasted half the day already. We need to get set up in here and get going on this case."

"Good luck with that," Buck said. "No one in the building knows exactly where Clem's office is or what his work hours are. You better try phoning the main GSA number first." He handed over the courthouse directory to David and then turned to Johnson.

"Come on, Johnson. I need you to help me carry boxes of O'Shea's files to storage."

"I don't work for you, Buck."

"I'll buy you lunch at Big Ted's at City Market as long as you don't order more than one lunch plate. C'mon, you love that place. Biscuits, chicken, butter beans, fried okra, squash—"

"You're on, but I get dessert too."

Buck and Johnson left the agents mournfully trying to find some bars for internet reception.

* * *

They'd just ordered the daily specials with double biscuits when Katie came into the restaurant. Spotting the two, she threaded her way through wooden tables covered by red and white checked cloths to their table in the corner. The decorating theme was country farmer, with a lot of sharp farm implements dangling overhead, but many of the area's top politicians came in for breakfast or lunch when in the capital city. Yellow sunflowers in clear glass vases brightened up the dining area.

"Hey, Katie, I thought you were finishing up with the reports." Buck stood up and pulled her chair out for her. He could have sworn she blushed.

"Yes, I was. I skimmed the main ones and made copies for the FBI agents because one of them called earlier squawking about getting them pronto. You met the agents yet?"

"You bet. Those two acted like the IQ average in the room slid into low double digits when Johnson and I showed up. The worst thing they did was insult Clem."

"Uh-oh. Their days in the courthouse are numbered. I think the last person to mouth off to Clem was one of the capital police officers. That guy got bounced back to bicycle duty. They wouldn't let him apply for horse patrol until a year later."

"Yeah," Johnson said, "the last tenant to insult Clem was there during the Bush son's administration. Because of that, the tenant's space was all but condemned. No garbage service. No running water. Sporadic mail service. Was that Homeland Security? Or whatever they call themselves these days."

"No," said Buck, "that was the one-term senator who had her token office space in the building. One of the electrical sockets shorted out not long after she moved in and nearly burned down the left corner of the building. Tough to get the GSA to come in after that. Johnson, you're thinking of the small agency that got into trouble for bringing prostitutes in after office hours. What was that?"

Johnson didn't answer. He was mesmerized by the heaping plate of food being set down in front of him: cornbread, barbeque pork, lima beans, black-eyed peas, and mashed potatoes. Buck's plate was heaped just as high with fried chicken, mashed potatoes, and greens.

Katie told the waitress she wanted what he was having. She broke open a biscuit, and the butter oozed out. Wiping her hand with a napkin, Katie said, "There were some disturbing images on O'Shea's computers and phone. I'll bring y'all up to speed at the same time I meet with the agents and judges. Judge Foster said it'd be okay to meet in his conference room at 2:00 p.m. since he doesn't have afternoon court. Can y'all get the agents to the right place?"

"You're thinking child pornography? No way. Well, damn. Anything that helps us with the investigation into his murder?" Johnson asked.

"I'm still trying to figure it out. The lab techs are sorting out the photos into those with identical backgrounds. I want to tell everybody some of what we've found so they can be prepared for it and for the media blitz when the media gets hold of it."

"You going to turn the case over to the FBI now? I'm not sure those guys can change a light bulb, but maybe they're good at investigating."

"It's up to the Sheriff. I've not reviewed the reports with him yet. I know, Johnson, you've got the marijuana grow case back home now and a couple other drug cases. I'm pretty clear until the Hancock murder trial, but this case is frustrating. There haven't been any clear leads until now, and they're still only a maybe."

Johnson had cleared half his plate and was looking for the waitress. "Wait a minute, Johnson," Buck said, "why do you need the waitress? I'm only buying you one lunch."

"I know it. I need to order dessert before they run out of something. I'm trying to decide between the banana pudding and the strawberry shortcake."

Katie smiled at Buck when Johnson got up to find the waitress to put in his dessert order. "I'm free later this week, Buck, if you still want to go out to dinner."

"I'd like that. Is it easier for you to go out in Raleigh or at home?"

"Probably home if you don't mind. I try to brief the Sheriff at the end of most days, and I also have to check my desk for anything that's come in on any of my other cases."

"No, that's great. Friday night work for you?"

"That's perfect."

Johnson came back to the table with a plate of chocolate cake in his left hand and a bowl of banana pudding in his right. "Now that's a nice waitress. She said they ran out of the shortcake, so I could have both of these for the price of one. Since you're paying, Buck, I thought you'd appreciate the deal. She'll be right over to add it to your tab."

"Thanks, Johnson. I appreciate the way you spend my money."

"I'm going on back to run the report copies. See you at the meeting," Katie said, pushing back from the table.

Johnson, with his mouth full of cake, waved goodbye without looking up.

"We'll see you there if Johnson ever quits eating."

Johnson wrapped up the last two biscuits in a paper napkin. "Come on, Buck. These will be great on the long drive home tonight."

Buck stood in line to pay the clerk at the ancient cash register. The old manual showed the final amount in numbers that popped up through the glass at the top. Toothpicks were prominently displayed beside it. Ancient advertisements for auto repair and grass mowing taped to the counter fluttered in the breeze from the open door.

CHAPTER TWELVE

gents David and Thompson were the last to arrive for the 2:00 meeting. Looking tense, they quietly slid into the burgundy leather seats. Judge Foster nodded to Lt. O'Connor to begin.

"Thank you, Judge Foster, for getting us get together. I've appreciated the court's cooperation in this case. The court has accommodated us in their space, and we've met with the clerk's staff too. I'll provide the group here with some general information that still needs to remain within these walls. I'll only be sharing sensitive information with the FBI and other law enforcement to protect the integrity of the investigation."

"Understood, Lieutenant. What can you tell us?" Judge Foster asked. In addition to him, O'Connor, and the two agents, Judge Evans and Buck sat at the old mahogany table.

"There was nothing of obvious evidentiary value, that we could see, on the computer belonging to Mrs. O'Shea. However, there were some deleted files dated shortly before Judge O'Shea's death. So, we'll need further forensic review to retrieve those files and examine them. There were some pretty scalding emails sent by Mrs. O'Shea to the judge. We've assigned Det. Johnson to further review these. But, at first glance, they appear to be of a domestic nature. By that,

I mean arguments about dividing up the marital estate. After Johnson's review, he'll interview Mrs. O'Shea."

"I've had a lot of domestic cases get pretty ugly," Buck said interrupting. "It didn't matter what the folks fought about, just as long as they could bicker about it. Even the 'nicest' people turn savage in these cases. My worst case was the stalemate over the disposition of a china cat. Finally, I went to Walmart during a lunch break and bought a replica so we could finish up the mediation and go home. Do you think their arguments went beyond verbal? Any physical threats?"

O'Connor shook her head. "I don't know at this point. Johnson will work with forensics on the missing files and on the hundreds of emails. He'll report back to me before confronting Mrs. O'Shea."

"For God's sake, I think we should get the computer back from the Crime Lab and look at it ourselves," Agent David whined. "Both Thompson and I have had forensic computer training. You're spending a lot of time on nothing."

"Johnson has already started the review, but we can move him to your space. Are you set up for internet?"

"No, goddamnit," David shouted. "I can't find anyone from GSA. I've tried the main number over and over. I can't find anyone in the hall that works for GSA. I've no idea how to get on the wireless or if there is a wireless network in this seventies monolith."

"Okay, then," Katie nodded, "I'll give you Johnson's cell number before I go, and you can call him when you are up and running."

Agent David glared at Buck. "Buck, how about getting your friend back to help us out?"

"I'll be glad to try him." Buck knew if Clem did not want to be found, no one could find him unless they stood at the front door at 6:30 a.m.

"As for the other electronic devices, I've turned the camera over to a forensic expert at the SBI, which is now the North

Carolina State Crime Laboratory," Katie continued. "All I can tell you about it is that there were some troubling images on the camera. I've put in a rush request. It still will take about forty-eight hours."

"We'll need to see it ourselves," sniped Agent David.

"Absolutely. When the SBI is finished, they'll let you know. I gave them your contact information."

Judge Foster interrupted. "I don't understand. What're these troubling images?"

"Sir, I'll explain what I can, but what I cannot explain, due to the sensitive nature of the investigation, I'll need to discuss solely with law enforcement. I don't want to compromise the case. I hope that you understand."

"Yes, but I find all of this very frustrating. I don't want to hinder you, or the investigation, but I'm concerned for the court family and what this might mean."

"Right, sir. I'll try to be less cryptic. Some images on the camera have the courthouse office space as background. The persons in the photos are not fully clothed. I don't want to jump to conclusions..." Katie's expression turned grim, "... but it's possible the photographs are of adolescent children. My concern is that the children in the photos are not over sixteen. In fact, some look quite young."

"You mean child pornography? You found child pornography on Judge O'Shea's camera? Oh, my God. I can't believe it. This is a disaster!"

"No, sir, I'm not saying that. I need a forensic examiner and a medical expert to look at the images to help determine if the persons featured in the photos are over sixteen. Even if they are, what were they doing in the court's office space? Who brought them here and photographed them? And, for what purpose?"

Judge Evans said, "How horrible there are any images of any child or young adult taken in the courthouse. Have you identified any of the people in the photographs?"

"Your Honor, I'm not able to answer that question now as it is the crux of this part of the investigation," Katie said. "If I may, I'll move on to the other items. The cell phones and the computers I've mentioned all have been turned over to the SBI and one went to Quantico. What this means is the forensic examiner did a brief look, and having located something that may have evidentiary value, he cut the phone or the computer off and sealed it up for delivery to the lab."

"Did these get a rush too?" Judge Evans asked.

"Yes. Each item collected had a corresponding rush request submitted to the lab. The forensic examiners know to contact Agent David directly once the exam is complete. I must caution you—there also were financial irregularities that appeared on the computer for Judge O'Shea's accounts. Is there any special court account over which he had control?" she asked as she turned to Judge Foster.

"No, none of us had a separate account under our sole control. Judge Evans, can you think of any reason for Judge O'Shea to have any such account?"

"No, I can't think of any situation," Judge Evans replied. "Money related to a judgment in a case is handled through the clerk's office, not through the judge's office. Maybe the accounts were all personal accounts?"

"I can call a forensic accountant who can try to straighten all of this out. There were large sums going in and out of the accounts I saw on bank statements dated not long before his death. Judge Foster, can I get the information for his monthly check so that I can strike that off as a regular payment, or the paying agency?"

"Certainly," Judge Foster said. "I'll get that to you later this afternoon. Do you want an email with the information or hard copy?"

"A hard copy is fine."

Judge Evans momentarily covered her face with her hands before she turned back to the Lieutenant. "I can assure you the deposit will not be a large sum of money. No one becomes a judge for the salary. It can be a lonely vocation too. Since we must remain impartial and appear to be impartial in all things, there aren't a lot of people who most judges feel comfortable associating with regularly."

Glancing at her watch, she said, "I'm sorry, but I need to use the conference room for a meeting with the attorneys in Judge O'Shea's 1983 case. Thank you for updating us on your progress, Lieutenant O'Connor. Judge Foster and I look forward to hearing from you when you can share the details with us."

Katie and the rest stood. She said, "Thank you for giving us some time to meet. I will let you know what we have on the devices. I need to notify the Administrative Office of the Courts about the accounts too."

After the law enforcement officers left, Judge Evans said to Buck, "Can you get Philip and the file with Judge O'Shea's notes on the 1983 violation of civil rights case? I'd like for you two to sit in on the conference instead of my law clerk since y'all are more familiar with it. Is that okay with you?"

"Absolutely, Your Honor. I'll grab Philip and the judge's file of notes."

Buck left to find Philip who'd been scarce these past few days. Buck found him in his office where, seeing Buck standing in his doorway, he hastily put down his office phone.

"What's going on?" Phillip asked.

"Judge Evans is going to meet with the attorneys in the 1983 case and wants us to sit in with her. Do you have Judge O'Shea's file?" He looked at Phillip's desk and floor which were littered with files, legal pads, and case reporters.

"Yeah, yeah, I got it here somewhere. Am I supposed to talk at the meeting?" Phillip asked as he stood up and rifled through the files on his desk. A couple of empty coffee cups fell off the desk and onto the floor. His blue button down was rumpled and his tie was missing. If possible, he looked thinner than Buck remembered.

"No, I don't think so. I think Judge Evans just wants to have us there to take notes and to make sure we bring the clerk's file and Judge O'Shea's note file. Hey, man, are you feeling okay? You look a little tired."

Philip gave him a slight smile, then a bigger one as he unearthed the file Judge Evans needed. "Yeah, I'm okay. I just miss Jennifer, and it's a bit lonely back here. I'm trying to get the files in some kind of order."

"Look, let me know if you need help. I just took down a bunch of files to storage, and I have some time. I can help you sort through them if you want my help."

"No, really. I'm fine. I'll feel better when I find out if Judge Evans or Judge Foster will take me on for the rest of my clerkship. I don't have much more time to serve, but I just started interviewing for a job when all this happened. I need to find out if the court can keep me on until I find something else."

Looking at Philip's wall of diplomas, he said, "You shouldn't have a bit of trouble finding something you like. Davidson College, *magna cum laude*, Duke Law School…"

"I don't know. There's a lot of competition out there for associates' positions in the big or even medium-sized Raleigh firms. But Judge Evans and Judge Foster said they'd write a letter of recommendation, so I have that going for me." He shrugged into his jacket hanging on the back of his chair and looked only slightly less wrinkled. He felt around for his tie on his desk, but then found it laying on the floor under the largest pile of files.

Phillip and Buck walked back to the reception area outside of chambers and the conference room to wait on the parties' attorneys. They did not have long to wait. Loud raised voices down the hall preceded the group of attorneys, all dressed in dark suits and white shirts. Three of the four men sported red ties, and the fourth a blue tie, in the tradition of Al Gore. Each was swinging an expensive-looking briefcase.

Out of their hearing, Buck said, "Uh-oh."

"What?"

Buck looked down at the afternoon calendar in his hands before he replied. "I forgot all counsel was from New York," he said under his breath. Buck extended his hand to the attorney who made it to them one-half step ahead of the others.

"Gentlemen, I'm Buck Davis and this is Judge O'Shea's clerk, Phillip. We're here to take you to the conference room, behind the security door, where Judge Evans is waiting for you. Before we go in though, does anyone have any questions about the general procedure this afternoon?"

Not wanting to be outdone by the attorney shaking hands first, the second attorney said, "Yeah. How much of the case is Judge Evans going to get into? Will he hear the motions this afternoon? My client is after me to move this case along."

"Judge Evans will talk to you all about the legal issues and *her* plan going forward. You are on this afternoon's calendar for motions. It will be up to Judge Evans as to how you proceed today."

Attorney two winced at the female pronoun and glared at his companion as if his associate had made the blunder.

Attorneys one and four, working together, smirked. "Thanks, Buck," attorney one said, smiling at attorneys two and three in obvious triumph.

Buck punched in the security code and ushered all four into the inner reception area. "If you gentlemen will wait here for a moment, I'll let Judge Evans know you have arrived and are ready for the conference. May I get anyone a bottle of water?"

All four said "yes" at the same time. *Probably their only agreement today.*

"I'll get the attorneys the water if you'll let Judge Evans know the parties are ready," Phillip said.

During the meeting in the conference room, Buck sat in a conference chair in the corner of the room. He watched the attorneys and team two's local counsel closely. The arguing ebbed and flowed monotonously. *It's going to be a long afternoon, especially if these attorneys keep trying to one-up the other, and over nothing.*

Judge Evans interrupted his thoughts and the four attorneys bickering amongst themselves.

"Gentlemen," she said, "what I want from each of you is a proposed scheduling order for remaining motions, a preliminary conference date, and agreed-upon trial dates within ten days from today if the Court does not grant the plaintiff's motion for summary judgment today. We've already spent thirty minutes in here and have made little progress. Additionally, someone in this case has tried to have unpermitted contact with Judge O'Shea. The Court regards those communications as threatening. You'll be provided a copy of the correspondence but should not share it with anyone else. Please advise your clients and any witnesses any *ex parte* communications with the Court are not permitted and threatening communications will be dealt with by a member of the FBI. Further, to safeguard the integrity of the proceedings, each of you will be contacted by the FBI in the New York district office. I expect each of you to cooperate fully with those agents."

After a moment of stunned silence, attorney one began to try to deny his client's involvement and to ingratiate himself with the judge.

"Really, counsel," Judge Evans said. "I've heard enough. I'll see you in the courtroom in twenty minutes to hear you on the pending motions. Thank you."

All the attorneys rose in a swish of Armani fabric as Judge Evans left the conference room. One rushed to open the door for her, but he quickly stepped aside when she eyed him and reached for the brass knob herself.

Buck said, "Okay, gentlemen. Phillip will take you to the courtroom, which should be open now. Just a reminder: When Judge Evans says ten days, she means it should be in before the clerk's office closes on the tenth day, not at midnight." Subdued, the four attorneys followed Phillip out into the hall and across to the main courtroom.

A few minutes later, Buck headed to the courtroom. He looked for an empty chair in the back. It took a minute to find a comfortable position in the hard cracked leather chair. The judge had just taken the bench, and only the rustling of papers could be heard.

The Court addressed the plaintiff's side, the one suing under the 1983 act, first. "Counsel, I'd like to hear why you think your client is entitled to summary judgment."

"Thank you, Your Honor," attorney one said. "We contend there is no dispute on the facts in this case and my client is entitled to prevail as a matter of law. We believe the other side deprived my client of his rights and privileges under the Constitution. We believe we have easily met our burden of proof in this case."

Before he could continue, attorney two jumped up. "Your Honor, may we be heard?"

Judge Evans looked at him over her half glasses. "No, counsel, you may be heard at the end of the plaintiff's presentation. Also, please instruct your client's family members to not whisper in the courtroom. It's very distracting. They can go outside to have a conversation."

Attorney for the plaintiff continued. "Your Honor has read the briefs and affidavits, so I will not belabor the arguments in them. I do want to point out the officer abused my client and when that wasn't enough, violated his Constitutional rights. After conducting depositions, parts of which we have attached to our motions, there is no dispute as to what transpired. Based on that, we are entitled to judgment in our favor."

"Thank you, counsel," Judge Evans said. "I have read the briefs by both parties. Each was well-done and I commend counsel for that. Now, I will hear from counsel for the defendants in the order they are named in the case caption."

"Thank you, Your Honor," counsel began.

Suddenly, a large heavy-set man seated on the front row behind the defendant's side started cussing in a loud whisper, "This is bullshit." He stood up and started to enter the area with counsel tables in front of the bench. The court security officer lunged toward him and missed his arm. Agitated, the man kept moving forward, so the guard tackled him. The man struggled, thrashing on the ground. The other security officer hustled Judge Evans off the bench and out of the courtroom. Buck started out of his seat to help the guard when Agent Thompson ran in from the back and jumped on top of the man. After a half-hearted struggle, the man, sweating profusely, was cuffed and taken to a holding cell off the side entrance to the courtroom.

A few minutes later, Judge Evans reentered the courtroom. She icily eyed the litigants. "Counsel for the plaintiff, please begin again. Counsel for the defense, we will have a contempt hearing for your client after the hearing on your motion."

Buck left the courtroom to check on the agent and to let him know the man would need to be brought back for the contempt hearing.

He found Agent Thompson in the hall at the water fountain wiping his face. Thompson's shirt was out, and there were scratches on his right arm where his sleeve had ridden up. His blazer and tie were in a crumpled heap on the floor.

The guy in the holding cell was screaming obscenities that could be heard in the hall. After a few seconds of silence, repetitive banging and chanting started.

"Good work, Thompson. That was a mean half Nelson you put on him. Glad you were in the courtroom. What's up with that guy anyway?"

"I have no idea, but I'm getting ready to find out. Agent David is on his way up. We're going to ask him if he was the one sending those threats to Judge O'Shea. He's big enough and strong enough to have killed the judge. He's also one mean son of a bitch. Runs in the family. His brother went after one of the security officers in the hallway. A couple of other officers saw the ruckus on the security cameras and ran up."

After shrugging back into his blazer, he added, "It's going to be hard to interview him. He's screaming that he doesn't recognize the federal government and that he's his own sovereign nation. I'm not going to say what he yelled about Judge Evans and the court case."

The two looked up when Phillip came down the hall. Phillip looked stressed.

"How did the rest of the hearing go? Did Judge Evans grant the plaintiff summary judgment?" Buck asked.

"It was a train wreck. The attorneys were so focused on their upcoming date with the FBI that they had a hard time organizing the rest of their arguments. The judge was not happy. Each side would stop and start. Then the other side would interrupt. Right before the judge cut them off, one of the clients sitting at counsel table got agitated. The lawyer's face turned purple as he whisper-yelled at his guy to shut up."

"Is Judge Evans really upset? About the lawyers or the guy who lost it? The security guys and Thompson did a good job shutting it down. Lockup is pretty full."

"Yes, she's livid. She was shaking when she left the bench this time. She's mad at the lawyers' lack of professionalism and the family members acting like they were raised in a zoo. I better get started on her research. Fortunately, I did some on the same issue in another case for Judge O'Shea, so it shouldn't take me too long. I just wanted to let Agent Thompson know she'll expect that guy in the courtroom at 4:00 p.m. for a contempt hearing."

"Okay. Agent David and I will come assist. I'm not sure he's going to stay quiet though. I better get with the defendant's attorney and see if he can talk some sense into him."

Buck turned to walk back to chambers with Phillip. "I'll go check in with Judge Evans's legal assistant and make sure the judge is okay. Got to be proud of Thompson getting in there and helping out. Who knew he had it in him?"

"Better him than Johnson. If he'd seen the guy talking to the judge that way, he'd have crushed him. He and the judge are old friends. I think they grew up together, or her sister grew up with him, one or the other," Phillip said.

"You're right. Johnson can really move when he wants to move. He was a starter for our local high school's football team. He's a force when set in motion."

While Buck was talking with Judge Evans's assistant, the judge came out from her office. "I'm okay. Thanks for asking about me though. You have a minute?"

"Sure. Do you want me to help with the contempt research?"

"No. I want to talk to you about Lt. O'Connor's announcement earlier today. I've been really worried. Do you think she found photos of Jennifer on the camera? Jennifer's attorney has been asking about the search warrant whenever he calls in to check if we are holding her job for her. Finding photographs of her on the judge's laptop would be horrible. She would be devastated."

"I don't know. I think Lt. O'Connor will say anything until after the forensic guys have done their part. While he was alive, did you notice O'Shea worked odd hours so he would be in the courthouse alone a lot?"

"I stayed pretty much to my side of the courthouse. Judge O'Shea and I did not have a lot to talk about. We had a civil relationship, but that was it. You know about him and Angela, right?"

"I heard he was the prosecutor on her rape case and did a terrible job. I remember you were a huge support for Angela. I also heard you tried to get the elected DA to change the prosecutor assignment but he wouldn't. So, you tried to help him out. You took notes every day during pretrial hearings and tried to hand them to O'Shea, and he refused to look at them. You gained a lot of people's respect for not giving up even when the case disintegrated."

"O'Shea was an asshole. Worse, he was an idiot. The court reporter could've done a better job prosecuting Angela's attacker than he did. My sister did not get justice that day, nor any day thereafter."

"I know, and I'm really sorry. How is she doing now?"

"She is back here for a visit. I don't know for how long. She still has nightmares but has found a counselor that she likes. I feel pretty helpless when she gets so low."

"Jeb said he knew Angela."

"Yes. I think they met during one of her stays in a treatment center. Angela thought your brother was very sweet."

"Jeb is a really good guy. I just wish *he* knew it. He's home now after working on some fruit farms down south. I miss him when he travels."

Judge Evans's clerk poked her head into the office. "Judge Evans, the bailiff wants to know if you're ready to start back in court."

"Tell him to give me about fifteen minutes," she said. "I've got to get with Phillip before we go back in for the last session."

"I'll call him and tell him you're ready to meet with him now," Buck said. Just after calling Phillip from the legal assistant's desk, his cell rang.

Katie's name lit up his screen. "Hey Buck, you by yourself?" Her voice was tense.

"Yes, I'm stepping out into the hall now. What's up?"

"I'm down here with Johnson in the FBI hole on second. The emails are pretty bad. He's found a few where Mrs.

O'Shea has threatened to kill the judge if he did not give her the house. But there's something else I need you to see. Can you come down?"

Buck texted Phillip he was going down to the FBI office. He took the narrow stairs at a run, too impatient to wait on the geriatric elevator, and passed Clem on the way down.

"Hey, Clem, how's it going?" he asked.

"Pretty good, pretty good. I'm on my way to see the heating and air guys. There's always something wrong with the dadburn system."

Buck waved back over his shoulder and hit the second-floor door harder than he meant to and rubbed his shoulder. Everyone in the room looked up.

Katie brushed her hair back from her flushed face. Johnson looked up, his face grim. "What's going on?"

"I've got to get a forensic accountant in here." Katie said. "There are some big withdrawals from the judge's account. I can see where his salary is being deposited, but I can't figure out where the other income is coming from and why so much went out right before he died. Could he have had a side business?"

"Not that I ever heard of, but you can ask Judge Foster. I thought the missus had all the cash."

Johnson said, "She sure didn't give him any those last several days, and they fought about it like cats. Her money was hers, and his money was hers. She emailed him from Paris and told him he was going to sign the goddamned separation papers or else. She refused to pay their mortgage."

Katie's shoulders were slumped as she hooked her leg over the side of an old wooden chair. Her long pants slid up to reveal socks with multi-colored polka dots. "I'm worried about what else we're going to find on the electronics. Some of those pictures had some pretty young-looking kids. I'm going to have to hire a physician to look at some of them or consult with the SBI. Just one more thing to look into, and I don't know how much this helps get us closer to finding his killer. What the hell was going on in his life?"

"Have you called over to the lab this afternoon?" Buck asked.

"Yeah. It's going to take two days or twenty days, depending on the analyst that picks up the phone. We're getting nowhere."

Johnson said, "Come on, LT. We still have Mrs. O'Shea to interview again, and the lab will come through."

"You have another suspect in lockup," Buck chimed in. "One of the clients in the 1983 case had a meltdown in court. The FBI is going to try to interview him and his family to see if they sent the threatening letters to Judge O'Shea. The average height in that guy's whole family is six-foot-three and weight is 250. Thompson thinks the guy could have hung O'Shea up by himself pretty easily if he was as mad as he was in court today."

Chapter Thirteen

Katie scanned the Oak Room for Buck. She'd told him she'd meet him there to give herself a chance to change, maybe even dress up. Slipping on her nicest pair of pants and the one shirt she had that showed a bit of cleavage, Katie felt almost pretty. She'd even curled her hair.

Buck stood up from the back corner booth and waved. He had changed into dress pants and a new shirt. He bobbled the water jug as he stepped aside to let her into the booth. "Whoops," he said.

Katie laughed. "What happened to the famous hands that made dribbling an art at Webb High School?"

"They are a lot slower, but still have some magic."

Katie blushed and picked up the menu.

"What's the special tonight?"

Buck craned his head to look at the blackboard located behind the Petron and Fireball signs.

"Looks like the ribeye with collards and mashed potatoes. Jeb and I had that last week. It was pretty good. The collards were cooked down to not much. I think we got the last servings."

Wanda sauntered up and took the pencil from behind her ear. "What will you two have?" she asked, balancing her weight on one polyester-clad hip.

"Hey, Wanda," Buck said. "Where's your wine list?"

"Red or white?"

"Katie?"

Katie said, "I'd like to look at your list of red wines."

Wanda studied her for a minute. "I mean red or white. That's the choice."

"Oh. Well, red then."

"I'll take a Stella," Buck said, but seeing Wanda frowning down at him made him follow up with, "Okay, then. I'll have a Miller."

Wanda scribbled something on her pad and strolled away. She hollered to the bartender, "One red, one champagne."

Katie said, "I didn't know they served champagne."

"No. She meant the Miller. You know, champagne of beers."

A few minutes later Wanda strolled up with the glass of red in one hand and a bottle of beer in the other. "Glass?" Wanda said to Buck.

"No, thanks."

Each ordered the special and tried to sort through topics of conversation that were not work and case related as Wanda screamed their orders back to the cook. Both turned in relief to the front door when it banged open.

"Oh, crap," they said in unison.

Tall and thin, the newcomer made sure all eyes were on her and her man. She wore stiletto heels and a skintight dress showing off every curve. He had on a bespoke suit and tooled cowboy boots. Sliding down in the booth, Katie and Buck hid behind their flimsy menus.

"Hi there, Buck. Long time no see," purred the blonde clamping her hand onto Buck's shoulder. The glint off the saucer-sized diamond nearly blinded Katie. Buck manfully tried to get to his feet.

"Aw, honey, don't stand up. Me and TJ were just coming in for a quick drink." Ignoring Katie, the platinum girl turned her head slightly to tell TJ to get a Stoli on the rocks for her. "How's Charles?" she asked.

"Charles is good. Jeb's home now, so I don't see much of him. He and Jeb are usually out tossing the ball or sticks in the yard. That Lab loves Jeb.

"Charlene, you remember Katie O'Connor don't you?"

Barely turning her head, she said, "Katie, you haven't changed a bit. Same old tomboy running around in pants and sensible shoes. Let's see, now. You're one of those women wrestlers, right?"

Katie did not trust herself to speak, so she sipped her wine. Or what passed for wine. The glass had smudges that were best not examined in the light.

Buck saw the look on her face and tried to pry Charlene from his shoulder. "Great to see you, Charlene, you and TJ, but I think our dinner's coming out now." Charlene smiled and twitched her hips as she walked over to TJ and the bar.

"Whoa!" Katie exploded.

"Sorry about that, but I owe TJ one. If he hadn't eloped with her on prom night, I'd be married to her. Thankfully, she saw a future with TJ playing in the bright lights of the NFL and decided that was far better than hitching her wagon to a college basketball player with a bum knee."

Wanda slid their plates onto the table. "Here ya go." Wanda paused. "Buck?"

"Yes, Wanda?"

She switched her unlit cigarette from one ear over to the other. "You're well shed of that one there." She tossed her head back in the direction of the bar. "This gal here, she seems nice. And, she has some manners." Wanda patted Katie on the hand and left.

* * *

Early the next morning, Detective Johnson nudged Buck in the shoulder. Buck jolted awake. He'd fallen asleep at Judge

O'Shea's desk. He glanced at the brass clock. He'd been out for over an hour.

"Buck, what the hell, man? You stay up all night? Better not have taken advantage of the Lieutenant, or—" The threat hung between them. Johnson stood close, almost snarling into his ear.

"No, Johnson. I did not sully one hair on her head. We just went out for a nice meal, by which I mean something edible I did not have to cook."

Johnson glared at him and then sat down in one of the red leather client chairs. He put one foot up on the desk until Buck frowned it down. "Heard the bitch is back."

"Yeah. Who'd you hear that from?"

"My younger sister sits Wanda's kids sometimes. What the hell are she and TJ doing in town?"

"I don't know, and I didn't ask. Hopefully they're leaving soon."

"I came up here to get you. We're going over to the North Carolina State Crime Lab. The forensics are back but the lab doesn't want to release the computers and electronic devices back to the sheriff's department. That's a bad sign."

"Well, damn. Can I go over there with you?"

"Okay, but LT said don't touch nothing and don't ask anybody anything. Hard for a lawyer, I know. But those are the orders."

Buck grabbed his coat and turned off the lights. He'd not gotten too far in the files today. Fortunately, it was the last stack to go through before turning them over to the clerk's office.

* * *

Johnson turned up the Gap Band as Buck winced at the thumping music. It all but drowned out the damaged muffler on Johnson's banged up sheriff's car.

"Johnson, your car is nowhere near legal. Why doesn't the sheriff fix it?"

He laughed. "The sheriff won't pay no undercover time-and-a-half, so I'm not worried about working undercover. Sometimes at dusk, I ease this baby down an old gravel road near town. I let the dope dealers hear I'm coming, so they scatter. Then, the DEA boys scoop 'em up out of the woods. They usually call in wildlife officers 'cause them drug boys hunt when they ain't selling drugs. Works like a charm every time."

"That's harsh, man. You should give those guys a fighting chance."

"Hell, no. Those guys deserve everything they get. They're out there poisoning our kids."

"You got a point."

Johnson wheeled the old car into the state crime lab's parking lot. Law enforcement had reserved spaces up front. Visitors parked a few blocks away. The lab was in a large stone building housing the state's drug labs, computer forensic labs, and DNA labs. Ballistics and latent prints were over in a temporary mobile home parked next door.

Katie met them inside at the reception desk. Agents David and Thompson were silently standing by. A brisk walk down the corridor and a right turn led them to a large utilitarian conference room. The plastic seats screeched as they were rolled out.

A young technician came in and asked if anyone wanted water. *This is going to be bad. No one here has ever offered me water.* Another tech came in and pushed a couple of buttons. The lights dimmed, and a screen dropped down. Agent David shot his cuffs while Agent Thompson rolled his chair down a few inches away from David. Johnson sat between Buck and Katie. He stretched out his neck and shoulder muscles, making sure Buck saw he still was in shape.

A few minutes later, a young woman walked into the room followed by an older man. After introducing themselves as computer forensic technicians, they explained the setup of the room. The young woman spoke, "Since you had so many people, we decided the screen was the best way to present what we've located. While we've not finished our review, we understand it's a murder investigation and you might need the information." The man stood up and pushed a few more buttons. Images began to fill the screen.

"Je-sus," Johnson said as an image of a very young male, partly clothed and standing next to a man that looked like O'Shea, appeared on the screen. There were video files as well.

Agent David sprang up as if scalded. "You need to turn that goddamned thing off right now. I'll take custody of the computer for the FBI. I appreciate your work, but this, but it needs to be kept under wraps. I mean, this is a federal judge we're talking about." His voice ended up a few octaves higher and a few decibels louder.

The tech, unperturbed, shook her head.

"I'm sorry, agent. But, these crimes, if that's what they are, happened here in our state, and I have been directed by the Attorney General not to release the computers. Not to you. Not to anyone. I've been instructed to provide you with a forensic copy and help you with locating any files on it, but the computers are not leaving the lab."

"We'll see about that," David said, grabbing all of the discs on the table and jamming them into his shoulder bag. I'll be back today with a warrant or a court order. Better have the Attorney General with you. Come on, Thompson, we're done here."

Thompson wished everyone a good day and followed an almost trotting David down the hallway back to reception.

Katie lifted up her arm where she'd salvaged a disc. "Sorry about that," she said. "Before he gets whatever he's going to get, can you walk us through the forensic review?"

Images of young boys and young girls flashed on the screen.

According to the tech, these pictures were on O'Shea's computer in an "erased" file. Efforts were being made to determine how and when the images were loaded and where they were taken. The Center for Missing and Exploited Children has been contacted to find out if any images or videos were of children who had already been reported as abused. Due to the number of images, a representative was flying in to perform their own review.

"So, you see why I cannot let the originals go," the tech said. "Also, you need to meet with a forensic accountant. We saw numerous bank and financial reports stored on your disc, but we don't have anyone available here for that type of work."

"Thanks so much for meeting with us. Do you want us to hang around until the FBI gets back? It might get a bit… uncomfortable," Katie said.

The tech stood. "No, thanks. The deputy Attorney General is on his way over from downtown. He loves a good screaming match. I texted him earlier to give him a heads up I thought the FBI would be back with a subpoena or court order. I could hardly get him off the phone he was so mad about the feds being on his turf. He's rounding up some of the State Bureau of Investigation agents. I'm just going to head out to lunch and take my time getting back."

Johnson, Buck, and Katie followed her out of the building and then stood out in the parking lot. The sun was shining through the branches of the dogwoods. The breeze was just low enough in humidity to feel good.

"Shame to miss this—" Buck started.

"No way," Katie said. "We're getting out of here. We'll head to the CPA's office tomorrow. I want to know who was paying whom and if our killer can be dug up out of these files. Johnson, drop Buck back off at the courthouse and meet me over at Margaret's in the morning."

Johnson snorted. "You still use that old lady? She's damn near a hundred."

"That 'old lady' caught the mayor using the town clerk's account as her personal shopping fund. She also sniffed out the deposits of the Front Street Boys gang at those local banks for most of their large drug sales, and we were able to seize all of it. She's a pistol, but nothing gets by her.

"I'm heading back to the office to pull off just the financials from the disc. I don't want her to stumble on those pictures. Those were god awful."

Katie climbed into a new silver Dodge Charger sporting the Granville County Sheriff's logo and sped away. Buck and Johnson walked to Johnson's car. "Let's burn rubber," Johnson said. Buck waded through the Bojangles wrappers on the floorboards and buckled his seat belt.

* * *

Buck opened the courthouse door at the front of the federal building. The demonstrators had moved on as it was well past lunch, so he had no problem getting into the building. Normally, it was like a rugby scrimmage. The demonstrators yelled at him hoping that he was the senator they despised. Then they yelled at him because he wasn't.

Depending on the day, the placards decried health care, social security, the military, and even animal rights for fish one day. The fish placards were the best because someone had hung the carcasses of a Spanish mackerel and a blue fish on sticks. The smell lingered for days.

He was looking forward to finishing up O'Shea's personal files and getting back to his law practice. He saw Phillip downstairs in the post office and waited to go up with him.

"How's it going? Getting your pile of files summarized for Judge Evans to take over the cases?" Buck asked.

"Yeah. I think I am getting close, but I have an interview with a law firm this afternoon, so I'm going to head out in a minute. That okay?"

"Sure thing. I might drive back to Oxford in a little while. The ADA called my office and wants me to try to dispose of some of Trooper Graham's cases this week. His assigned court date is coming up, and he has a lot of old ones on the docket. I only have a few of the trooper's left, so I may get those knocked out if I can get a good plea."

They passed by the court security officers and stepped into the elevator.

"You heard from Jennifer lately?" Buck asked as they rode up in the shaky contraption.

"No. I think she's back at her mom and dad's now. She's out of the evaluation facility—Cherry Hill. Judge Evans said that's what her parents told her. Judge Evans calls them every couple of days."

"Johnson may go back to talk to Jennifer. I want someone to check on her and see how she's doing. Think Jennifer would be okay with that?"

"Probably. I just don't think she's talking much."

The two split off, going to their respective offices. At the last minute, Buck went by O'Shea's door and headed to Judge Evans's chambers. He rang the security buzzer and pushed the door after it clicked open.

* * *

The shotgun pointed at his chest did not move—unlike the guy holding it who was whippet thin and shaking like a leaf. His bifocals slid down his nose, and his voice quavered, "What the fuck are you doing here, boy?"

Buck took one small step back on the sagging front porch. The shotgun stepped forward. "Jennifer's dad? Are you Jennifer's dad?" Buck asked trying to stop his voice from squeaking.

"Dad! Dad! What are you doing? Put that down," Jennifer squeezed around her father and near Buck. "This is Buck, I told you. He works for Judge Foster."

The shotgun lowered. "You can't be too careful. Sorry, Buck. Didn't know you. Come on into the house. I'm Jim, Jennifer's dad." He did not offer his hand.

Jennifer's parents temporarily had rented the small wood frame house on the edge of a mobile home park while Jennifer had been in treatment in Cherry Hill. Next door, children played near a lone tire swing and a few dozen dogs. The painted tire buried in the yard served double duty as a hobby horse for one of the younger ones. Semis blew past on the two-lane highway, ruffling their hair.

Jennifer called out for her mother as Buck closed the screen door. Her mom offered iced tea to Buck and went back into the kitchen to bring some glasses. She disappeared after serving the drinks.

Gingerly sitting down on the overstuffed couch, narrowly missing two orange cats, Buck asked, "Jennifer, how are you doing? Everyone at the courthouse asked me to tell you hello."

"That's so nice. Tell everyone hello back for me. I really miss working with the clerks and Phil too. Has he found a new job yet?"

"Not yet. He had an interview the other day, but I forgot to ask him about it when I saw him earlier. Judge Evans said she would like to stop by for a visit soon if that is okay with you."

"I'd love to see her. Please tell her yes, and I'll make sure Dad behaves."

Jim looked sheepish but said, "We're not taking any chances here. Jennifer's been through a tough time and…" he blew his nose on a wadded-up handkerchief he took out of his jeans pocket, "we weren't here to protect her from that rat bastard judge, but we're here now, and by God we're going to look after her." His hands shook as he wiped the moisture from his eyes.

"Oh, Dad. You can't blame yourself for what that monster did. I'd like to go back and finish out my clerkship. I only have a few more weeks left."

Buck awkwardly started petting one of the cats to give Jim a moment. The other ginger had jumped down and now regarded him balefully from under the scarred coffee table.

"Are you feeling up to coming back? Judge Foster and Judge Evans would understand if you were more comfortable checking out a laptop from IT and working from home. Give

Judge Evans a call whatever you decide or talk it over with her. I'm getting ready to finish up at the courthouse but wanted to stop by and see how you were getting along. I can't put my law practice on hold for much longer. I've had a couple new civil cases come in I need to deal with before we consider filing suit."

"Lawyers," Jim snorted. "We tried to talk Jennifer into being a schoolteacher. She was so good at all of her subjects, but she wanted to go to law school. Cannot imagine why. She ain't got a mean bone in her body. Her mama and I raised her to be polite. And she is."

"Dad, Buck doesn't want to hear this. I didn't want to teach at all. I hated my student teaching classes. Easier to go up against another lawyer than a sixteen-year-old middle schooler. At least it's a fair fight with the other lawyer."

Buck stood, smoothing the light-colored fur off his pants and thanked her parents for the iced tea. The cat on the sofa ignored him.

"If you feel up to it, meet me and Phil for lunch one day next week. He has a good courtroom story about the litigants in the civil rights case. One of them is sitting in jail. I'll pick you up if you need a ride."

"Nope. I'll give her a ride into town if she wants to go. Got my Ram truck out there on the side drive. Gotta keep it away from them kids out there, or they'd be all up on it. We can meet you when and if she says." Jim's shotgun gleamed in the sun as he carried it to the screen door, waiting for Buck to leave.

"Thanks for stopping by. I'll call you or Phil next week," she said.

Buck tried not to leap off the porch as he headed for his car. One of the next-door neighbor's dogs stared him down through matted fur. He could feel the shotgun barrel track him into the driver's seat. He glanced back over his shoulder, but the porch was empty.

* * *

The setting sun turned the sky pink, then purple. The golden beams hit Buck in the eyes and had him squinting as he drove the road over Falls Lake. Heading back to Oxford, it was almost cool enough to roll down the windows. Buck passed by the closed old country store on the right just before the bridge over the Tar River. A black object hurtled at his passenger side, colliding with the front bumper. The impact jarred him into the driver's side door frame. Buck slammed on the brakes as the deer slid over the hood. It limped into the woods. Two more quickly followed. He pulled the car over onto the grass and got out to examine the damage. The front bumper was dented, the wheel well caved in, and the tire was flat.

"Damnit," Buck said. He pulled out his cell phone to call his legal assistant, Emma Jean. Remembering it was Wednesday night, he cursed again. Emma Jean would be at church and have her phone turned off. A fervent member of the Oxford Grace Church, Emma Jean attended every service and potluck supper.

Jeb answered after a couple of rings. "What's up?"

"Man, some deer hit my car. I'm out just past the mobile home park on 15, next to the bridge. Can you get a ride out? I'm going to call AAA, but who knows who'll show up. James Albert had the contract but lost it to Sammy. I heard Sammy lost it when he got pulled for running liquor without a license."

Jeb sighed. "Yeah, okay. I'll get someone to pick you up. Give me a few minutes to roust up somebody."

"Thanks. Where are you?"

"I'm just getting back from Mom's. I helped her cut the grass and use the weed eater. She cooked baked chicken and sent some home for you."

Buck felt awful. Since he'd been in Raleigh, he'd completely forgotten to do Mom's yardwork. "Damn. I owe you. Thanks for helping her out. I haven't seen her in a couple of weeks."

"She knows you're busy. Look, I'll get somebody out there."

Jeb had not had a driver's license for a while. He surrendered it to the DMV before going into rehab the last time. The surrender kept a driving-while-impaired conviction off his record. He'd promised Buck he'd go to the DMV and try to get it reinstated. He just had not gone yet.

Fifteen minutes later, Trooper Graham pulled up behind Buck leaving his lights on bright. He got out of the silver patrol car and strolled up. He took his time circling the car, then looking at the trail of blood disappearing into the tree line. "Looks like I'm going to have to cite you for injury to wildlife. The rabbit sheriff said to tell you he's on his way. He said to tell you to hold tight."

"Goddamnit, Graham. There was nothing I could do. The buck came out of nowhere and hit me. I'm lucky it didn't push me into the river."

Graham started laughing. Jeb stepped out of the front passenger side door of the patrol car and grinned.

"Very funny. Jeb, is this the only guy you could call?"

Jeb shrugged. "Yeah. I figured he's supposed to protect the citizens on the highways."

"Let me get my briefcase and jacket. Triple A has a recording, and I haven't heard back. I'll just leave the car here."

Buck started to get into the front seat of the patrol car.

"Ho, man. I got front. You gotta sit in the back," Jeb said.

Buck waited as Graham unlocked the back doors. He got in and stared balefully at the wire cage that separated him from the front.

"Thanks for the ride. I appreciate the hell out of it.'

Graham and Jeb laughed louder. "This is small payback for all the shit you pull in my cases," Graham said. "You get the tickets I write pled down or dismissed. I'm tired of coming to court every other week and putting up with your whining. My arrests arc solid," Graham added, snorting.

"Go to hell, Graham. What about that bogus seat belt ticket you gave to Mrs. Oakley? She nearly had a heart attack when you pulled her over. That lady's been teaching Sunday school since you were a toddler. She never drives her car. And what about old man Branch? You gave him a speeding ticket a foot after the 35 mile per hour zone changed into a 25 mile per hour zone. That's just bullshit."

"I can turn the sirens on if you want to make sure folks see you sitting back there."

"No, Goddamnit. Just get me home."

Jeb snickered and said something to Graham but Buck couldn't hear it. He could only get so mad at them.

Surprisingly, Graham had been one of the few solid supporters for Jeb when he went back to rehab in Wilmington. Graham had come to the house off-duty and talked to both of them in the dark hours before the scheduled commitment. He'd brought coffee and solace. He'd talked of his own dad, a confirmed alcoholic, dedicated to drink until the end. Opening up about what he'd felt like as a boy, seeing his dad kill himself with it, Buck and Jeb had appreciated his honesty and his offer to go with them down to the coast the next day. Jeb had struggled after his first admission, trying to find a job, trying to find his center. He'd relapsed only six months after getting out of treatment. Going back was tougher than the first time.

They all owed Graham Jeb's life. If Graham hadn't had the naloxone in his patrol car, Jeb would be gone. Accidentally overdosing on heroin, Jeb was slumped over in his car when Graham had spotted the car idling outside the downtown bar on Main Street in the early morning hours. Afterwards, he'd gone by to see Jeb in the hospital and then every day after until Jeb left. Sometimes he talked to his brother, but most times they sat together quietly reading or doing crosswords. He never preached to or advised him on what he should do. Jeb looked Graham up after he got back to town.

"Here ya go," Graham said stopping in front of the house. Jeb got out and opened the back door for Buck. There were no inside handles in the back, which prevents prisoners from escaping after arrest.

"Thanks, Graham. Want to come in?"

"Naw. I got a hot date tonight."

"Really, who is that desperate?"

"*Game of Thrones*. See you." He sped off, making sure the next-door neighbors heard the patrol car.

"Sorry about your car. Want to take mine to Raleigh tomorrow? I think it has enough gas to get you to the gas station." Jeb said. "I know, I know. I still haven't gone to the DMV. I hate those people. They're total dicks."

"Thanks for offering. I might do it. I'm almost done in Raleigh. Has it been inspected?"

"Yeah, Mom had it inspected for me a few days ago."

"Well, thanks. Want me to go with you to the DMV sometime?"

"Yeah, maybe. I don't know. I don't really want to drive just yet."

"Okay. Let me know when you're ready, and I'll go with you. Oh, I saw Angela today over at the courthouse."

"Oh God. Is she in trouble again? I really hope not. That'd be awful," said Jeb.

"Judge Evans said Angela's in Raleigh now but didn't mention she was in any trouble. The judge didn't say why Angela was there or what her plans were."

"I've talked to her a couple of times. Mostly we talked about the rehab place and some people we knew there who she's kept up with more than I have. She knew some different people than me, too. She did the group PTSD therapy, so I really didn't get to see her as much there except at lunch and dinner. I saw her a while back though. She looked good. I think the private therapist she has now has really helped her. Of course, O'Shea dying helped her too."

"Yeah. What a tool. He was a total asshole to her and her family during the rape trial. The elected DA was spineless.

He refused to replace O'Shea when anybody could see he was unprepared and incompetent to try to the case," Buck said.

"Yeah. We talked about that some because being back at any courthouse brings back those bad feelings. She'd been angrier at O'Shea than at the guy who attacked her because O'Shea made all these promises at the beginning of the case, but he wouldn't meet with her after that. The guy who attacked her had mental health issues, but O'Shea wouldn't negotiate with his lawyer or try to work it out. Angela didn't want to testify, and O'Shea just ignored her."

"That's really awful. She didn't need to be treated like dirt by O'Shea after trying to deal with the attack. Judge Evans couldn't stand how he treated Angela, and they were barely cordial."

Charles bounded from one to the other when Buck opened the front door. The Lab ran to his food bowl in the kitchen. He sighed contentedly after forcing each to scratch him behind his ears by rubbing his big golden head against their thighs. Buck said, "I'll walk down for takeout if you feed Charles."

"Deal."

* * *

The next morning, after all but cussing out AAA for the ruinous cost of the tow, Buck drove over to Margaret's to meet with her and Katie. In a folder on the front passenger seat, he had the last few months' approved deposits and expenditures for O'Shea that he'd gotten from Judge Foster.

Margaret lived in a lovely old Victorian house on College Street, not far from the Masonic orphanage. The house was painted yellow with white gingerbread trim and sat up to survey the town on the lot's small hill. Next to an elementary school, the two turrets rose up to the sky and the sun porch sat shady and cool off to one side. Large elms grew between the sidewalk and the wide street.

Margaret had been running her solitary CPA firm from the house for years through all of the zoning efforts and laws prohibiting businesses from running in the residential area. No one messed with Margaret if they wanted to avoid an IRS audit or worse.

Opening the huge front door threaded on each side with lead vines dividing the panes of beveled glass, Margaret greeted Buck. "Glad to see you. How have you been? How's your Mama and Jeb? Tell them 'hello' from me. I remember teaching you Geometry in eighth grade. Boy, you were awful at it."

Stepping into a lovely pastel pink drawing room, his feet felt too large for the dainty chairs and knickknacks. "Fine, fine. Everybody's fine. Thank you, Miss Margaret."

Buck thought she'd been a tough old bird back in middle school, trying to cram his head full of isosceles triangles and equations. Jeb had sailed through her class like he was Einstein's twin. Her calls to their mom sang Jeb's praises and bemoaned Buck's ineptitude. He'd had to go back for tutoring after school and before basketball practice twice a week.

He couldn't imagine what she was going to do with the computer discs and financial records. He hoped Katie knew what she was doing, handing off the complex materials to Margaret.

Following her slender frame to the back of the house through a dark hallway that smelled of lavender, he narrowly missed toppling a spindly mahogany table inlaid with walnut. The tiny paper weights and figurines shuddered as he passed. Glancing around, he spotted an oil painting of a handsome Civil War general. *Probably her dad.*

Margaret stopped at a door festooned with elaborate molding. "Come on in. Katie and Walter are here. Now that Walter, I mean Detective Johnson, he was a quick learner. I always hoped he'd take the higher math courses, but he chose football over academics." She sniffed at the injustice of it.

Margaret swept into a room with more computers, printers, desks, and electronics than NASA. Johnson looked uncomfortable in a low cane-backed chair angled into the corner. His arms and legs spilled over the sides. Katie appeared at home in an upright Martha Washington chair pulled up to a computer. She asked Buck, "You brought O'Shea's approved financials, right?"

He nodded, unsure of where to stand. Margaret took the file from his hands and hummed as she swiftly reviewed the papers inside, wetting her finger first to scroll through them. She was a petite woman with snowy white hair and a ramrod straight back. "Buck, you're making me nervous standing there. Go sit over there by Detective Johnson." Buck eased his backside onto the seat, praying for the chair to not crumble.

Katie quickly outlined the forensic report for Margaret. "There were a lot of bank accounts on the computer. The accounts were either mentioned in emails or found in some online transactions." Katie gave Margaret the list of account names and numbers she'd pried out of Mary Francis O'Shea.

"What looked irregular to us, at first glance, is the money moving into and out of the judge's bank account that he used for the direct deposit for his paycheck and the few direct withdrawals he'd set up for things like additional life insurance and a car payment.

"At this point, we don't know what the motive for his murder was, and it may have been financial. We need a picture of who was getting what and how often. Was someone blackmailing him? Did he have financial problems? We know his wife, Mary Francis, kept him on a tight financial leash and was anxious to finalize the divorce and the division of property. I don't think they had a pre-nup, and she is worth a lot of old family money."

Margaret listened intently and then leaned down to look at the screen where Katie was pointing out the bank account statement. "Yes, I see what you mean. Odd. Well, leave it all with me and I will look into it. If I need more information on origin of accounts and the holder, I assume you have the subpoena power to get it for me from the financial institutions?"

"Absolutely," Katie said. "Call me or Johnson with whatever you need. If you think you need something the district court may have, give Buck a call, and he'll let me know if it is something the court cannot voluntarily release. Now, as for the FBI partnering with us on the murder case, I'd like to send your contact information to them. Is that okay?"

Margaret thought a minute. "Yes, dear. Do that. But give them my phone and email. I'll be far too busy for a visit from the feds. Although, I've worked hand-in-glove with the FBI in the past. Let me think, was that Hoover? Oh, well, I really can't remember. Tell them I prefer a phone call should they need to make an appointment."

The group left Margaret in the room of whirring and beeping computers and printers. As they closed the door, she was typing furiously onto one of the screens, her glasses perched on her nose with the chain around her neck. Turning, Johnson snagged his sleeve on a huge English secretary sitting with its back to the end of the hall. He caught the lovely cranberry vase filled with roses before it hit the floor. "Nice catch, Johnson," Buck said.

"Jesus," Johnson said. "It's like a museum. My paycheck wouldn't cover the first thing I broke in here." He minced his way out the front door as Buck threaded his way between the front room's peony pink velvet settee and the walnut tea table.

Chapter Fourteen

Two days after Johnson dropped off the financials with Margaret, she presented her forensic financial report to both the FBI and SBI agents back at the North Carolina State Crime Laboratory in Raleigh. Buck, Lt. Katie O'Connor, and Detective Johnson were permitted by the FBI to sit in a dark corner of the same room where they had met with the crime techs earlier in the week. After thirty seconds of stunned silence from Margaret's analysis of account transactions that took place after O'Shea's death, all hell broke loose.

Agent David screamed at the State Bureau of Investigation head, Jason Roberts, that the report was to remain confidential and sealed and that he'd get a federal order to keep it that way. The SBI head screamed at David that his state agents were taking over the financial part if Margaret could show the transactions in any way affected North Carolina taxpayers or violated its tax laws.

Roberts was a squat, florid-faced man whose accent disintegrated from Episcopal prep school to broad eastern Johnston County the angrier he got. David screamed back that the Internal Revenue Service would be called in to see about any violations, and that they had jurisdiction and the state should sit back and shut up. The noise volume rose as each agent weighed in until finally Margaret said, "Enough!" Her schoolteacher voice cut like a blade of ice through the shrill squawking.

Standing in a sharp navy suit at the podium centered in the stuffy room, Margaret stated, "Look, gentleman. I have more to report, but if you want to sit here bickering like a bunch of old hens at the bingo parlor, I'll step out. I've got a project due for the big eight accounting firm down the road, but I moved this one up because I was told it was important."

Chairs scraped back into place and ties were adjusted while Margaret eyed the group. Buck slid further back in his chair placed in the center of the room while Lt. O'Connor and Det. Johnson tried to avoid her baleful stare.

"Okay, then. As I was saying, there were a few transactions that posted after Judge O'Shea's date of death. You can issue subpoenas for the bank records, including his investment account records, and that might give you a good place to start. If you need me to review the records, I'll be glad to do so."

"I'm on it. I'll get those out today. What else?" David asked.

Roberts interrupted, "Hell, no, now wait just a doggone minute. Margaret, were those North Carolina banks you're talking about?"

She replied, "From what I can tell, the banks are state credit unions and both regional and national institutions. You'll know a lot more about the when and the where if you get the records."

"That's what we'll do. What's the amount of the transactions?" Roberts asked.

"From what I saw in the few months of records, it totals about one million dollars."

Roberts whistled, "Goddamn! Sorry, Margaret, ma'am." He turned to Agent David. "What in the hell are you people playing at? You've got a goddamned unsolved murder, and somebody's screwing with the judge's bank accounts. That sounds like what we all at the SBI would call a *clue*." The state agents snickered. One muttered, "Hell, yeah."

Agent David slammed his laptop on the table. "Shut the hell up, Roberts. You don't know what the fuck you are talking about. All I've heard from you is just a bunch of chin music. And you won't get subpoenas, I will. I can get them a hell of a lot faster."

"Fine, but we want access to the records," Roberts said.

"I don't have to agree to a damn thing, but I'll give you guys copies of the state credit union records to review. If you know some of the heads of these places, you can serve those subpoenas—it might go smoother."

"We'll do it. Give us a list and we'll serve them today," Roberts said.

Margaret cleared her throat. "There are a few more issues I can see from what I have been given. I believe some of the transactions, right before and after the judge's death, involve a few foreign countries and the Cayman Islands."

There was a collective groan.

"Yes, you see the problem," she said. "Offshore accounts are the devil to obtain. It's all but impossible to get those institutions to cooperate. Now, a few of the foreign countries' banks may be more amenable to providing records depending on who's asking."

"I'll get the IRS to help out on that one," David said. "The agency may have some good contacts depending on the bank and on the country. Was the money going out or coming in?"

"Mainly out, as far as I can tell. I'm going to need to get another six months of the judge's financials to get a real grasp on this thing. I want to prepare a thorough analysis for you. Any chance of getting more records? Can I get the tax returns or his accountant's name?"

From the far corner of the room, Buck said, "I'll talk to Judge Foster about the court's or the Administrative Office of the Court's position and let you know today."

Margaret took her glasses off, placed them in their case, and snapped it shut. "I'll leave my draft report with you for now. Let me know if you get any more documents."

* * *

Charles de Gaulle airport held a heaving mass of sweaty, angry people—not the least of which was Agent David. Only twelve hours ago, he'd gotten the call from higher up that an agent was needed in Paris, and pronto.

The passport control line snaked around the room's cordoned off lines an agonizing twenty times prior to arriving at the end of the security line. He hit the FaceTime button on his government cell phone and waited impatiently for the connection. His "companion" alternately snarled then simpered at him. He shoved his carry-on ahead of him as they agonizingly advanced.

"Come on, come on," he muttered. He shook his cell like a rattle, and then looked at the top of his phone. Of course—no internet connection in one of the world's busiest airports in one of the world's largest cities. Earlier, he'd requested a female agent meet him at the airport for assistance in transport. He was assured in both French and in English an agent would meet him there. So far, no agent.

He shut his phone off and then turned it on again. His "collar," the livid Mrs. O'Shea, struck out at him, "I think you have made a dreadful mistake and one you are going to regret. I know most of the federal judges and they will put you in jail for this…this outrage!" Mary Frances O'Shea said.

Agent David started sweating harder if that were possible. The boiling angry sea of humans called out their grievances to the airport personnel passing by in jaunty orange. Some distracted the attendants so much that parts of lines squeezed through and broke in line up front.

"Look, Mrs. O'Shea. I'm just doing my job. You're wanted back in Raleigh for some questions related to Judge O'Shea's death. You would not return phone calls and ignored the subpoenas."

"I want my lawyer. Give me that phone so I can call him. You had no right to take my cell phone. You have treated me like a common criminal."

"Mrs. O'Shea, I have to follow procedure. You can call him after we get through this morass. No problem."

She crossed her arms and turned her back on Agent David.

A few minutes later, there was a slight explosion of French at his elbow.

"*Bonjour*, Agent David. I have been sent from the office to assist you in the transportation of Madame O'Shea." A dark-haired young woman stood at his elbow close enough to talk to his jacket's lapel. He had no idea what office and did not want to ask, but he'd risk almost anything to hand off Mrs. O'Shea. If he ever got the darn cell phone working, he'd get the information himself.

"My name is Margot, and I will go with you on the flight," said the charming young woman in heavily accented English.

Mary Frances turned on her heel and looked the new agent up and down. "Whatever," she said. Margot addressed her in French which seemed to mollify Mrs. O'Shea somewhat since she knew Agent David understood not a word. Mary Frances inclined her head to something Margot said.

"We're never getting through this line in time to make our flight. This is ridiculous," Agent David said.

"Nice planning," Mary Frances sneered.

Margot pulled out a cell phone from the pocket of her expertly tailored black pants. She tapped on it, paused, then tapped again. "*Mais oui*," she said. "Agent David, we will see you on the other side, at the gate. I am permitted to take Madame O'Shea through a separate line but can only take her." Mary Frances smirked at him as she picked up her Louis Vuitton carryall. "Ta ta," she said as she followed in the petite agent's path toward security.

Agent David's collar was heavy with sweat, irritating his poorly shaved neck. Yesterday, he'd jumped on the opportunity to go to Paris and pick her up. He'd never been out of the country. Now, jet lagged and smelling like a week-old hamper, he blindly shuffled along the never-ending line.

* * *

Mary Frances refused to look at or talk to the investigators. She appeared fresh and crisp in a periwinkle boucle suit. Her pair of attorneys, however, looked frazzled. They'd been unable to get her to utter one syllable. The group was seated in the largest interview room at the new chrome and glass FBI building in Cary, North Carolina. Cary, located just outside of Raleigh, catered to the nouveau riche and to the Yankees who'd stopped on their way to Florida and failed to move on south.

"Look, Mrs. O'Shea, we've been talking in circles for an hour. I mean us, not you. Why won't you help us with these financial records? At least look at them? We'll leave you in here with your attorneys if that would help," Agent Thompson said. Agent David, seated the furthest away, nodded, barely awake.

"Mrs. O'Shea, can you help the agents at least rule out transactions related to your accounts?" Buck asked. "To any money you sent to or received from Judge O'Shea? I have his papers here for you to look at." Buck had picked up the documents that morning from the court and gotten permission from Lt. O'Connor to attend the meeting. She had to go back to the North Carolina Crime Lab to ask for better copies of the photographs on the computer to meet with a representative from the National Center for Missing and Exploited Children and the county's representative from Child Protective Services.

Mary Frances begrudgingly turned to face him. "You guys get out. I want to talk to my attorneys." The attorneys seemed surprised. She'd not treated them any better than the agents. They each preened a little under her glare.

The agents and Buck gratefully scrambled to their feet. The room progressively had gotten hotter, and they'd gotten exactly nowhere with this interview.

The agents went back to their offices and Buck hung out in the narrow hall. An administrative assistant brought him a bottle of water. He smiled his thanks and began checking messages on his phone.

Suddenly, the door swung open. "She's ready to help," said one of the attorneys. Buck told him he'd be right back. He started looking into offices and then on the main floor for the agents. They were in side-by-side cubicles. David was asleep and Thompson was on his computer.

"She's ready to talk," Buck said.

Thompson closed his screen and put his jacket back on. He went over and nudged David's feet off his desk. David jolted awake. "Let's go," Thompson said, "Mary Frances has seen the light." Wordlessly, David dragged on his coat and followed them back down the hallway.

Her attorneys looked ready for action. They'd taken the tops off their identical Montblanc pens and straightened up their legal pads. Mary Frances sat between them. She arched a brow at the oldest, and he said, "Okay, here are the ground rules. She will identify her personal transactions with Judge O'Shea, but that's it. They've been separated for over a year, and she does not know what all he was into. They'd owned some rental properties together and she'll identify those for you and provide the name and contact information of the managing agency."

Thompson started to speak, but the attorney held up his hand. "That's it. That's all she's willing to do. She wants to make a preliminary statement, against our advice. Mrs. O'Shea?"

She looked around the room, openly relishing center stage. "I have never been so embarrassed in my life. Two days ago, I was sitting at the lovely bar in the George V, Four Seasons, when that agent," pointing at David, "strode in and started braying my name. Everyone in the bar stopped talking and looked at me. He came over and grabbed my arm like I was a common criminal. He announced my name in a loud voice and pulled me out of my seat. I was humiliated. My companion tried to help me, but Agent David rudely told him I was wanted by the FBI. My companion looked at me in horror. Agent David hustled me out of there so fast my companion had to run after him with my wrap and my Chanel bag. The only consideration I was shown came from a foreign agent, a French agent named Margot.

"Now, I will answer questions within the parameters outlined by my attorneys. I will then meet with the resident agent in charge of the FBI and tell him what happened and demand he fire you." With her last words, she pointed one beautifully lacquered fingernail at David.

David slowly got up from his chair and wordlessly stared out the window into the courtyard, fuming. After a few seconds he growled, "I've got to be somewhere else." The door closed with a soft snick. Thompson looked over at Buck and shrugged.

"Okay, Mrs. O'Shea. I understand your position. Can you help us out? We'd like to make some headway on these records," said Thompson.

She pulled her Chanel readers from her bag and folded her hands in front like a schoolgirl. "Go for it," she said.

Buck had to hand it to her. She reviewed records for two solid hours, answered questions, and looked just as fresh as she did when she'd arrived. He, Thompson, and the attorneys had first taken off jackets, and then rolled up sleeves, and then opened the door to the hall, trying to get some air circulating. The older attorney's hair stood straight up where he'd run his hands through it over and over.

She placed the final piece of paper back down onto the table. "Nothing on this statement. I don't see where I sent him anything from my account, and I don't see where half the rents were deposited."

The first thirty minutes had been spent in providing details of her account locations and numbers and the managing company's accounts and contact numbers. She next wordlessly reviewed the stacks of paper. The only sound she'd uttered was when she expressed surprise over the foreign transactions, especially those in the Cayman Islands. Her concern seemed genuine.

Buck had made a few notes for Katie, but Mary Frances's information about monthly payments for O'Shea excluded certain transactions as unusual. She'd given Judge O'Shea $10,000.00 to deposit monthly, and the rental deposits rarely varied in amount.

Mary Frances caught Buck's eye. "There's one more thing I have to say," she said. Her attorneys murmured negatively and shuffled the papers in front of them. She shook off the hand the older one had placed on her wrist.

"No, I must." She continued to look at Buck. "Just as I told you when you and Lt. O'Connor first came to my house, I had nothing to do with my husband's—my *estranged* husband's death. The money I gave him helped with his living expenses. His salary as a judge was a mere fraction of what it had been at the New York law firm, but he'd agreed to move south for me. I felt it was the right thing to do."

She gathered up her purse and her soft leather briefcase and stood. Her attorneys scrambled to stand. "That's it then. I am going to meet with the resident agent in charge." She looked at her attorneys. "I won't need you for this. Send me the bill."

* * *

That night, Buck put their dishes in the sink. He'd tried to cook dinner for himself and Katie with fairly disastrous results. The grill ran out of propane halfway through and the baked potatoes were raw in the middle. The remainder of the cooking was done in the microwave. Katie had told him it was delicious, but she was just being kind. Even the dusty candles he'd dug out of the seldom-used walnut buffet could not hide the raw meat.

Jeb was at a twelve-step meeting at the Episcopal church, so they had the house to themselves. The hurried search for heartburn medicine ended the beginnings of a romantic evening. Now, they each lay on matching couch and settee in the glow of candlelight with one arm over their eyes.

Jeb crashed open the front door stumbling over Charles whose tail beat a tattoo of welcome on the walls. "What the hell?" he said as he tripped over Katie's shoes kicked off in the entry. "Whose shoes are these? Hey Buck," he hollered. "Are these your high heels?"

Buck and Katie groaned in unison as their peace was shattered. Seeing motion on the couch, Charles licked Buck's face while Jeb turned on the light. "What are you guys doing?"

Buck said, "We are trying to recover from a near fatal date with death. Those steaks in the freezer were awful. The grill gave out. I think we ate them raw. You may have to take us to the hospital."

Jeb said, "What steaks. Oh…"

Buck said, "What do you mean, *oh*?"

Katie lifted her head a fraction off the settee and chimed in, "Yeah, what do you mean? What was wrong with them?"

Jeb scratched Charles behind his ears as he sat down in their grandmother's delicately carved chair. "Those steaks in the freezer were in there when I left for Florida in the spring. They're not cow meat."

Katie clutched her stomach. "What were they?" she whispered. Talking seemed to increase the pain.

"Graham brought those over last fall after he'd gone hunting. He had more than he could use, so he brought some meat over here. I'd completely forgotten about them."

"What the hell were they?" Buck softly shouted.

"I think some kind of game rolled together. Maybe possum and deer or deer and bear? I don't know. I wasn't going to eat them. I was in my vegan stage. I meant to throw those suckers out. Hey, you guys don't look so good. Let me call the doctor. Old Doc Harris still makes house calls."

"Dear God, no," Buck said. "He can't see to get down his own front porch stairs. Last time I had an appointment, he tried to shove a pencil in my mouth to take my temperature. We don't have enough liability insurance for him to come over." Katie whimpered.

Jeb headed to the kitchen. "I'll make some tea. That'll help settle your stomachs. Come on, Charles, leave Buck alone." Charles stopped licking Buck's limp hand and trotted after Jeb.

Some color had returned to their faces a half hour later. Jeb returned with another round of hot tea. He had set the formal silver tea things on their aunt's silver tray and placed it on their mom's beloved tea table. At any other time, Buck would have admired his brother's efforts.

"How was your meeting?" Buck asked.

Jeb said, "Alright. Not one of the better ones. Only a few people shared, and it was the same ones as last week. Our members keep dropping out."

"Sorry to hear it," Buck said. "Did your sponsor make it?"

"Yeah, he did. He's pretty faithful. Oh, and the cookies there were stale. Bummer."

Buck glared at Jeb. Jeb said, "Oops, sorry man. Look, I'd completely forgotten. If you all are going to make it, I'm heading downstairs. Night." Charles followed at his heels as Jeb took the tray back into the kitchen then opened the door to the basement.

"Let's please change the subject," said Katie. "How was Mary Frances? Did she help at all?"

"Not bad," Buck said. She seems to have had a small part of a heart because she put money in Judge O'Shea's account each month even when they were separated. She's still pissed at Agent David about hauling her back from France and is trying to get him fired."

"That's decent of her to have given O'Shea money and to help try to figure out where it went in and out. What about the overseas transactions?"

"No help there. They'd had separate accounts for a while. She doesn't know anything about what he did with the money after she sent it to him. How about you? How was the meeting with the folks from the National Center for Missing and Exploited Children?"

"Pretty awful. They think that they can identify real children in some of the photos. What I mean is that these are children that they've already identified before as victims of child pornography in other cases."

"What will they do now? Will they go through all of the images?"

"I think they have identified a few of the children by the names on the files that were transferred and compared the photos to the known victims. They have matches based on prior investigations. I left the forensic report with them and the SBI. The SBI is a great resource for tracking the sender and the recipient of images. Our office doesn't have anyone certified to do that. We barely have enough in the budget to pay deputies much less send somebody for computer forensic training."

"What happens next? Do they think O'Shea manufactured the images, or was he the conduit to receive or to post them?"

Katie thought a moment. "No one would say. I think they want to get their hands on the material and review everything to make an educated determination. They also don't want to start slinging guesses around since this involves a federal judge. They're not sure because some of the background in a few images looks like one of the courtrooms. From the looks I caught going around the room to each other, I think they all suspect he was the conduit, that he either sent it on or he requested the materials. Either way, getting or sending each image is a federal and a state felony.

"Since we have a murder investigation, they separated into teams to work the case around the clock. Each team has someone from the center, a Child Protective Services member, and an agent with the SBI. The first set of teams were ramped up scrolling through when I left.

"Those photos and videos are horrible, beyond horrible. Every one of those children lost their childhood and their innocence. That's motive enough for murder."

Buck moved over to sit on the floor beside her settee. He took her hand and gently rubbed it. "You deserved a nice quiet evening after dealing with that. I'm sorry I nearly poisoned you. Who leaves disgusting game parts in their freezer? Give me a chance to make it up to you?"

She smiled at him and patted down his cowlick. "I would love to see you again. Next time, I'll cook."

Chapter Fifteen

Angela confronted her sister in chambers. "The hell I will, Loretta. I've stayed here too long this time anyway. You know that."

Loretta looked at her sister in equal parts sympathy and exasperation. "Angela, I'm just asking for a few more days. Give the new therapist a chance. He comes highly recommended in the area of anxiety and PTSD. You said you liked him."

"Jesus. I do like him, but that's not the point. I just can't stay here. After a couple of days, all of the bad memories start coming back. I can't sleep, I'm more anxious. I keep thinking about it."

The judge got up from her desk and hugged her sister. "I know. I know," she said softly, rocking them back and forth. "I'm being selfish. I miss you when you're not here. Can you wait a few days? I can cancel court and take tomorrow off. We'll do something fun."

Tear-stained, Angela regarded her sister in silence. "Two more days. I'll go to the doctor's appointment this afternoon. Tomorrow, we can go to a double feature."

"Oh, God, no. You'll pick out some violent action movie, or, worse, some animated art movie with subtitles I won't understand."

"Probably. But it's my day, so you'll just have to get a bucket of popcorn and load up on candy. Besides, you need a dose of art. You don't get it in this place."

Judge Evans looked around the paper-strewn office. Files were piled in one client chair and on the floor beside the other. Legal pads, federal reporters, and law review books took up the small conference table on the far side of the room. One stack listed to one side with messages and memos on top. Since O'Shea's death, the piles of work had grown steadily higher.

A soft knock at the door had both turning in tandem.

"I'm sorry to interrupt Your Honor, but the one o'clock pretrial conference call is set up on line two," her law clerk said.

"Thank you, Brenda. Tell the parties I'll be right with them."

Angela said goodbye and left her sister alone in her office. She yelled back, "Love you!" just as Judge Evans punched line two.

* * *

Buck mashed down on the last bit of tape on O'Shea's box of files. Clem had offered to bring him a cart so he could put the boxes in storage in the basement of the federal building. He attached the contents summary to the outside in case the FBI or the clerk's office wanted to find a particular file.

Standing up, he felt the arthritis in his right knee and cursed it. Johnson came through the door and shoved a cup of coffee in his hand. "Damn, boy, you look like a crippled dog. How're you gonna keep up with the lovely lieutenant moving like that?"

"The same way you chase those drug dealers—slow and steady. And with a lot of Aleve."

Johnson snorted. "The lieutenant's too good for your sorry ass, but you've put a smile on her face, so that's okay. You ever disappoint her, you better find a rock to hide under. There won't be a deputy in the county who won't come after you."

"You sound like some third-rate hitman. You need some new lines. So, where are we headed today, the lab or Margaret's for the financial update?" Buck asked.

"Neither," Johnson replied. "The FBI and the IRS want to meet. LT said you can sit in on it, but same deal as last time. You don't speak."

Buck shrugged back into his navy blazer and cut the storage room light off. "Fine. Tell me it's not Agent David, but Thompson leading it."

"Agent David all day long."

"Better stop for some more coffee. You're driving. My damn knee is killing me."

Johnson cuffed him on the shoulder almost sending him into the concrete wall. "Quit whining, man. We'll get this thing solved soon. We'll be shed of him and the Bureau. He ain't in it for the long haul."

* * *

Agent David and two others sat in the FBI conference room. They looked up when Buck and Johnson came in but did not stand up. Legal pads were perfectly aligned in front of the two across from David.

David smirked at them, then introduced them to the two female IRS agents. "I'm disappointed Lt. O'Connor did not come. We'll try to dumb it down for you."

Johnson, amazingly, kept his composure. "Sure, David. We'll take back anything you tell us. The lieutenant is reviewing the computer images over at the state crime lab. She's looking at the photos and videos and hoping to God she does not see a child she recognizes in some unnatural sex act with an adult—hoping she does not have to then drive over to a friend's house and tell them their child has been defiled by the worst kind of monster."

The two IRS agents looked sick. David cleared his throat. "Well okay then, I just thought…" He shoved a memo across the table at Johnson and Buck.

"Here's the summary the agents prepared after reviewing the last two years of tax returns and then Margaret's financial analysis. Ladies, go ahead and tell Detective Johnson what you found." Both IRS agents glared at David.

The agent with half glasses perched on her nose said, "We found some financial abnormalities. The income Judge O'Shea reported is off from the income he reported as received. The deductions taken are mostly straightforward, but there is an LLC in which he did not declare his interest and involvement in for tax purposes. We're focusing on the LLC first. Then we'll look at these offshore transactions you saw and Margaret analyzed. Basically, there is some type of fraud here, and we're trying to get to the bottom of it."

Agent David smugly looked at Johnson and Buck as if he were the proud parent of a gifted student. He leaned back in his chair. "So then, gentlemen, I think you can tell the lieutenant she is barking up the wrong tree. We find the other owners of the LLC, and we have our killer."

The IRS agents stared at the agent in horror. The youngest started stuffing papers into her briefcase.

"What? What am I missing?"

"Agent David, we are simply gathering and analyzing the financial records that have been found and associated with Judge O'Shea. We're looking for tax and financial abnormalities as the bureau requested. It seems a big leap between our research and finding a killer."

Agent David waved her off. "You ladies do your bit and I'll do mine, but I need you to hurry it up. This is a federal judge we are talking about. His killer needs to be brought to justice."

Johnson rolled his eyes at Buck while David turned away, delivering his orders to the IRS agents. David continued on even as the IRS agent stood to go, "… you know, love, revenge, greed, those are motives for murder. So, I'm betting greed based on what you gals found."

Buck winced at the "you gals."

The IRS agents sidled toward the door, but not before the elder turned a scathing glare at Agent David. "You'll get your analysis as soon as it's complete. We're putting in extra hours and assigning extra staff to it. You just do your job."

Agent David snickered as they swept from the room.

"Hope you got a good CPA," Johnson said.

"What for?"

"You're about to get audited by the IRS. I'm guessing every year for the next ten years, or until one of those agents retires."

"What the hell you talking about, Johnson? The older gal had the hots for me. Didn't you see her? She smiled when she talked to me."

"I'm guessing your last assignment and the twenty before that were at a desk, am I right?"

"Well, I worked some complicated financial crimes in DC. I also investigated some abnormalities in the transportation areas."

"Told you. You don't know how to talk to people is your problem."

David stood up and slammed his legal pad back down on to the table. Weighing little, it made no sound but skittered off.

"What the fuck you telling me how to do my job, detective? I don't work in a podunk-ass department in BFE. Most of the people you deal with have an eighth-grade education. They don't even know where the nation's capital is. They probably think it's still in Richmond."

"You can insult me, but don't you talk about the decent, honest people of Granville County, dipshit. You're not fit to wipe their boots. You're a sorry excuse for an agent and a human being," Johnson said, two inches from David's face. The veins in Johnson's linebacker neck throbbed and his shoulders all but hid the smaller agent.

Buck grabbed Johnson by one of those shoulders and tugged.

"Come on, man. Let's get out of here. Later, David," Buck said as he slowly moved Johnson toward the door. He'd put his body between the two hoping to defuse whatever was about to happen.

David, seeing he was not going to get hit, squeaked out, in a high thin voice, "I'm calling your superior, Johnson. You'll be sorry for this."

Johnson shook his head and grinned all the way down the long FBI corridor. Buck walked quickly after him despite his throbbing knee.

"Damn it, Johnson, wait up."

When they cleared the door, Buck rounded on him. "What the fuck was that back there? You're gonna get yourself fired."

Johnson snorted and got into the Dodge Charger. He put the air conditioning on blast and put his phone on speaker.

"FBI," a pleasant voice answered.

"Hey Crystal, how you doing, girl?"

Crystal purred, "I heard you were here and didn't even come by to see me."

"Yeah, I'm sorry about that. You know I wanted to."

"Who you need to talk to?"

"Is the RAC in?"

"Yeah, he's here. I'll put him on. You come back and see me now."

"You know I will, and thanks."

A few seconds later, a male voice came on the phone. "Yo, Johnson. What the fuck you do to Agent David? He's all but sobbing at his desk. Hey, man, whatever it is, don't tell me. I can't wait to get rid of his ass. I don't want to have to do anymore paperwork though."

"Sorry. Look, he's going to call the LT about it, which is okay. But he was a complete dick to those IRS agents."

A sigh came down the line. "Goddamn it. I cannot keep babysitting this guy. I'll call over to Karen at the IRS and try to smooth it over. Thanks for letting me know. We don't need to chap off the IRS, that's for sure. We'll be doing audits from here to Sunday if we piss those agents off.

"Hey, how're the Webb Warriors looking? A good football season this year, or more of the same?"

He and Johnson dissected the upcoming football season for J.F. Webb High School. The RAC had played high school ball against the Warriors when Johnson had been a senior at Webb.

After they hung up, Buck said, "Well damn, Johnson. I didn't know you knew the RAC."

"Yeah, we work out sometimes when I come over here to the bureau. That dude was a fast wide receiver. Not as fast as me, but fast.

"He's a good guy. Hell, most of those guys are. They just got a bad draw in David. He's gonna cost them if they can't get rid of him soon. The FBI's going to have to promise the IRS all kinds of shit because of that asshole."

"You're right.

"I hope Katie's finished up at the lab. Call her and see if she can meet up with us."

"You just want to see your lady love. I see where this is going."

"Shut up, Johnson. I'm getting ready to head back to Oxford this afternoon, but I hope she's got some solid leads. Judge Foster will ask me when I check back in with him.

* * *

Buck opened the door to Katie's knock. She was picking him up for dinner since Jeb was taking his car, with his new driver's license, to the church's twelve-step program. She brushed past him, sat down on the velvet settee, and burst into tears. Jeb looked helplessly at Buck. He grabbed the car keys and headed out the back. Buck sat silently beside Katie for a few minutes, then pulled her onto his lap. Her sobs muffled against his neck. He could feel her tears slide down and pool into his collar bone.

"Want to talk about it?" he asked.

She pushed back and sat up, hiccupped a couple of times and pushed the hair out of her eyes. She slid back over onto the cushion and looked up at him.

"I don't know if talking about it will make it better or worse. I'm sorry I soaked your shirt. I really thought I had it together before coming over here."

"Katie. Johnson told me where you were today. I can't imagine going through those images. Looking at those would bother anyone, but especially someone as kindhearted as you are. I know you try to keep up the tough image to lead your squad, but no one expects you to be made of iron."

"Oh, you know what they say about me. I'm a tough old bird."

"They say no such thing—especially not in Johnson's hearing. He'd rip them limb from limb."

"Can you point me to the ladies room? I need to put some cold water on my face. I'd even worn makeup for you. That's a lost cause."

He hugged her to him for a few minutes. "Katie, don't beat yourself up. You're a great detective and a wonderful human being. You're going to get the bastard who ruined those kids' lives. I've no doubt."

He watched Katie walk to what his mom always called his aunt's "powder room." As a child, he'd lifted up every container and opened the cabinets looking for the powder. A few minutes later, Katie came out, shaky but with a watery smile.

"Walk to the Oak Room for dinner? Hey, where's Jeb? Does he want to go too?"

"Sure. Let me get my coat. No, Jeb headed out to the twelve-step. He goes somewhere every day."

"Good for him. He's putting on a little weight too, isn't he?"

"Yep. I'd say it was my cooking, but you know better. It's great having him here even if only for a little while."

Katie slid her arm through his as they stepped off the wide front porch. Charles looked at them mournfully from the gap in the lace curtains lining the front window. They walked in silence the few blocks to the Oak Room. Opening the outside door, the heat and smells of charred steak hit them in the face.

The hostess escorted them to the back booth. It took a while to negotiate the greetings and good-natured joking from the people already seated. Handing them gargantuan menus, the hostess shrugged and said, "This is the boss's idea of a new and improved menu."

After they'd ordered and were alone, Katie said, "I've never felt so helpless as I did looking at those children suffering. I just can't get the images out of my mind. If I can't, how can they? Ever?"

"The best thing you can do is to use the images and the anger as fuel to get the monster or monsters who victimized them. So you can tell the children and their parents the monster won't hurt anyone else again."

They were quiet a minute.

"I helped a child in a civil suit against someone who had violated her," Buck said. "It was one of the hardest and most rewarding cases I'd ever had. All that child wanted was for the guy to admit to the world what he'd done to her. He agreed to it. When he finally did in open court, his family left him standing alone in the courtroom. The child smiled, getting the affirmation she needed. He valued his money more than the words she needed him to say."

"How do you deal with the horrors she went through?"

"I try to remember it was her struggle and she chose not to want my sympathy, but she did choose me to expose his sins to the light. To the community. To let people know just what kind of asshole he was."

"Vindication?"

"Vindication and affirmation she told the truth, as ugly as it was. That he did not make her who she was going to become. That *his* vile acts did not define *her*."

The waitress slid their plates onto the table with one deft motion. She refilled their iced tea glasses. "Anything else, hon?"

"We're good, thanks," Buck said, eyeing his all but charred rib eye he'd ordered medium rare. "Well, I hate to ask, but is this medium rare?"

She looked at the steak and then swooped it back up. "That damn new chef, he read medium well where I clearly wrote medium rare, see that big *R*?" She pointed to the handwritten check she'd put on their table.

"Okay. Yeah, I see it."

She turned to Katie. "How 'bout you, hon? Is yours right?"

Katie nodded.

"Be back in a flash. I'll get you some of those corn muffins. On the house."

Before Buck could protest, she was off, power walking to the back to the hapless chef.

"Do you want part of my salmon?" Katie asked.

"No thanks. I'm afraid of what she'd do to me after she's gotten in the chef's face on my order."

"Okay. How'd you think the meeting went with IRS? All Johnson would say is that it was a shit show."

"Can't disagree with him. Agent David was back in fine form, insulting everyone in the room. The IRS pinpointed irregularities they are going to pursue. The resident agent in charge is going to try to smooth things over so the IRS doesn't show up in Cary with subpoenas for the FBI's financials."

"Good Lord. Agent Thompson offered to go with me to review the forensic images on the judge's computer. I sent him over to O'Shea's house to photograph the rooms to check for backgrounds in the images. He had to deal with Mary Frances and her lawyer. Figured that would take some finesse.

"I don't see how he can stand David. The guy's a complete train wreck."

"I think David is the FBI's cross to bear. Something about the FBI in North Carolina sending an agent to D.C. last year that totally pissed off the Vice President. David's some kind of odd payback," Buck said.

"Jesus, we're trying to solve a murder case of a federal judge. Not play games with people's lives."

The waitress slid the big plate in front of Buck. "Cut into that," she said.

Buck gathered up his utensils and cut into the center. "Perfect."

She sashayed away with a look of triumph and back to the kitchen from where Buck and Katie could hear a lot of plates crashing and invectives in four languages.

"What're you doing tomorrow? Back to Raleigh?" he asked.

"No, I'm staying put and going over the notes I made and Margaret's analysis. I'm comparing hers to the IRS report I got today so I can issue subpoenas. I'm beginning to get an idea."

"I'm not going to ask where you're headed with it. I'll be in my office here in Oxford, if you need something, though."

"I'll call you if I can. I feel like we're getting close. How's the office, by the way? Emma Jean burn it down while you were away?"

"That would be funny if it wasn't so close to the truth. Emma Jean took a day off while I was in Raleigh, but she came in Friday to catch up on my phone calls. She heard some beeping she thought was coming from the waiting area's smoke detector. She used her lighter to check it and ended up soaking wet when the sprinklers went off. My files did too."

Katie tried not to laugh. "What did Cal say?"

"According to Cal, he chased her out the front door with a broom and told her not to come back. Of course, he really just yelled at her and told her to clean it up before I get back tomorrow."

"Poor Emma Jean."

"Poor Emma Jean? My insurance rates have tripled while she's been there.

"Cal is glad to quit covering my cases for me. He hates going to court. He doesn't mind the estate or real estate work, but he threatened to end the partnership if he had to talk to one more domestic client or go to court on one more speeding ticket."

The pair shared a gooey chocolate dessert and then walked back to Buck's house. While they were kissing on the porch, Jeb turned the light on. He poked his head out the heavy front door, "Hey guys, thought you'd like to be able to see out there."

"Good night, Buck. Thanks for dinner."

Buck gave his brother a look.

"Oh. Okay. Sorry." Jeb disappeared back into the house.

"Good night, Katie. I'll walk you to your car."

"It's right here in front."

Buck was going to kill his brother. He watched her get safely in her car, and then he jerked open the front door.

"Jeb!" he yelled.

Jeb, wisely, played least in sight and left Charles sitting in the hall smiling his doggy smile at Buck. Buck squatted down and scratched behind Charles's ears.

"I don't forgive him," he told the dog.

Buck ambushed Jeb in the kitchen while he was quietly opening a can of Coke. The sound of their running footsteps thudded all over the house then pounded outside. "I give, I give!" Jeb yelled.

Winded, Buck let him go. "Okay, dumbass. You turned the lights on us like Mom! You can get yourself back in my good graces by playing a game of HORSE."

"Beating the crap out of you helps me how?"

"Ha. Just get the ball, and I'll get the lights."

The sound of the basketball thudding against the pavement was a rhythm that soothed both.

Buck drained Jeb's Coke and let one fly over his shoulder from fifteen feet. Swoosh.

"Damn, Buck. Pretty good for an old dude."

Jeb matched the shot and then moved out farther out for one on the angle.

"You're losing your touch."

Buck bent over with hands on his knees breathing heavily. Almost harder than dealing with Jeb's addiction were the good times like these—when his brother was back with him. It wouldn't last, but there was pure joy in his heart while it did. In celebration, he knocked in the shot and then cut his brother's legs out from under him, hoping to hit the back door before Jeb did.

Chapter Sixteen

The New York lawyers were back. Each group sat stiffly by their client's side at the walnut tables, which were polished to a high gloss. Dark suits set off red ties at one table and blue ties at the other. Pencils and pens marched in military precision in front of each litigant. The attorneys were bright-eyed and expectant. Their clients slumped next to each team and looked markedly less confident.

Judge Evans took the bench, and court began.

"Here are the ground rules," she said, looking at each side for a beat. "Only the attorneys will speak or argue. There'll be no outbursts or unseemly behavior by anyone. If there is, you'll be watching the hearing from a holding cell. Any questions?"

Neither side wanted to piss her off, but each senior attorney wanted to talk, to show her how smart and obedient he was. Billing by the hour, it would be a crime to let the chance to address the court pass by.

The senior attorney for the plaintiff preened as he rose to his feet. "Harvey Thurgood Marshal for the plaintiff, Your Honor. Thank you for this opportunity. We do not wish to address the court at this time."

The senior attorney for the defendant shot to his feet jostling his client in his haste. "No questions here, Your Honor. We continue to appreciate the court's indulgence."

"Jesus God," Judge Evans muttered so only Phillip could hear. Phillip smiled and covered his snort with a cough. This would be his last hearing as a law clerk, and it was bitter-sweet. The bitter was the New York lawyers, and the sweet was the chance to write an opinion the judge would submit for publication.

The defendant, the client who'd previously been held in contempt of court for an earlier outburst, avoided eye contact. Agent Thompson sat next to the bench and balefully stared him down. Since the disruption in the courtroom, Agent Thompson followed Judge Evans wherever she went.

An hour later, each side had argued their remaining motions and replied to their opponent's arguments. "Thank you, gentlemen. I will recess for a few minutes, then return with my decision," Judge Evans said.

"All rise," intoned the bailiff. The attorneys prodded their owl-eyed clients into a standing position as she exited the courtroom.

Unzipping her robe, she gratefully sipped from the can of Diet Coke her assistant Brenda had thoughtfully left for her on her desk blotter.

"Well, Phillip? What do you think?"

Seeing Agent Thompson walk into her office, she said, "I think I'm okay here behind the security door."

"Absolutely, ma'am. I'll be outside when you're ready to reconvene court."

Phillip waited until the agent had left and said, "I told you he's sweet on you."

"Get serious, Phillip. The man's just doing his job. Now, let's talk about structuring the three parts of the opinion."

* * *

Silence hung like a pall over the courtroom. The court reporter's fingers were poised over her machine. The clerk readied the exhibit notebook on the bench and poured a glass of water for the judge. The blue-gray carpet absorbed all of the small rustles as people shifted and cleared their throats in anticipation of the ruling.

Judge Evans entered.

"Please be seated, everyone. After hearing from the parties and after giving this case and the matters before the court much thought, these will be my findings of fact and conclusions of law."

The judge began to recite the list of facts adopted by the court. When she moved on to the conclusions, the client at the table for the defendant, Earl Wilkerson, began to speak in angry loud whispers to his attorney. His face reddened as his attorney tried to placate him first with hand gestures and then in equally sharp whispers. The plaintiff won the motion for summary judgment.

The families in the audience either cheered or booed the decision, depending on their side. Court security officers hastily sent the hecklers outside, but their loud voices could be heard in the courtroom.

Wilkerson stood up, threw over the table, and hit his attorney in the jaw with a meaty "whap." Then, all hell broke loose. Wilkerson hitched up his pants and started striding towards the bench. His stunned attorney weakly slapped at his arm, but Wilkerson shook him off.

Launching himself from beside the bench, Agent Thompson tackled him below the knees. Judge Evans searched blindly behind her for the knob to the door that would allow her and Philip to exit back to safety. The defendant kept screaming, "I want to talk to the judge! Get off me! I want to talk to the judge! She's made a big mistake!" Flailing on the floor, he turned his vitriol toward the winning party and his counsel.

"Goddamnit, I'll get you for this. You lying sack of shit!"

The two began scrabbling on top of the desk—grabbing papers and pads—and avoiding further eye contact. Court security officers pushed them out of the courtroom and radioed for backup.

Wilkerson was under the agent hissing with choked breath, "Get off me, you bastard. Get off me." Despite his lack of oxygen, he continued to throw his arms around to avoid the cuffs. His attorney stood open-mouthed but away from the escalating struggle. His jaw bloomed red and purple where he'd been hit.

Every time Thompson grabbed Wilkerson's arm, he jerked it away. The cuffs kept clanging around. Only grunting and heavy breathing could be heard as the two struggled towards the doors to the lobby.

For a minute, Wilkerson stopped struggling enough to eye his attorney who was mincing his way toward the exit.

"You piece of shit, where are you going? What did you do? You spent my money and promised me O'Shea would hear this case, no problem. That bitch ought to be where O'Shea is now."

His attorney slowly backed away never taking his eyes off his rabid client. Using his briefcase as a shield, he pushed the courtroom door open with his hip and was gone.

"Yeah, run, you coward. You piece of shit. You made me send big money to the judge, and I got nothing for it! You said this would never go to trial, you goddamn liar," Wilkerson screamed. Suddenly, he went limp. The agent rolled him over to make sure he was still breathing. Satisfied he was, Thompson put the cuffs on him and helped him get to his feet. He assured the man he would get to make a phone call and he could get a court-appointed lawyer if he wanted one.

"Look, man, do you want to talk to me about what you said back there? About O'Shea?"

Wilkerson spat at his feet, then closed his eyes and leaned back against the court bench. "Nope."

Deputies from the Wake County Sheriff's Office arrived and offered to take the prisoner down to the county jail.

Thompson agreed and released him into their custody. After a few minutes and a few phone calls, the Wake County sheriff, Raleigh Police, and FBI negotiated jurisdiction.

"Man, that could have been a real shit storm. Wilkerson was big son-of-a-gun," Thompson broke off muttering to himself and massaged his sore shoulder. Maybe the FBI would get a lead on O'Shea's killer after all.

Thompson found the court reporter shaking in the lobby to Judge Evans's chambers. Judge Evans was seated beside her and talking quietly about the recorder. She'd found out the reporter had left the recorder on when she'd run from the courtroom. Wilkerson's statements about Evans and O'Shea would be on the tape. Buck brought the reporter a cup of water, and she settled down enough to go back into the courtroom with a deputy U.S. Marshal and began listening for the parts the agent wanted transcribed.

From chambers, Agent Thompson called the TSA at the Raleigh Durham International airport. Judge Evans sat lost in thought while he made the call.

"Jason? Hey, this is Thompson. Yeah, man. Still here in Raleigh. Can you do me a favor? Keep this guy from New York from boarding the plane back up. In fact, I'll email you a list of New Yorkers that need to be put in a room and interviewed. It'll be me or David. Yeah, I know. I'll try to get there myself. See ya."

His last calls were to the United States Attorney's Office for the Eastern District of North Carolina and to the United States Marshal Service. The marshals agreed to transport the guy in holding and the assistant United States Attorney agreed to set up his initial appearance before the magistrate judge for later that afternoon for a criminal contempt charge. Once the guy was appointed an attorney, or waived the appointment, he'd interview him. He'd send Agent David to the airport to interview the New Yorkers.

* * *

Angela sat with her sister Loretta, Phillip, and Buck back in chambers. They'd gathered there before walking out to Phillip's farewell lunch. Loretta's hands were shaking, but she forced a smile to her lips.

"Phillip, I hate to see you leave, but congratulations on your new job. You'll be working a lot of hours, but I have every confidence you'll make partner in record time. You'll make a fantastic associate with your research and writing skills."

"Thank you, Judge Evans. It's been an honor working here. I've learned so much during my clerkship. I appreciate you giving me the chance to work for you after Judge O'Shea died. I'll miss you all."

"When do you start at the firm?" Buck asked.

"I've started working part-time so I can get the law firm benefits and finish up the one remaining order for Judge Evans. The firm still hasn't decided if I'll work on white collar crime or be assigned to their bankruptcy section, or both. I should know that much by tomorrow."

"That's a great opportunity. You'll do well there." Turning to Loretta, Buck asked, "Judge, are you up to going out, or do you want to postpone lunch until tomorrow?"

"No, I'd like to celebrate with Phillip today. Let me clear it with Agent Thompson, then we can head out. It may take a few minutes to find him. I can meet y'all in the lobby."

Angela protested. "Are you sure you're okay? You were really upset when you came back from court. Phillip won't mind if we wait one more day, will you?"

"No. Absolutely not. Really, it's okay. Judge Evans, I've got to draft the opinion for you from today's case. Plus, I'm back here for a half day tomorrow, and we can go then if you'd feel better about it."

"No, guys, I'm fine. Let's go."

Judge Evans got Agent Thompson's approval to leave the courthouse on the condition she take along a deputy marshal escort. A deputy trailed the group while they walked over to

Big Ted's. Another deputy marshal walked in front, scanning the sidewalks and city park for potential threats.

At lunch, talk naturally returned back to the court proceedings and the money supposedly given to O'Shea.

"I don't think the IRS found any big cash deposits, but I'll call them or Katie after lunch to see if the FBI gave them a heads up. Seems like they'd have latched onto that sort of thing pretty quickly," Buck said.

"That came out of left field. Thompson said his attorney just stood there stunned. They're holding up the attorneys from New York at the airport to find out what they know about it. He said the lawyers wouldn't quit screaming at each other, so they were put in separate rooms." Judge Evans sighed.

"Hope they brought an overnight bag. Those guys are gonna be here awhile. Admitting to bribing a federal judge is damn serious," Buck said.

The group of four took pictures in front of the restaurant on everyone's phone before heading back to the courthouse. Phillip asked the judge as they wound through the large trees in Moore Square Park, "Did you decide if you want me to work on an order or an opinion to publish?"

She laughed. "Phillip, trust you to stay focused even in your final hours. Let's do an order given the new developments."

Angela said goodbye in front of the courthouse and headed off to her last appointment with the new therapist. Phillip left Loretta and Buck outside on the benches enjoying their Styrofoam containers of banana pudding. The sun shone brightly on the square concrete planters filled with marigolds waving in the slight breeze. The court security officers stood a few feet away discreetly watching the streets in front and beside them.

"Buck, I'll miss seeing you over here too. I've enjoyed having you around to chat about cases. But I bet your law partner will be glad when you're back in the office.

"Guess I'll also need to hire a new law clerk. I've put off interviewing anyone. I don't know why."

"It's hard to move on after something as traumatic as O'Shea's death. Now it looks like the events before his death are pretty sordid," Buck said. "That's a lot to deal with in a short span. You'll find someone as good as Phillip and one you'll like just as well as Jennifer. With five law schools in the state, you'll have your pick of a great clerk."

"I guess so. Did you know O'Shea snagged him before I could get him in for an interview? I made the mistake of telling him Phillip was on my list of top two. Telling him was like waving a flag in front of a bull. I should have guessed he'd go after who I wanted just for spite."

Buck leaned back and turned toward to the deputy marshal sitting at the adjoining bench. "You want any pudding, deputy?"

The deputy shook his head, unsmiling and continued to maintain a watchful silence behind his mirrored aviators.

* * *

The gloomy small holding cell was crammed full. The men sat knee to knee. Thompson ushered Wilkerson into the adjoining smaller cell. The FBI agents were uncomfortably seated in gray plastic chairs. Wilkerson sat down and slumped on the hard metal bench next to his new lawyer. The new lawyer's suit was shiny and looked worn in spots.

Miranda rights were read and signed off on. Silence and cherry disinfectant did not mask the smell of remorse or the odor of stale urine.

The man shuffled his feet. "Okay. Okay, I'll tell you what you want to know. That New York attorney told me I'd get O'Shea to hear my case if I paid more. So, I had to pay on top of the huge attorney fees. Then things started going bad with my case, and I had to pay so O'Shea would not hear my case. I paid the last installment near the time the guy died. I want immunity."

His new young attorney chimed in, "He wants immunity. This is good stuff, you guys." The attorney looked around as eagerly as a retriever who'd managed to find and return the ball he'd been thrown.

His client glared at him. "God help me," he muttered.

The agents leaned back in their chairs in tandem. The plastic chairs protested, squeaking on the hard concrete floor. They communicated silently then one of them said, "Okay, we'll call the U.S. Attorney's office." The other agent left, and after a few minutes returned.

"The U.S. attorney will give you immunity from prosecution on the bribe to O'Shea if you are truthful, if you give us details we can corroborate, and if you tell us your whole involvement in this, and anyone else's."

Wilkerson looked hard at his court-appointed attorney who was still smiling at everyone. "I want it in writing."

The attorney's smile slipped a bit. "He wants it in writing," he repeated.

Another screech, and the agent disappeared for longer this time. He returned with a signed letter of immunity on the U.S. Attorney's Office letterhead. The guy read it over and handed it to his attorney. "Hold on to this." The attorney put it into his briefcase and snapped it closed.

"Okay. Here's the way it went down. That New York lawyer said he'd gone to school with O'Shea and that we needed O'Shea on the case. So, I had to write a big check. Then he called me later and said, "No, you have to do this in smaller amounts." So, I tore up the check and wrote three smaller checks."

Thompson interrupted. "What bank were you using? Was it your personal or business account?"

"I used my personal checking account. My wife has the stubs. You'll get copies. I told her to go to the bank today and get them."

His attorney's head bobbed. "Today," he said.

Wilkerson looked at him in disgust. "Okay, like I was saying, a few weeks after I retained him the attorney called back and said he needed more money, but this time he wanted cash. I'm like "What the fuck for?" He asked me, did I want to win the case or not. So, I went down to the bank. I gave the courier for the lawyer the money in a bank deposit bag. I got a receipt from him. About a week later he said that things went wrong and I had to pay more money. I had to write another check to get the case transferred away from O'Shea. Something like he had friends on the other side who were suing me, from the town where he'd prosecuted before. Anyway, I told the guy—the lawyer—I couldn't get that kind of cash immediately, and it'd have to be a check. Then O'Shea died before he got the money or deposited it, I guess. I really don't know."

Agent Thompson fired off, "Did you write the last check? Did your check clear? What account did you use?"

"I wrote one on a Bank of America account. The first time, before the lawyer called me back wanting cash, I had to do three checks to keep each amount under ten thousand. I mailed them to O'Shea's chambers and marked the envelope "personal." My attorney told me how to do it and for how much.

I couldn't afford to lose the lawsuit. The publicity would've killed my business. For someone to get away with calling me a "racist"—that didn't sit well either. I'm not. I'm a businessman. Hell, over half of my customers are Black farmers."

Thompson interrupted him. "Who told you O'Shea would be interested in this kind of a deal?"

"My attorney. That asshole." He glared at his new one who shrank back along the metal bench.

"Anyone else present during the conversations? Any other member of the law firm?"

He thought a minute. 'No, I don't think so. Wait, maybe one of those younger lawyers was there. An associate. Look, I got tractor and farm dealerships up and down the east coast, including one in Oxford. I don't need this thing to go south."

"So, you thought it'd be a good idea to bribe a federal judge?"

"Well, no. My attorney did. But, then it started sounding good. Then the bastard up and died. I tried calling the lawyers. Then I tried calling the other side's lawyer. No one would talk to me or return my calls. What I wanna know is where's my goddamn money?"

"That is the least of your problems. How much money, and when were the installments paid?"

"Twenty-five thousand for the first checks and thirty thousand for the rest. That's a lot of money. The first time was around when the 1983 suit was filed. The rest right before the judge died."

Thompson looked at Wilkerson's appointed attorney. The attorney was beaming back at him as if his client had just won the national spelling bee.

"What address did you use? Or did the firm handle the first installment? Any type of letter or note added for the first payment?"

"Other than what I told you, how the hell would I know? Ask my lawyer. Not you, ace," he said to the new one.

"We intend to. Is that all you can tell us?"

"Yeah. My wife will let you have my checkbook, check register, and withdrawal slips. I kept all that shit. I also took a photo of the envelope I mailed out. My lawyer here can give her a call. Look I didn't mean that lady judge any harm. I wouldn't have laid a finger on her. You gotta believe me. I was just pissed off about my case and my money."

"That's a whole separate issue. We're not going to talk to you about what happened today. Your detention hearing is in three days. In the meantime, we'll see if the documents you have back up what you say."

The agents left the cell. Wilkerson turned to his attorney. "Okay, Hester. Go earn your money. Call my wife and get those documents to these guys today."

Crestfallen, his attorney said, "My name's not Hester."

"I know, kid. Just try not to fuck this up. I need to cooperate and fast with those agents. You need me, you know where I'll be." He banged on the door for the deputy marshal.

CHAPTER SEVENTEEN

Katie threw the cuffs into her top desk drawer. She leaned back stretching out the kinks in her back. Her pony tail stuck up on top of her head like a mast. She'd brushed the dried dirt off her khaki pants as best she could before sitting down in her office chair. The old relic had been borrowed from the magistrate's office down the hall around the time when most folks rode their horses into town.

Johnson strolled in with two Styrofoam cups of coffee. Each was stamped Sunny's Biscuits, so at least she knew it wasn't the black goop from the breakroom. Finding one old chair that wasn't piled high with files, he sat down and sighed. Sipping from his cup, Johnson turned to face Katie. The butterfly suture over his eye did not deflect from the huge shiner under it growing bigger by the minute.

"That was a good day's work, LT," Johnson said. "How many is that total? Did you check in with the last two deputies? Those two had the southern end of the county. I think they got some good leads on a few men on our list."

"Seven arrested in all," Katie said.

She flipped through the papers in the nearest stack. "That last guy put up a hell of a fight. He hit you hard with that beer bottle. Your eye looks like Tyson took a swing at you and connected. Is it hurting you?"

"Nah, I'm alright. It'll leave a bruise is all. I don't know what got into him. Most of these sex offenders are scrawny, nerdy-looking white dudes. That guy didn't get the memo. He packed a wallop."

Johnson had grabbed the guy by his turkey wattle neck before he could swing the busted Bud Lite bottle a second time. The offender clawed at Johnson's ham-sized arms for air and then for the ground once Johnson lifted him up. His mom stood by throwing pots and pans and screaming into Johnson's ear that her "baby ain't had nothing to do with a damn thing."

"Aren't you going to get that shiner checked out at the hospital? I know Doc sewed you up, but you might need X-rays."

"Naw. A little ice will fix it. I want to see this thing through—charge the bastards with violating their probation and with the filth we found in their bedrooms."

"You're doing the paperwork for all this?" Katie asked. "The rest of the shift are over at the magistrate's office getting bond set for the ones we arrested. Old man Thorp is the magistrate, so they'll have no chance to make any bond he sets when he sees the charges."

Johnson snorted. "You got that right. Hopefully none of the district court judges will monkey with the bond when the pervs go to court for their first appearances tomorrow." He drained his cup and stood. "I'll go type up the reports."

"Are you heading home after?" Katie asked.

"No. I've got to call the federal agents that were working on the rest of the sex offender roundup. They collared some guy in Raleigh who looked like a possible fit to receiving some of the more recent photos on the judge's computer. I want to find out if he talked about anything."

"Later then. Don't stay all night."

Johnson shrugged into his lightweight jacket and headed for his office in the gloomy basement of the building. The sheriff had offered him one upstairs when he'd made sergeant, but he preferred the cool and quiet to the upstairs offices, which were subject to the public—angry girlfriends, angry wives, angry boyfriends, and angry husbands—wandering in unannounced. Johnson liked the relative calm downstairs where he could play his Darius Rucker CDs unmolested.

Upstairs, Katie turned on her small iPod and put her ear buds in. The strains of Jason Aldean's new song helped her to relax. A few minutes later, she called Buck.

"Hey, I was thinking about you," she began.

"I was thinking about you, too."

"I can't come over tonight. I gotta call the locals in Raleigh. Johnson's calling the feds. They each caught a few perverts in the round up. We got a few ourselves. Can I come over tomorrow?"

"Yeah, sure. Jeb's got a meeting, so we should have the house to ourselves for a little while. I promise not to cook."

"Deal. I'll pick up something on the way over."

"Miss you."

"I miss you, too."

After Katie hung up, she indulged in a few minutes of feeling sorry for herself. Afterwards, she grabbed a chocolate from her faux crystal candy dish. "Let's get this the hell over with," she mumbled around the caramel.

She'd talked to Sally in the DA's office earlier. After hearing the descriptions of some of the photos retrieved off the sex offenders' phones and iPads, Sally agreed to charge a felony for each sordid, sickening image of the children pictured. The judge might be pissed off with all the paperwork. Sally didn't care. She promised to not back down and to take on the cases the federal government did not take.

Katie picked up the photo of her dad off her desk. He looked so young and handsome in his uniform. The picture was taken right before a drunk driver had run him and his patrol car off the road and into a ditch. "Oh, Dad. I don't have your instincts. I don't have your strength. But please look out for me from up there and help me to help these poor children."

* * *

Early the next day, Buck was staring into space while sitting at his desk in Oxford. The sunlight filtered in through white Irish lace curtains his mom had insisted lent the office the right gravitas. Emma Jean miraculously had made it in on time and put the day's files in the center of the massive piece of furniture he'd inherited from his Aunt Tilley. He'd reviewed half of the files but stopped when he realized he'd read the same paragraph three times over. Hearing raised voices, he stepped out into the hall, closer to the reception area.

Mary Frances O'Shea, in this season's mint green Chanel suit, was standing one inch away from Emma Jean's pert nose. "I told you, miss," drawing the sound out like a huge serpent, "that I want to see Buck, and I'll see him now." She stuck a hand on her hip for emphasis.

It took a lot to get Emma Jean riled, but that did it.

"Listen here, you. You need an appointment, and I don't care who you are. That's the way it is." Emma Jean's face was almost puce. "But since you drove up from Raleigh, if you will sit down, I will buzz Mr. Davis and see if he can work you in before court. If he can't, you've got to hoof it." Emma Jean swished her skirt out of the way to sit at the reception desk but waited until Mary Frances had retreated to her corner of the office and was seated before calling Buck.

Buck sprinted back into his office to avoid being caught eavesdropping and grabbed the phone on the last ring. Emma Jean said, "There's some woman out here to see you. She doesn't have an appointment. She says she is Mrs. O'Shea." Her tone nearly froze the receiver.

"Okay, thanks, Emma Jean, I'll be out in a few minutes. Thanks for letting me know."

Buck waited a good ten minutes to appease his assistant. When he ushered Mary Frances into his office, she was fuming. It didn't help that Charles chose that moment to share his chewed-up pink bunny rabbit with her and her suit.

"Dreadful filthy creature," she muttered, whipping out a pristine monogrammed handkerchief to dab at the drooled-upon skirt.

"Well, I don't think Emma Jean's all that bad. She can be a bit crabby some days, but overall she's pretty great."

She stared at him. "No, you idiot. Your dog."

"Oh, Charles. Well, he's pretty great too."

"Look, I came here to show you my recent bank records where someone has gotten into my accounts. They said the lieutenant was out this morning, so I'm leaving them with you. I didn't want to give them to one of her underlings. It's under ten thousand each time, but there are a lot of withdrawals. I left a copy with my attorney to hand over to his counterpart at the FBI. I'm heading back to France, and I wanted to make sure I handled this personally. Could it be the person who killed the judge? Why would they keep targeting me?"

Her voice began to shake and she lowered it, "I need to put this all behind me. His death, the nightmare about the money, the allegations his law clerk is making about being forced, about being…"

She trailed off and stood staring into space. Buck gave her time to compose herself.

Shoving the files on his desk to one side, she spread out the documents she'd brought with her. She'd circled the unauthorized transactions in red.

"These are the strange ones I can't account for in any way. I left a power of attorney with my attorney. If you all want any of the paper documents related to the accounts, just ask him to get them to Lt. O'Connor or the FBI. It adds up to over $200,000.00."

Absently, she placed her hand on Charles's big head. He'd crept closer while she was talking. He thumped his tail into the side of the desk.

"I hope you catch whoever is responsible. No one deserves to die like that. Not even the judge, up there swinging from the chandelier. Oh, it's just too horrible."

She pulled out a sodden handkerchief and dabbed at her eyes. Recoiling from the mild doggy smell, she wadded it up and threw it in the wooden wastepaper basket.

"He wasn't a bad man. He had his faults like anyone else. We didn't really have a marriage for a long time before this. I think, well, I know when we found out we couldn't have children, we just drifted apart. There were no real bad feelings. Just a coldness, an absence of caring, but he deserves justice like anyone else. I hope his killer rots in prison."

"I'm so sorry for your loss. I know getting closure is important to you. The officers and agents are working hard on getting it solved, I promise you. I'll make sure Katie—the LT—gets your papers today, Mrs. O'Shea. She'll appreciate you driving them here for her. Is someone with you? I'd hate for you to have to drive back by yourself."

"Yes, I've got Guillaume. He's studying at State and does odd jobs for me at the house when he's not in class. I'll be fine," she said more briskly. "I froze my accounts and have an appointment this afternoon at the bank to open new ones."

"Send me your new address or your attorney's number. I'll make sure Katie gets it so you don't have to go back down to the sheriff's office."

Her black low-heeled Ferragamos made distinct clicks on the hardwood as she left. Buck barely got there in time to open the firm's door for her. He watched her slide into a large dark town car double parked at the curb. People walking by stopped what they were doing to take in the sight.

Mildred, his octogenarian former speeding ticket client, ambled over from the shade of the Western Auto's awning next door and asked Buck, "Was that a movie star? She looked a bit like Grace Kelly. Is it someone I'd know?" She obviously hoped to share the details of her "sighting" with all of the other "girls" at bridge.

"No, ma'am. She's just visiting for a minute."

She persisted. "Now, are you sure it's no one famous? Is she in one of the magazines like *Vanity Fair*? She looked real familiar."

"No, she's not a movie star. Mildred, I'm heading on over to court, but I have time for a quick cup of coffee. Can I treat you to one?"

He held out his arm for her and escorted her over to the wrought iron bench knowing she eschewed the walker she'd been prescribed.

Mildred beamed up at him. "Sure, that'd be nice, Buck. And me here in my casual clothes. I guess it's early though. There won't be anyone to see me dressed like this."

She smoothed down her blue rinsed hair, lightly toned with Angel's Delight hair dye, and peered up at him from under her very few lashes.

"You've made my day. Let me grab those files and my jacket. I'll be right back."

The two jaywalked across Main Street and sat down at the drug store counter. He knew Mildred would have preferred a table in the front window, but all of the tables were full. A few people stopped at the counter and spoke to them as they were leaving the store. Mildred patted her hair.

"How's your brother Jeb doing? I loved having him in my art class in high school. Could always depend on him to be creative and not draw the same old tired bowl of fruit. Except that one time he 'overdrew' Michelangelo's statue of David. I couldn't stay mad too long. He shocked that temporary principal we had so bad she had to lie down for the rest of the day in the nurse's room. That lady didn't come back to work for a week."

"Oh, he's fine. He's been home a few weeks now. I like having him around. He's been over to Mom's a good bit to help her with the yard. It's the darnedest thing. He can make anything grow. He's got the old wisteria back blooming. And, last week, he dug her a goldfish pond and put some water lilies in it. Used the stones from the woods. Mom loves it."

"If he gets the blues again, just call me. I'd like to spend some time with him." She added more quietly, "You know, my Albert got the blues a lot toward the end. He said me being there made him feel a bit better. He just couldn't turn loose of the alcohol, or it wouldn't turn loose of him. He was a sweet gentle man. Reminds me a bit of Jeb."

Buck put some bills down in front of their coffee cups. "Thank you. I'll call you if he needs a friendly ear. I gotta run next door to court. Hope you beat the ladies on Wednesday and bring home the big pot of money."

She gave a girlish giggle. "Now Buck, you know us Baptist gals ain't into no gambling. Well, the winner does get to take the leftover dessert home."

He laughed, gathered up his files, and headed toward the red brick three-story courthouse. The trim around the huge wooden double doors was painted white, and the cupola on top was a verdigris. A couple of men standing in a group on the small porch nodded or called out to Buck as he passed by.

Buck had a couple of afternoon court appearances. He checked the calendar outside the courtroom to make sure they'd not switched up judges or the ADA on him.

His two clients were in the six by four holding cell beating on the window. Little Curtis was in there too, yelling to see him. The old bailiff finally found the right key and let Little Curtis out with leg shackles on to talk to him.

"Hey, man. What's happening?" asked Little Curtis.

"You tell me. Why are you back in?"

"Aw shit. My girl got mad at me and called the cops. She told them I had an AR-15 and an AK-47. But that was bull-shit—and call me *Cee*."

"So why are you in?"

"Well, I had a gun hidden up under the toilet tank and this time they came in with a search warrant. Found the damn thing. There was one good thing though."

"What's that?"

"They forgot to take my sack of crack I had in the kitchen. Had it by a stack of money up on the top of the kitchen cabinet. They did take my damn money."

"Dammit, Cee. They're going to take you federal if you keep this up."

"Whatever. Look, man. Heard you were looking for some freaks."

"What do you mean?"

"You know, them kiddie fiddlers."

"What do you know about it?"

"I got a cousin who's into some of that shit. He just ain't right. You want me to get him to talk to you? Will that get me in good with the sheriff's people?"

"It might, but I can't promise. Lt. O'Connor and Johnson are in charge of the sheriff's investigation. I can see if they'll get up with you. Who's your attorney for the new charge?"

Cee stared at Buck.

"Oh no. I just got your bond reduced earlier because the visiting judge made me represent you that day. I can't handle your case unless I'm retained. Sorry, Cee."

"Aw c'mon. Y'all represented my daddy and my brother. Why can't you represent me? I'll get you some money. My girl ain't mad anymore and she'll bring it to you."

"I'll talk to Lt. O'Connor or Johnson, but that's it. I'm sorry. I gotta meet with the two other guys in the cell before court starts."

"I'll get my girl to bring you $25,000."

"She brings it, we'll talk again, but no promises."

"Thanks. 'preciate it."

Chapter Eighteen

In the FBI's cramped conference room at the federal courthouse, the main sounds were the rustling of paper and the scratching of pens. Periodically, someone typing on his or her iPad interrupted the gloom with a barked question. The deputies huddled in one corner passing around mug shots of the suspects from the sexual offender roundup. In another corner, Margaret and the IRS agents talked quietly. Fingers flew across calculator buttons. Spreadsheets draped over their table softly blowing in the puffs of air-conditioning.

Johnson, Katie, and Buck stepped out into the hallway with Agents David and Thompson at David's request.

David spoke first. "I don't know why we're wasting time on the perverts when you know the culprit is the guy with the money. That Wilkerson guy or someone he paid. Buck, go downstairs and get the printout from the clerk's office for O'Shea's expenses and payments for the last five years and the list of his cases where restitution was ordered. I told them I needed to get it from them last night."

Buck started to move toward the stairs, but Katie held up her hand to stop him.

"Look, David. I know you think it's all about the money, but I'm not sure I buy that. Plus, it's Saturday. The clerk's office is not going to be open."

"Look, sweetie, you're out of your depth here. Why don't you run along to lunch with Buck and Johnson and leave this case to the trained investigators?"

"Oh boy," Johnson muttered. He wedged himself between Katie and David and spoke before she could grind out a response.

"I don't know how they do things up where you come from, agent, but we work together down here. And, as for 'trained investigators,' the LT here has been trained by the best. Five times, she's been detailed to the State Bureau of Investigation on specific request of the Governor to help solve complicated murder cases and to the FBI for violent crimes. You're just trying to get rid of us because you think you're close to solving the murder and you're a glory hound. You need to head back to DC or wherever and quit interfering with the officers who're actually working. And quit insulting the women officers and agents with your sexist comments. They're worth a whole hell of a lot more than you are."

"I'm fucking calling the sheriff," David snarled back. "You're done here. You and your little band of yokels. This is my investigation, so get the hell out. All of you."

Wordlessly, the trio moved towards the stairs. Katie paused and then headed back into the conference room. Thompson whispered furiously to David further down the hall.

"Deputies," she announced to the room. "The FBI does not want our help. Go home to your families and enjoy the rest of your Saturday. I really appreciate the overtime you've put in and will tell each of your supervisors how helpful y'all have been. I really appreciate it."

Margaret and the two IRS agents looked up from their table and fell silent. Then, in one accord, they picked up their handbags.

The deputies wordlessly filed out past the FBI agents, followed by Margaret and the IRS. Johnson invited each one to lunch, but they declined, wanting to get on the road home.

"There you go, Agent David. Lock up the courthouse when you leave."

"Goddamnit, lieutenant. You instigated a mutiny. What kind of officer are you?"

"I don't have to answer to you, thank God. If the sheriff wants me back, I'll be back. Right now, I'm going to enjoy what's left of the weekend. C'mon, guys."

* * *

An hour later, after Katie got the go ahead from the Sheriff, they reconvened in O'Shea's suite of rooms. A couple of the deputies had gone home, but some stayed, diligently going through the photos. Margaret and the IRS agents used O'Shea's chambers while Katie, Johnson, and the deputies used the reception area. Buck stayed in Phillip's office trying to get the clerk on the phone.

One of the deputies held up a copy of an image taken off the computer owned by the man who'd hit Johnson. "I'll be damned," he said. He shuffled through the pile of photos taken off O'Shea's computer and compared them. They were almost identical.

He called out, "Hey, LT. Think I got something here." Katie leaned over his shoulder after putting on pink-striped readers. She studied the photos for a few minutes and then called Johnson over.

"No doubt," Johnson said. "That's the same image. Do we know the child in the picture?"

"I'll go back to the list, but I don't think this child has ever been identified. The image looks fairly dated, doesn't it?"

"What do you mean?"

"The clothing on the floor. The shirt style and logo—that band folded pretty quickly after their first album. More of a 1980s look I'd say than current day."

"I see what you mean. Yeah, you're right.

"I'll call the Center for Missing and Exploited Children. Maybe someone's working today."

Katie turned to the deputy. "Good work. Let me know if you see anything else in your stack. So, this came from the last guy we arrested in Granville County, in Oxford?"

"Yes, ma'am. From the guy that smacked Johnson a big one upside his head."

Johnson glared at the deputy.

"Do we have anything on the photo to identify it as his?" asked Katie.

"No, but I'll write the suspect and location on the back of it. We're each working on downloads from separate suspects."

"Great. Call out if y'all see anything else we can check out."

Johnson walked over. "Hey, Katie, I spoke to Cee, you know, Little Curtis Hockaday. His guy, his creep, wasn't one we picked up. Found out today the son of a gun died from a drug overdose last night. Whatever he knew, he took with him," Johnson said.

"Thanks for following up on it. Little Curtis Hockaday will be disappointed he can't get some help on his charges. I heard the feds are coming in this week to look at the reports in his case. I think the ATF is sending Larry Bradsher, some task force agent. He's from down Rocky Mount way."

"Little Curtis is gonna be pissed."

"Yeah, well, it's his own damn fault. His girl also tried to slip him a gun during visiting hours today at the jail, but the revolver got tangled up in her hair so the deputies booked her," said Katie. "I think she took it out to use on him because they'd gotten into a fight. He'd called her the 'H' word."

Johnson thought for a minute.

"What's the 'H' word?" Johnson asked.

"'Ho.'"

Johnson shook his head and walked back over to his desk.

A few minutes later, Margaret came out of chambers to talk to Katie.

"I think we've found something. We've been going through the bank records and looking through check registers and bank statements. We've found Wilkerson's money in an account we didn't know about. The subpoenas for records went to all of the nearby banks just in case. One of those was the local federal credit union. That's where Wilkerson's money ended up, but it went back out pretty quickly after deposit. That's our next step. To figure out where it went next. The IRS has better resources to get the follow up documents. They're going by the credit union tomorrow. I know it's none of my business, but don't let that FBI agent intimidate you. You're doing all of the right things here."

"Thanks, Margaret, for the hours you've spent on these records and for the words of support. I appreciate it."

Chapter Nineteen

Buck thought Phillip had left the small law clerk's office fairly neat for a lawyer. A few legal pads were on the table along with a smattering of pens, paper clips, and staples. He started shelving the file boxes on the empty bookshelves. *United States v. Santos* took up an entire shelf on its own. *United States v. Peterson* and *United States v. Warren* took up only half a box. The boxes were marked in black permanent marker and filled with the next docket's court cases set to begin in two weeks. He'd spent a few late nights organizing and summarizing the files for the visiting judge who would be assigned to hear some of them.

Buck flipped off the light switch and began to pull the door closed. A small stack of files and papers were in the corner on the floor. A couple of pieces of paper were wedged between the baseboard and the wall nearest the door jamb. He stooped to pick everything up. The biggest piece wedged in the baseboard was an old photograph of a group of folks. The papers next to it were case notes on the 1983 case. Phillip must have overlooked these when he loaded up his car. Buck threw everything in his briefcase, planning to drop it and another file folder off to Phillip sometime next week. He caught himself whistling as he headed to the exit. Tonight, he planned to redeem himself and his culinary skills with Katie over a romantic homemade dinner. He'd even bought new placemats to replace the aqua horrors his Aunt Tilley had used every day. They'd matched the Frigidaire, as she had called it.

* * *

Charles greeted him with a cold nose but refused to look at him. *Uh-oh.* "Charles," he said, "what is going on? What did you do?" Charles turned his head away and stood still. Buck headed to the kitchen, slinging his briefcase and jacket onto the nearest chair. The briefcase fell and popped open on the floor.

"Jesus," Buck stopped at the entrance to the kitchen. Steak bits were strewn everywhere as well as what looked like broccoli, tomatoes, carrots, and lumpish yellow bits. "Charles! What the hell?!" Charles whined and backpedaled to the front door.

Dinner for Katie was a bust. The smell was bad enough that he opened all the windows and back door to the porch. Apparently, the dog had not liked the gourmet meal and had returned it.

The front door slammed shut. Jeb ambled in. "Dang, man. What is that smell?" Pulling his t-shirt up and over his mouth and nose he said, "Oh, gross. Did you get into a food fight with Charles?"

"No, your damn dog opened up the fridge and ate half of everything I planned to cook for Katie. Look! Here's a half a stick of butter!"

The mangled butter had prominent teeth marks and an unknown wet substance on it. Buck wiped his hands on his pants without thinking. "Goddamnit! Now I've got to go change. Clear this mess up! He's your damn dog!"

"Whoa, man. *Now* he's my dog? You two have been living here thick as two thieves until today. I'll help you, but he's your dog too!" Jeb shouted.

Charles whimpered trying to edge under the chintz loveseat, knocking over knickknacks they'd never bothered to move or replace. He wedged himself halfway under, but his back legs and tail were still out.

"I'm supposed to cook for Katie tonight—now this?! This place smells like a slaughterhouse, but worse!" Buck's gorge started to rise, and he ran out the back for some air.

Jeb got a broom and a mop out of the pantry. A few minutes later, Charles came back into the room and lay down next to Jeb's feet when he sat down to take a smoke break. Jeb scratched his head. "Damn, Charles, you really want to stay in here?" Charles yawned and put his head on Jeb's shoe. "Come on, I'd better finish up or Buck will be even more pissed."

Jeb headed to the den to pick up the papers from the floor and put them into Buck's briefcase. Buck was taking a shower before his date. He'd calmed down and even threw the ball for Charles when he went outside to wait for Katie to pull up.

Jeb squinted and held the papers closer trying to tell the difference between the law papers and the bills that had fallen off onto the floor. He'd ignored all pleas by his mom to go to the eye doctor for his nearsightedness.

Buck came in toweling his hair with another towel wrapped around his waist. "Hey, thanks for cleaning up the mess. Katie's fine with meeting me at the Oak Room. Her food will probably be better than my meal. Want to come with us? I owe you."

Jeb shook his head. "Nah, that's alright. I'm thinking about heading out and over to Raleigh tonight with some friends. Hear a band we like. Thanks anyway. Hey, where'd you get this picture?" He handed the stack over to Buck.

"That was in Phillip's office. You know the old law clerk? Why?"

"It looks like something I've seen before, in the background. I don't know. Maybe I'm making this up. Just something familiar is all." He continued to study it.

"Stick it back in the briefcase when you're done with it."

"Yeah, okay. You and Katie have fun. Don't be home late," he snickered.

* * *

Judge Evans closed the outer office door and jumped when Agent Thompson emerged from the gloom. She dropped her purse and he hurried forward to pick it up.

"You scared me."

"Really sorry, judge."

They laughed as they both talked at the same time.

"What can I do for you Agent Thompson?"

"Your Honor, well, I wondered if you would go to dinner with me tonight. Or sometime?"

"Agent Thompson, I'm flattered, but I am not sure it would be appropriate. You're working on Judge O'Shea's case. I guess we're all considered suspects until the murder's solved?"

"You're not a suspect. You never were. I'd like to take you to dinner and get to know you. If that's alright."

"Not a suspect? You know my sister Angela's issue with O'Shea, right? I could've killed him back then for sure…" she trailed off in thought.

She looked up into the agent's kind eyes. "Look, agent, that's awfully nice, but I don't know. I mean you and I both work at the courthouse. You're ten—no, five— years younger."

He shook his head and put a hand on her elbow. "Please, I think it'd be nice to get to know you. We'll just have a nice time talking about something other than the courthouse. I'm really tired of eating by myself or with Agent David. Agent David has one emotion—anger. It's hard on the digestion."

She looked at him for a minute. "Haven't the local agents adopted you? I thought I saw a big group of y'all outside eating lunch yesterday."

He shrugged. "They're okay I guess. Most of them have families to get home to at night."

He seemed sincere and a little unsure of himself. Lunch had been a long time ago, and she was starving.

"You know, I'd enjoy a dinner that's not microwaved and eaten on a tray in front of the news. Let me think. There are not a whole lot of restaurants open downtown tonight, but there are some good restaurants near Glenwood."

A few minutes later, an Uber deposited them at Sullivan's steakhouse. The two were seated at a small table in the corner of the room. The dim restaurant was almost full of downtown workers and couples on their own.

Thompson pulled out Loretta's chair and offered her the wine menu. She raised her eyebrows. "Maybe one glass of red. How about you?"

"Sean. My first name is Sean. I'm named after my granddad."

"Okay, Sean. Do you care for any wine?"

"I'll take a red too. You pick out one for both of us."

The waiter gave them the nightly specials. After they'd ordered, he asked her, "How are your cases going now that you've picked up some of O'Shea's? You've got to be exhausted adding those to your normal caseload."

"I thought we weren't talking shop? But you're right. It's been a struggle, but I just got a new clerk—Jennifer. Have you met her? She was O'Shea's law clerk before. Well, before she went on personal leave."

"I've met her just the once. She's friendly and seems smart and mature. She certainly looks up to you. She talked about you a lot."

"Thanks. She's very bright and really has had a tough time of it."

The waiter placed their red wine down in front of them, and each took an appreciative sip.

"How did you decide to become a lawyer and then a judge? Was someone in your family a lawyer?" he asked.

"No, I'm the first. I started out wanting to be a teacher like my mom. Then, well, then I watched a trial in state court. I wanted to do what the lawyers were doing—standing up and presenting a case, prosecuting people, defending people, arguing to the court." She laughed. "I sound like I couldn't make up my mind—prosecutor or defense attorney—but the truth is, I just wanted to be able to research and argue my case. I'm a type A, and I like things organized. I thought I could do a better job than either of the two lawyers I saw in state court."

"I've spent a lot of time in a lot of courts, and I think you're one of the most patient and astute judges I've seen."

She waved his words away, but her eyes shone a little brighter.

"How about you? How did you get into law enforcement? Family tradition?" she asked.

"Heck no. My family primarily belongs to the other side of the law. My dad wasn't around much and then died when I was thirteen. And my older brother," he shrugged. "My brother thought stealing things and selling them was a great idea. He served some years and then went right back in when he started stealing again. Cars, the last time. He is up to have his probation revoked again in a few weeks. My mom just didn't give a damn. She had her own problems with the bottle and couldn't or wouldn't keep up with two teenaged boys."

"I'm so sorry to hear that," she said.

"Thanks. It's easier now than it was then. My coach talked me into applying to the police academy. I'd been staying with him and his family for a couple of years. So I listened and worked as a cop for a few years in Chicago and then applied to the bureau. And here I am today, enjoying your company—without Agent David anywhere within five miles."

Loretta looked down, twining her fingers around the stem of her glass. "That's really sweet, but you know, this is just two friends having dinner, right?"

He reached over and gently took her hand. "That is what *you* want it to be. Me? I'm going to try and woo you and hope you'll give me a chance."

"I don't want to ruin dinner. This has been so nice, but we're from very different worlds. I just don't see it. I'm sorry."

"You mean because you're a judge and I'm just a cop?"

"Really? You think that's it?"

"Now don't give me one of your stink eyes the defendants get in court."

She looked around at all the couples in the darkened corners enjoying whispered conversations in the candlelight. "No. It's because I'm Black and from a small town and you're white from a metropolitan city. Two very different people."

"You're beautiful because of that and more. You are patient with people and take an interest in everyone around you. You take pride in what you do. That's tough to resist."

"What do you think my mama would say if I brought you home? Do you think she'd welcome you with open arms?"

"I hope so. But if not, if she's as smart as her daughter, she'll give me a chance to prove to her I'm a good guy."

"You're persistent."

"You're stubborn."

"If you think you can take on my mama and my family, you're going to need all of your strength, patience, humor, and maybe the rest of the bureau as backup."

He smiled. "Just give me a chance."

She clinked her almost empty glass with his. "Best of luck.

* * *

Loretta walked into her townhouse around 10:00 p.m. A modest two bedroom, it was like an old sweater, comfortable and familiar. It'd been an interesting dinner. Oh, who was she kidding? It'd been wonderful having a nice man pay attention to her and seem sincere in his interest.

She hadn't been out with anyone in at least—oh, at least nine months. It was hard finding someone who wasn't intimidated by or who wanted to take advantage of her position. She'd finally told her mother to quit trying to set her up with everyone's cousin, nephew, or grandson. The last "wonderful guy" from home had chewed with his mouth open, and his only topic of conversation was *The Fast and the Furious* movies.

She drew on her long wide-legged pajama pants and picked up her book. She put it down again. Sean had been, well, different. He was flirtatious but not over the line, and he was funny. He'd had her laughing so hard she could hardly cut up her steak. He worked hard at his job, appreciated his life, and didn't take anything for granted.

Would he survive a trip to Oxford to meet her family? She wasn't sure. The last guy to make the trip—a lawyer—had started sweating before he reached the driveway. Mama had shaken his hand and not so discreetly wiped hers off on her apron. Her date felt compelled to fill the silence and had talked nonstop. Her mother's raised eyebrows kept climbing during the meal. Even her cousin, Brendaice, had looked over at her with a "what's this?" look. The men. Oh, the men. They were worse. They started talking about crops and tractors and farm equipment, leaving her guy out. He'd tried to join in, but they shouldered him out of the backyard conversation, not even looking at him. And *he* was Black.

What in the hell would her family do when—no, if—she brought Sean home. When? Oh no. She really liked him and had since she'd met him. His bravery in the courtroom on her behalf had not hurt his stock. If he could make it through a home visit, they might have a chance. She'd have to talk Uncle Otis Lee into putting up his shotgun and moonshine he kept calling his "tonic" when he thought she was around—and get Grandma Hazel to wear a bra. She was forgetful these days, especially in the personal grooming department.

Hoping to dream of men who carried badges and a gun, she cut the light off and snuggled down deep into her bed.

Angela interrupted her dreams by calling early the next morning.

"Loretta, Loretta, are you awake?"

"I am now. What's up? Where are you? Do you need a ride?"

"Never mind. Are you going to be in your office today?"

"I have court this morning but am in the office this afternoon. Want to go to lunch?"

"Yeah, let's meet at the Stone Street Café. Around 1:00?"

"Okay. It'll be good to see you. I've missed you. Where have you—"

Angela cut her off. "Yeah, I'll see you there."

* * *

Later that morning, it was a little awkward seeing Sean smiling at her in the hallway. He all but tipped a nonexistent hat toward her and then called out "Good morning." She mumbled "Good morning" and then hid behind her chambers' door.

Brenda looked up at Judge Evans in concern.

"Are you okay, Judge? Is anyone bothering you?"

"No, Brenda. Sorry, just not awake yet. I need coffee. Let me get some started and I'll put myself back together."

She quickly scuttled into her office. *Am I really hiding from him? This is ridiculous.* She chided herself for acting like a high school student and straightened her shoulders. *Get a grip, you're a grown woman. Besides, he's just a kid. He can't be serious.* She put on her robe after she'd gulped down the first cup of coffee, scalding her mouth.

He was serious. He stood behind her at every court session and only took breaks when she took breaks. He didn't stare at her, but she was very aware of him. At the lunch break, she called him up to the bench.

"Look, Agent Thompson, I really don't need you in the courtroom all day. The deputy marshals and I will be fine. Wilkerson is still in lockup. If you want to be here the day he is brought over, great. Otherwise, there's no need for you to spend your time in here."

"I don't mind at all. Plus, I just think the FBI would want me to ensure your safety during these tense times."

"Are you leaving the murder investigation to Agent David?"

"No. The locals, SBI, and Agent David are rounding up some guys in possession of child pornography for interviews. They think there's a link there to O'Shea. Who knows, maybe one of them knows about the murder."

"Honestly, go. I will be fine here."

"With due respect, no way, ma'am. I can't just leave you here by yourself. I will after this business with Wilkerson is concluded, but until then, I'm with you."

She gave him a dark look. "Oh, whatever. You'll be bored I promise you. There's two antitrust cases this afternoon."

"That's fine. I'll be here." He backed out of the courtroom and threw her a wink.

No one else was in the courtroom. She started laughing. *Good for him.*

* * *

Jeb came into the kitchen early the next morning. His jeans rode low on his skinny hips. He had on an unbuttoned flannel shirt with the sleeves rolled up ready to start cooking breakfast.

He stopped cold when he saw Katie in the kitchen. "Morning, Katie."

Flustered to see Jeb so early and in a pair of Buck's Wake Forest sweatpants, she said, "Good morning, Jeb. How was Raleigh? Was the band decent?"

"It was pretty good. I have a friend who works as their grip, and he got us in for free. How was dinner last night? Sorry Charles ruined your dinner here."

"The Oak Room was surprisingly good. And we ran into Johnson and his extended family, so it was fun. Sorry you couldn't go with us."

With his head in the fridge, he said, "Where are the eggs? I thought I just bought a carton."

Katie pushed the carton over on the counter. "There's bacon near the range. Do you want me to cook some for you?"

"Nah, I like to cook. I'm a whole lot better at it than some people."

Buck came in and kissed Katie on the cheek. "Don't listen to him. He can barely boil water. Where are you headed to today?"

"I'll be in the office typing up my interviews and collecting interviews from the other detectives from yesterday. Johnson's going to talk to Junior. The FBI and I are going to exchange them sometime later today. We found some of the same child pornography on the suspects' computers that O'Shea had on his computer, but none of the suspects we interviewed claimed to know him. The SBI is checking the child porn against the Missing and Exploited Children database, but it didn't recognize any of the images right off. The FBI is making noise about leaving in a few days but then they turn around and start yelling about how the case needs to be solved. I get the feeling that the 'higher ups' aren't too happy with Agent David."

Jeb shuddered. "How can you look at that stuff? That's so sick. I couldn't do it."

"Most of us have had some training in this area, but it doesn't make it any easier. We don't want to see this, and we've divided it up so no one has to see a lot of images. On the good side, each image is a state class I felony, so we need to charge it if the guy has it. This means a guy with a shitload of images gets a shitload of charges."

Flipping his eggs, Jeb pointed to the pan, "You want breakfast, Buck?"

"Yeah, that'd be great. Two over easy? Bacon?"

"Coming up. Hey Buck, you need to get that briefcase fixed. Charles got back into it and started chewing on some papers and stuff. I tried putting it all back in there, but some of it was soggy so I put it on the back porch to dry."

Buck sighed. "Damn. Most all of those belonged to Phillip. Did the papers get mauled?"

"Yeah. Well, only a little. Remember when I went to that place in Wilmington? There's a photo looks like it was taken in the family meeting room they had at the rehabilitation place. You know—where the family came to visit with their relatives in rehab?"

Buck got up and opened the screen door. He brought several slightly damp pictures back to the kitchen table. "Show me which part you're talking about."

"See, on the right side, where that door is, and you can see the blue curtains with the sailboats on them? I hated those curtains. Anyway, that's the family room at that place."

Buck handed the photo over to Katie. "This was in Phillip's office?" she asked.

"Yeah, I found it stuck to the baseboard yesterday. Thought I'd return it and his other papers to him when I get a chance. I guess we shouldn't be riffling through his things though."

Katie said, "You're probably right. He may have had a family member or friend there and wouldn't want to violate their trust."

Buck shrugged. "Yeah, he never mentioned anything about it. Hey, Jeb, did you ever take photos there? I can't remember."

"No, I fucking hated that place and the staff. A bunch of fake smiles and talk. All they really wanted was a weekly paycheck."

"I remember you liked the group meetings and the guys in your cabin or bungalow."

"Yeah, they were okay. I keep up with a couple of them, but the place itself stank. Too many of the staff trying to sell drugs to the people staying there who were fucking trying to get well. That just sucks."

"They should raid that place."

"They did a few times, but I think one of the dealers had an inside track to the local cops because there'd be a lot of bed making, sweeping, trash throwing, and runs to the employee cars right before the raids. Plus, those raids scared the shit out of most of the residents who were just kids."

"That's terrible if the cops conspired with those losers," Katie said. "And to victimize those guys who were trying to overcome their problems is criminal."

Jeb shrugged. "Those residents didn't have any control over it, and they were paying the freight which was huge."

Katie said, "Sorry to have to leave you guys. I'm heading to the shower. Buck, will I see you at lunch?"

"No. I've got nine or ten hearings with Trooper Graham today I have to handle. The DA's office demanded I come to court. I've dodged the trooper long enough. But there are a couple of good cases in the mix I think I can win."

Buck followed her toward the bathroom and gave her a searing kiss. "See you tonight?" he whispered. Breathless, she nodded.

After breakfast, Buck opened the laptop and tried to find a photo of Phillip. After a few minutes, he said, "Jeb, I'll look harder for a picture of him this afternoon after court. You working today?"

"Yes, I'm going over to Mom's. She's gotten it in her head that a trellis with a vine growing roses could be nice near her back door. I have no idea how to set one up. Guess I'll learn. Her neighbor has one, and that's all she could talk about—the roses over at Mrs. Sturges's. I finally got the hint."

"Tell her I said hello."

"You ought to tell her yourself. But I'll be glad to fill her in on your sleepover. That will give her a real project. Getting you married. She'll have the church reserved and her dress picked out before you can blink. She'll come to your office every day with new ideas for the reception. She's been on me to date Mrs. Sturges's granddaughter. That girl thinks Led Zepplin is a lipstick color. I need Mom to focus on something else."

"Dammit Jeb. Come on. Don't rat me out."

"A little cash incentive to keep your sordid secrets will give me the appropriate level of amnesia. Enough money for some gas, a trellis, and one rose bush."

Buck started throwing bills from his wallet at Jeb. "Here, here, go buy what you need, and keep your mouth shut."

Jeb grinned, "Like the tomb."

CHAPTER TWENTY

Buck pushed open the door to his office late that afternoon. Emma Jean looked up from her filing—her nail filing, that is. "Oh, hey." She looked back down.

"Emma Jean. Did anyone call today?"

"Naw, not really. Oh, wait. There was this lady detective who called you but didn't leave her name. But I recognized her voice. She was in my brother's class. It's Katie. Oh, and Agent David called, but he was rude, so I hung up on him."

"Okay, I will take it from here," Buck said. "Here are the client files from today. Can you get the bills out tomorrow?"

Emma Jean snapped her gum once. "Yeah. I'll get them out first thing. How'd court go? Did you get everything tried?"

"Pretty well. I won a few trials and lost one. Trooper Graham was his usual pompous self. Fortunately, the judge let in only one roadside test, the HGN test, for one of the stops 'cause that's all the prosecutor had to offer. No bad driving. Just a taillight out. I couldn't win the one with the confession."

"Yeah, that was tough one. Did Emmett get pissed off when you lost?"

"You know Emmett. It was my goddamn fault he was caught driving at twenty-five miles per hour down I-85 in the seventy miles per hour zone. He gets arrested for driving while impaired. Then when the magistrate releases him, he gets in his car while no one is looking and does the exact same thing."

She laughed. "Gotta hand it to him. He's consistent."

Buck scrubbed his hair out of his face. "Yeah. That's his third DWI on the same stretch of 85."

Buck unpacked the remaining files of his clients who weren't tried and re-shelved them in his bookcase. He made a few calls to clients and then got a Coke from the minifridge hidden under the right part of his desk.

"Agent David? My assistant said you'd called?"

"Yes—did she also tell you she hung up on me? Are all of you uncivilized? You need a new assistant!"

Buck heard the last bit clearly even while holding the phone away from his ear.

"What did you want?"

"I want the SBI and the lieutenant's reports with the child pornographers. The bureau—the SBI—said the lieutenant had them and I can't reach her on her cell phone. I've called multiple times."

"She told me at lunch she was trying to finish them up. Give her an hour and I bet she'll be in contact."

"We need to meet with your friend Margaret again about the missing funds. I can't get her on the phone either."

"Margaret is probably at the IRS, and their cell phone reception there is pretty spotty. You know how paranoid federal agencies are."

David ignored his last comment. "You people are slowing this whole investigation down. We need to keep rolling. We're finally getting somewhere."

Buck pinched the bridge of his nose and counted to three. "Try the lieutenant and Margaret in about an hour. I feel sure they'll be in a place to talk to you."

"That's what happens when you put a bunch of women in charge—total chaos."

Buck stayed silent.

David charged on. "Wilkerson's back on the court docket tomorrow. You coming over for the hearing?"

"I plan on it. I'm about to finish up summarizing the last of O'Shea's files so I'll bring those over. Have you found out anything more on Wilkerson?"

"No. The big New York law firm is sandbagging us. Probably will send about thirty lawyers to the hearing tomorrow. A bunch of jackals in suits."

Buck wondered what subgroup of humanity Agent David actually liked.

"See you over there tomorrow."

David hung up without further conversation.

* * *

Angela didn't call. Loretta woke up worried about her sister but couldn't put a finger on what it was. The last few days Angela had seemed happier, more content than she'd seen her in a while.

She tried calling Angela's cell. It went straight to voicemail. She made a note on her iPhone calendar to call her again at lunch.

Today was the Wilkerson case. She dressed in her two-piece splurge suit—a St. John's black knit and a white shirt with a small ruffle at the neck. She eschewed her daily flats for patent leather pumps. Regardless of how it went, she wanted to present the face of confidence. She wanted to make sure he and the courtroom audience knew she was not rattled by his previous assault attempt. She hadn't been able to talk Agent Thompson—Sean—out of standing guard over her. He'd insisted and got Judge Foster in on it to direct her to accept extra security. Sean wouldn't be swayed by anything she'd said. It would make her feel safer to have him there. She just wasn't ready to show her vulnerable side to him yet. Maybe one day.

A contrite Wilkerson appeared in court with his appointed lawyer. The lawyer left the courtroom a short time later, crestfallen that Wilkerson had retained other counsel to represent him. Behind the scenes, Wilkerson had been cooperating, meeting almost daily with the FBI, and providing documents of payments from his bank. In exchange for his cooperation, Wilkerson had been moved to a single cell and been provided books and magazines. He was able to get personal products and snacks paid for by the bureau as well as unlimited calls home.

Two New York attorneys representing O'Shea's old firm sat at counsel table and appeared nervous. The firm had been requested to appear by the Court. There was a lot of throat clearing, pen wagging, and sibilant whispers from their counsel table, breaking into the otherwise sepulchral silence.

At 10:00 a.m. exactly, Judge Evans took her seat on the bench. She turned slightly to her right giving a small nod to Agent Thompson. He, in turn, remained facing forward, weight on the balls of his feet, ready for any disturbance.

"Mr. Wilkerson, I understand you have retained new counsel. Is that correct?"

Counsel for Wilkerson stood.

"Yes ma'am. I am Tommy Watkins, from the Wake County bar, here on behalf of Mr. Wilkerson. At the appropriate time, Your Honor, I'd like to approach the bench with opposing counsel to discuss a matter that's fairly sensitive."

"Good morning, Mr. Watkins. A pleasure to see you here again. We haven't seen much of you this year."

Turning her head toward the two New York lawyers, she asked, "Any objection to Mr. Watkins's request?"

"No sir—I mean, no ma'am Your Honor," said the shorter, wider attorney. He was visibly sweating even though the ancient air conditioning was purring away. His companion looked a little green.

"Counsel, please approach."

Agent Thompson stood where he was, watching Wilkerson, who would not look at him. The deputy marshal moved closer to the judge as counsel approached the bench. The court reporter picked up his machine trying to balance it so he could record the side bar. New York counsel had to be redirected to approach from the right side of the courtroom instead of following Watkins.

Judge Evans muted her microphone so the others in the courtroom would not hear it. "Mr. Watkins, what is the nature of your request?"

"Your Honor, my client is being cooperative with federal agencies, and we need more time. I was just retained a few days ago and need to get up to speed on the case. I filed my notice of appearance yesterday."

"What say you, counsel? And please introduce yourselves for the court record."

The shorter attorney said, in a nasal whine, "Your Honor, I'm Jonathan Bateman, and this is my partner, Jeff Hoffman. We've traveled all the way from New York—at great expense— to be here today. At the court's request, of course." Hoffman nodded vigorously. "We'd like to move forward with whatever is before the court today."

The judge looked at Wilkerson's counsel. "Mr. Watkins, what is your response?"

"Your Honor, Mr. Wilkerson has the right to have his choice of counsel represent him if it's early enough in the proceedings. I need additional time, but not a great deal. If it would be helpful to Your Honor and the two gentlemen from New York, perhaps we could agree on a convenient court date to reconvene?"

Hoffman spoke. "Surely you have all of the documents submitted by our firm and any from the FBI? What else do you need?"

"Mr. Hoffman, remarks should be directed to the court, not to opposing counsel," said Judge Evans.

Hoffman reddened. "I'm sorry, Your Honor."

"Now, gentlemen, please take a moment out in the hall and try to select a date you can agree on for the next hearing. If you can't, I will select a date for you."

To the marshal, she said, "We'll be at ease for a while."

After a few minutes, the three attorneys could be heard from inside the courtroom. Volleys of "your client," "the money," "O'Shea," and "bribe" reverberated throughout. Wilkerson turned his head toward the noise as the deputy marshal hustled to the door to quiet the attorneys down.

Finally, the three came back in and approached counsel table stone-faced.

"Mr. Watkins, have you and Mr. Hoffman and Mr. Bateman reached an agreement?" asked Judge Evans.

"Yes ma'am, we have. We have agreed to appear here thirty days from today."

"Mr. Bateman, Mr. Hoffman, do you agree?"

"Yes ma'am, Your Honor," Bateman said.

"Based on counsel's agreement, this case will be continued for thirty days. If there are any issues for the court to be resolved ahead of time, we'll have to set up a telephonic conference call a week ahead of the hearing. You'll do that with Judge Foster's office as I am recusing myself from hearing any additional matters related to this case. You'll receive a notice of the date and time of the next hearing through the mail and by email next week. Please approach my law clerk and give her your addresses so she may get them to Judge Foster. Anything else for today?"

Replying in the negative, each attorney and Wilkerson stood. Judge Evans said, "Court is adjourned until 2:00 p.m. today."

Agent David stepped from the shadows at the back of the courtroom and met the two New York attorneys at the door. "Mr. Bateman and Mr. Hoffman, you are under arrest for the felony of bribing a federal judge, in relation to Judge Patrick O'Shea, and obstruction of justice."

Wilkerson cackled, "How do you like that, you rat bastards?"

His attorney hustled him, still laughing, out of the courtroom through a side door that accessed the back hallway.

Judge Evans and Agent Thompson headed back to Judge Evans's chambers. "Time for lunch?" Thompson asked.

"I wish I could, but I need to get up with Angela and I have this afternoon's file to review. Not antitrust. Another time?"

"Sure, or dinner tonight?"

"That'd be nice but let me see if I can find Angela first. She needed to talk to me, but I'm having a hard time running her down. I'm getting concerned."

"I understand. Give me a call when you know your plans. I'm skipping this afternoon's case. Fighting over the number of fish collected in North Carolina waters is not in my top ten list of cases I'd like to hear."

She laughed. "The fishermen and the federal agency find it very stimulating.

"I'm headed down to see if Agent David needs help on the suspects they interviewed this week. I hope they've made progress and have reviewed all of the images."

Chapter Twenty-One

Katie, Buck, and Agent David were hunched over two rows of photographs when Agent Thompson pushed open the door to the FBI room.

"Thompson, come over here and look at these," David said. "The top row photos are from O'Shea's computer. The bottom row photos are from a guy they picked up in Granville County. Do they look the same to you?"

Thompson studied the two rows, trying not to linger over any one image of children and adults caught in horrific acts.

"I think they're the same, but the background—that looks like the courtroom here. Is that what y'all are thinking?"

"Pretty much, which of course means those children were brought here and violated. But by whom?"

"I think we should go back to the guy who had these on his computer and see if his alibi for the night O'Shea was killed holds up. He and O'Shea could have gotten into a fight about the kids, the pictures, who knows—maybe it was a blackmail situation."

Katie straightened up and stretched out her back. "Yeah, I think it's worth a second shot. I'll contact his lawyer and set it up for later today. I gotta tell you, though, I think it's just a matter of him having a series of photos that the judge also had. There's no evidence he and O'Shea were friends or acquaintances. I mean, c'mon, the guy lives with his mother in her basement, doesn't have a job, and has to borrow his mom's car to go anywhere. Plus, he must be five-foot-nine and 125 pounds. He's scrawny, underweight, and couldn't lift a dead body."

Buck nodded. "Yeah, I represented his mom on a worthless check charge and a couple of other minor crimes and got to know her son a little. He doesn't strike me as the type to leave Oxford much less murder a judge and then haul him up on a rope."

David pursed his lips. "Well, by all means, let's just eliminate people you know. That'll save us a lot of time."

Buck sighed. "That's not what I meant. Just thought you'd be wasting your time."

David said sarcastically, "I really appreciate it, but you're the law clerk here, and I'm the investigator. I'll decide who we interview and who we don't. Lieutenant, let's head out."

Katie rolled her eyes after David had gone through the door. Thompson followed wordlessly. "This is going to be a long, fruitless day."

"Good luck. I'm finally done with O'Shea's files. After I meet up with Judge Foster, I'm headed back to Oxford for good. Oh, wait, after I take Phillip his box of files and papers."

"If we arrest the guy after the interview, I'll let you know, but I think this is a huge waste."

"Look at it this way—at least you'll get to spend time with a trained investigator."

She punched him in the arm and they headed for the elevators. Furtively checking the hall for people first, Buck kissed Katie goodbye and headed to Judge Foster's.

* * *

Seated behind his office desk, Judge Foster had thanked Buck profusely for his work in overseeing the two law clerks and summarizing the rest of O'Shea's files. Handing him a small gift bag, which contained a new toy for Charles, Judge Foster invited him to come back for lunch at the Downtown City Club next month.

Lost in thought, Buck strode down Fayetteville Street mall toward Phillip's new firm. Housed in the elegant new multi-story BB&T building, the firm was ideally situated for the state and federal courts. The seventh-floor reception area was furnished with odd-shaped maroon leather chairs. The PNC and Red Hat buildings were visible in the afternoon sun.

"Buck?"

He turned and shook Phillip's outstretched hand. "Just enjoying the view. I hope you are getting settled into the new job."

"Yes, I am. I'm primarily focusing on corporate work or transactional work and find it challenging, in a good way. I work for two of the partners and they've been awfully understanding while I try to learn the ropes. Billable hours are a challenge since I'm so new, but one of the couriers we use just dropped off ten boxes for one client, so I think that's about to change."

"Good to hear. They miss you over at the courthouse. Judge Foster told me to tell you hello for him. Oh, here's a box of some papers you left and something from the Administrative Office of the Courts that came in after you left. I wanted to make sure you got all this since I'm headed home for good now."

Without glancing at the small box, Phillip said, "I really appreciate it. Sorry to hear you're leaving. That must mean you've finished up, and I know Judge Foster was anxious that it be organized for the visiting judge coming in this weekend."

"At one point, I didn't think we'd get it done, but you and Jennifer were a big help."

"I heard Jennifer is going to work for Judge Evans. That's great news. Jennifer's a good law clerk."

"Judge Evans can't wait. She's loaded up her desk."

"Any news on the investigation? Does the FBI have a suspect yet?"

"Not really. They're following up on the child porn and interviewing some guys the locals picked up in a roundup. I think Agent David's getting a lot of pressure to wrap it up. I heard Mrs. O'Shea's been calling the Governor and her senators about how long it's taking."

"I almost feel sorry for the guy," Phillip laughed.

"Good to see you again. Call me if your work brings you to Oxford."

"I will, thanks. And thank you for bringing these over."

Buck headed back down Fayetteville, stutter-stepping over two guys asleep on top of a grate. Neither stirred as he narrowly avoided stomping on one of their arms. Decentralization of the mental health system had done nothing to solve this problem. Buses dropped mental patients off downtown early each morning and made half-hearted attempts to pick them up at night.

He called Jeb on the way to his car. "Hey, you want to call a couple of the guys and shoot some hoops or play tennis in the park tonight, sometime after 6:00?"

"Sure. Ready to get your ass whipped again?"

"No way. Make sure you call the regular crew. Don't stick some short twelve-year-old on my team like you did last time."

"No problem. I'll get Trooper Graham and a couple more guys from the PD."

"You're on."

About an hour later, Buck changed out of his suit and walked over to the Oxford park where Jeb and some of the guys were shooting free throws.

Jeb saw him and whooped, "Look at those white legs!"

"Better than your scrawny sticks. Do we have an even number?"

Three on three took to the court. Once again Jeb tagged his brother's team with some slow PD rookie who looked like he'd blow away in the first good wind. *Nice kid, but he couldn't hit the backboard much less the net.*

Buck glared at Jeb after the rookie missed his third free throw.

Jeb laughed, grabbed the ball from the man outside the line, and swooshed another one into the basket.

Graham hollered, "You're hot as a two-dollar pistol tonight, Jeb!"

After what seemed like a long time to Buck, the score finished up at fifty-five to forty. It had gotten too dark to play.

Buck and Jeb walked back home. On the way, Buck said, "We better sneak in the back. Charles is going to be mad we didn't take him to the park. Uh-oh, there he is."

Charles had his back to the two brothers. He was sitting on his gray dog bed on the back screened porch. He refused to respond to his name.

Buck fell asleep in the "lady chair" by the rose-colored settee. It was an ornately carved spindly chair covered in green velvet. He woke up when Jeb smacked him with his towel.

"Jesus, Jeb."

"Where's that photo you had the other night? I got to head over to a meeting in a minute, but I wanted to look at it again."

"I took Phillip's papers back to him today."

"Okay. No problem."

"How'd the rose garden turn out for Mom?"

"Looking good. I put in two types of climbing roses. Mom seemed happy. I told her you might make use of it one day soon."

"What the hell are you talking about?"

"You know, to propose to your lady love?"

"Goddamnit Jeb, I hope you didn't say that to Mom. She'll be over here until she squeezes it out of me."

"Hah. I kept my mouth shut. I'm headed to the church. Want to come?"

Buck studied Jeb a minute. "Yeah, I'd like that. I haven't gone with you in a while. Let me change."

* * *

Buck called Katie later that night. "How was your interview with Purvis?"

"'Bout like you'd expect."

"He cried through the whole thing."

"Yep. Agent David got close to hitting him once he was so mad. That really sent up the water works."

"Not good."

She sighed. "Not good at all. We had to call EMS because Purvis had a spell. Thought David was going to have one too."

"Did Purvis give up anything?"

"Not on O'Shea. He had no idea who that was—and I believe him. He just wanted to go back to his mom's basement and cuddle up to his laptop. He doesn't like the local jail."

"That's awful."

"It is, and what's worse, I think he has some mild mental retardation in addition to a complete lack of socialization. No way could he plan or commit a murder like this."

"Poor guy."

"Yeah. I felt a little bit sorry for him. Then I remember those images, and the sympathy gets washed away by disgust."

"You're right. Some of those images are burned onto my retinas."

"You hear they arrested the two New York attorneys for federal bribery?"

"Yeah. David crowed about his big arrest. An arrest and an interview all in one day. You'd have thought he was a one-man FBI unit. He took credit for everything. They brought the local agents in to interview those guys—assuming they'll talk. I think the lawyers are toast. You don't represent either one, do you?"

"Naw. They'll bring in some big guns from New York. They won't trust anyone down here."

"You're right."

"Hey, where's Johnson?"

"He's been doing follow-up interviews on the roundup guys. No luck so far."

* * *

At Loretta's townhouse, after a late takeout dinner, Loretta and Sean were seated on her plush ivory couch. Loretta shook out a colorful handmade throw and spread it over her lap. "My niece made this for me. She knows I like bright colors."

"It's definitely bright." He hesitated, "Your family seems really close."

"We are. It's a blessing until we all get to talking at once. Then it's a bit of a curse. Everyone thinks they're right and stops listening to the others."

"I wish I'd had that experience. I love my coach, but sometimes I felt like I was the outsider."

"Did you and your family or you and coach's family attend church growing up?"

"Some. I was raised Catholic, and we went while my mom was living. The coach's family went to the big Baptist church, and we went less frequently, about once or twice a month and on the holidays."

"Our church is different because the extended family goes and participates in the celebration. The service is usually about two hours."

"Two hours!"

"Usually. We take our time and greet each other and have a lot of music during the service. We don't rush through it."

"Is the sermon long?"

"Not really. There's usually more music than sermon. The choir really puts their all into it."

"And you want me to go with you this Sunday?"

"I want you to go if you feel comfortable going with me."

"Can I bring something for lunch after?"

She pulled back from him in horror. "Oh, gosh, no. My Mom would be insulted. She and the aunts, nieces, and cousins like to do it up big. And for goodness sakes, don't compliment one cook's potato salad over another's. You'll make lifelong enemies that way."

"You're joking."

"I'm not joking. In fact, just say you love everything and take a little bit of each dish."

"But I hate beets."

"Those shouldn't show up. How do you feel about fried chicken, potato salad, green bean casserole, and pecan pie?"

"I like them all."

"Good. You'll be fine. If the guys are crappy to you, offer to do the dishes. That'll get them in a twist with their wives and girlfriends."

Sean laughed. "I don't want to get beaten up on my way to the car."

"I bet you can handle yourself. Haven't you been trained for all sorts of dangerous situations? This will just be one more."

* * *

Loretta and Sean met her family outside of the Bountiful Lord Church. He'd spent hours polishing his shoes and picking out his tie. His pant creases were up to military precision. It was worth it to see Loretta's smile when she picked him up. They parked in the row of cars on the gravel drive. She took him over to where a small group was gathered.

Loretta said, "Mama, Daddy, I'd like you to meet Sean."

There was silence. Then, Loretta's mom reached out a hand and patted his arm. "Good to meet you, Sean. I'm glad you got my baby girl up here for church."

Loretta's daddy shook his hand, taking time to look him over. "Nice to meet you, Sean." His grip tightened then he released his hand.

After a lot of greeting and hugs in the church, with a few squeals from Loretta's contemporaries, the service began. Sean was wedged in between Loretta and her daddy, Little Roy. He'd have hated to meet Big Roy. Her daddy, with every bit of his six-foot-four and 250-pound frame, was keeping him in his seat until it was time to stand for the Gospel.

Loretta enjoyed the service and within five minutes felt like she'd never left Oxford. Afterwards, family and friends came up to speak to her. Most looked sideways at Sean, before speaking to him or giving him a half hug or handshake.

Smiling at her in the car, he said, "Wow. That's a church service. The music with the instruments was terrific, and I really liked your lady preacher."

"That's Uncle Ezra on the bass. He and his wife, Undine, will be up at the house."

They arrived at the house with most of the other folks. The house was a white two-story frame with dark green shutters and a wide porch. It sat next to a pasture and in front of a field. The cars parked along the edge of the pasture in two rows, getting the shade from an old oak tree. Pitchers of iced tea sat on colorful trays with ice in glasses on a long wicker table. Rocking chairs were dotted along the edges.

Women carried covered dishes, and men took off jackets and ties. Children ran to the swing set in the back and the rope swing on the other side of the oak tree.

"You grew up here?" Sean asked.

"Yes, me and Angela. My other sisters were grown and out when we moved here. I hope she's here today so you can get to know her." She picked up a large Pyrex dish from the cooler in the back of her BMW SUV.

"Oooo. And the lady can cook too."

She laughed. "This is Death Salad—mandarin oranges, whipped cream, marshmallows, orange Jello."

"Sounds good. Why is it called Death Salad?"

"We take it over to folks who've had a death in their family. My aunt has the original recipe. It just caught on."

Loretta's mom came out on the porch. She put her hand on Sean's arm. "So nice of you to come. Welcome to our home."

Sean handed her a small bouquet of miniature roses and irises and said, "Thank you for having me."

"These are beautiful. Come on into the house with me."

Loretta shyly introduced him to the family in the living room, dining room, den, and kitchen. He charmed the women and left the men to stare at him awhile.

Little Roy pulled Loretta aside. "Ain't no flies on that one. He's already got your mama loading up his plate. Beats the heck out of that last guy."

Loretta laughed. "Sean can be very charming. The best part? It's real. He likes people. He didn't have a great family life growing up. I think he likes to belong, to fit in."

"Your mama puts much more on that plate, it's gonna break. Better go save him."

He put his big arm around her and continued in a low voice. "But look here, honey, if you like him, I like him. He treats you well, we'll have no problems. You're a bright, attractive woman, and you should pick someone who is going to cherish you."

"Love you, Daddy."

"Love you too, baby."

Sean caught her eye and smiled at her across the room. When she sat by him at a small table, he said, "If I don't get up soon, I won't be able to. Your Death Salad was great, by the way."

"Let's go out on the front porch and sit in the rockers. We can get some iced tea to wash it all down."

In a few minutes, her cousin Malcolm came over. He nodded at Sean. "Hey, you wanna join us for basketball?"

Loretta looked worried. "Malcolm…"

"It's cool, cousin. We just needed a fifth man. I don't think Uncle Ezra's gonna make it." He pointed over to a large shape in a rocker. A spread-out newspaper over his head halfway hid the snores.

Sean stood up. "Let me put my jacket and tie in the car, and I'll be right over. I think I have some basketball shoes back there too."

Loretta grabbed his hand. "You don't have to play if you don't want to. Those guys can be rough."

"I can handle a little game. If I can't, I'll holler for you to save me."

Loretta snorted. "You might be too whipped to holler but go on. Don't tell me I didn't warn you."

After he was dressed, he headed over to the garage where the hoop was set up. Eight unsmiling men greeted him. Then Malcolm broke the silence, "You ready to play?"

Malcolm's dad leaned over and said, "This ain't no girl's game. You sure you want to play?"

Sean felt every single blow to his ribs and shoulders as he dribbled and shot the ball. Over and over, the players reaching to steal the ball hit his arm or his hand with force. For a bunch of farmers and store owners, these guys were in shape and serious about it. He took most of it without a whimper, but the last blow hit his throat, and he went down. Looking up, he saw Malcolm's hand reaching down to help him and grabbed it.

"Let's take a break guys," Malcolm said. To Sean, he said, "Hey, dude, I'll get your iced tea. Rest here on the steps. Please tell me you take it sweetened and not Yankee-fied unsweet."

Sean muttered, "I just hope I can drink it at all."

Malcolm laughed and said, "You're alright. Be back in a minute."

Malcolm poured two glasses full and went over to Loretta. "Your dude's okay. He's hung in there."

"Don't kill him."

"Oh, no. We're going easy on him." He started to pick up the two iced teas and then turned back to her.

"Hey, Loretta?"

"Yes?"

"You know he's white, right?" Malcolm spun around and sprinted to the back before Loretta could get out of her seat.

A few minutes later the game ended, and Sean and Loretta prepared to head back to Raleigh. Angela came over to the car just as they were getting in to leave. Loretta got out and gave her sister a hug. "Angela, I want you to meet Sean. Sean, this is my sister, Angela."

Angela shyly said, "Hi. Good to meet you."

"Good to meet you too." Sean said.

Angela grabbed her sister's hand. "Can I talk to you a minute?"

Loretta said, "We've got to get back to Raleigh. Sean has to work tonight. Can I call you after I drop him off?"

"Fine," Angela said. "Call me tonight. Don't forget."

"I will. Or maybe you want to come over and watch a movie?" Loretta asked.

"No. I can't. Call me later. Bye, Sean."

"See you later, Angela."

"Your family has a great enthusiasm for basketball," Sean said, easing himself gingerly into the passenger seat. "Unfortunately, they hit me more often than they did the basket." He groaned putting on his seatbelt.

Loretta looked at him worriedly. "Did they hurt you? Oh, no. I'm really sorry."

"I'm fine, it's okay. It was a bonding experience. At least I think it was."

"They were just checking you out, trying to figure out your angle."

"I don't have an angle! I just want to go out with you. Is that so hard to understand?"

"Not to normal people. But my people are protective. They want to see what you're made of."

"Right now, bruises on top of bruises," Sean winced. "Malcolm's dad clipped me right below the ear during the one minute he played. My ear rang for a good thirty minutes."

"Good thing you didn't have to play the best player in the family this time," Loretta said.

"You're kidding. Who is that?"

"Me."

*　*　*

After she dropped Sean off at his hotel, Loretta headed to the Fresh Market and then home. Her mom had given her enough leftovers for a week, but she'd needed something green to offset the butter and sugar in most of the dishes.

Angela was waiting for her outside on the concrete bench. She hugged Loretta and helped her take in the bags of groceries.

"I really miss you sometimes, and I appreciate your support." Angela said. "You 'get' what I've been through, but you wait for me to bring it up if I need to. Thanks for being patient with me."

Loretta smiled at her sister. "Angela, you know I love you and want what's best for you. Are you still planning on stopping your sessions with the psychiatrist?"

"Yes. I've liked him, and he's helped me some, but he doesn't fit in with my plans right now," Angela said.

"What plans?" Loretta asked.

Angela stalled for time by folding up the throw and straightening up the couch pillows. "Oh, I'm hoping to move to a bigger place, but outside of Raleigh. Too many memories here and close to here."

Angela had refused to stay with Loretta very often and had stubbornly rented a small room at a "boarding house" in the worst part of town. Hookers, pimps, and drug dealers hung out at the stoops, doorways, and sidewalks around the building. The building was five stories tall, and its corridors consistently smelled of grease, wine, and despair. Angela was comfortable with all of the people hanging around, calling most by their first names.

Her "room" consisted of a tiny studio apartment. It had a threadbare rug, one miserly window and a dim overhead light. But it was hers and she'd been able to pick up a couple of decent pieces at thrift stores to decorate it. A walnut side table and a small oil painting of the Outer Banks were among her prized finds. Loretta had not been to the apartment in a while but knew their parents had sent over a new mattress and box spring. Angela took it to save her back from the drooping sofa bed with its one spring and musty covering.

Angela never asked their parents for help and normally refused their offers. She'd been unable to refuse the bed because the delivery guy wouldn't reload it in the truck after hoofing up the stairs with it.

Over the years, her parents had spent a lot of their savings on rehabilitation places and psychiatric visits for her. She couldn't pay them back but didn't want them to continue spending money on her. They said, "You can have the money now or after we're gone, but if you need it now, you should take it and get the help you need."

Rankled but never showing it, Angela had continued to refuse any help from them this year. She qualified for food stamps and other assistance before she landed a part-time job which was just enough to keep her bills current. Recently, she'd been reselling some of the thrift store finds which had boosted her confidence and bank account.

Angela stretched out on Loretta's sofa and softly said, "I want to start my grown-up life. I want everything to be new. So, I've been going to the library and searching for places."

"Is this smart? Your therapy support group is here. Mom, Dad, and me, we're here for you too. Don't you think staying close by is better?" Loretta asked.

Angela sat up and said, "I think it's time I tried to live the life I've wanted to live. I can't get rid of the PTSD or anxiety, but I can focus on moving forward, not dwelling in the past. It helps a little that O'Shea is dead."

"How does it help you?"

Angela thought for a moment and replied, "He was a man who betrayed me, and what was worse, he was someone I trusted, who acted like he cared about me and my case. When, really, all he cared about was not losing his case in court when he was challenged by my rapist's attorney. He only cared about himself."

"I know, baby. He was a total jerk for not consulting you on what he planned to do about the case and about that—that monster. But he's gone now and can't hurt you or anyone else."

"I know," Angela nodded. "It's just that I want a fresh start. I'm good at picking up things at yard sales and thrift stores and reselling them. I've been finding treasure and dusting it off so it shines. I've found a couple of consignment stores that ask me to hunt for particular things for them, and I've gotten lucky a few times."

"Take it slow," Loretta warned. "You know Mom and Dad are going to totally freak out, right?"

Angela sighed. "I know they will. I can't ever repay them for all of the treatment places, but at least I can try to stand on my own two feet now."

Angela then changed the subject. "What about the boyfriend?"

"What boyfriend?"

"That Sean guy. Y'all looked pretty cozy together at Mom and Dad's. How's that going?"

"Huh. It's going. I just am trying not to focus on the fact he is probably going to be reassigned soon. Once the O'Shea investigation wraps up, he'll have to go somewhere else. I don't know how I feel about a long-distance relationship. I'm not too wild about the idea, but who knows? It might work out. What'd the family think of him?"

"I think they're okay," Angela replied. "They liked him as a person, but they're withholding judgment for now."

"Our family? They never withhold judgment. Spill," Loretta demanded.

"Okay," Angela took and deep breath, and said, "Cousin Malcolm thinks he's nice but won't survive. Dad wants you to be happy. Mom was snowed because he praised her cooking. Uncle Otis and the male part of the family tried to kill him playing ball. And the aunts tried to kill him by overloading his plate.

"Sounds like he might make it. He beats the hell out of that last guy. He was a total ass—which I guess made him a good lawyer," Angela said with a laugh.

Loretta tweaked her sister's braids. "Okay, romantic advisor. Enough about Sean. Anyone out there caught your critical eye?"

Angela looked at her fingernails. "I'm not telling *you*. I don't want some nice guy putting up with all of the abuse."

"Not abuse. You've got to trot any guy you might be serious about before the family. I decided to take Sean early on because I wanted to see if he could be accepted or what. It went okay. Grandma Hazel lost her bra at dessert which was pretty alarming, but mom put a sweater on her before Sean got an eyeful. Oh, and cousin Tracy kept batting her five inches of store-bought eyelashes at him. He ignored her until one dropped onto the table and he killed it thinking it was a spider. She was so mad! He did give her ten dollars to replace it which I thought was sweet."

Angela couldn't quit laughing. "I hate I missed it! What did Uncle Otis do with his *tonic*? Did he hide it from you?"

Loretta rolled her eyes. "He hid it in the Y branch of the oak tree, but everyone over five feet could see it sitting there. Even some of the kids told him they could see it. He tried to tell everyone he kept going out there because he was an arborist, but he kept saying abortionist. I thought Aunt Garnett was going to faint. Mama called him out on it, so he changed it to tree lover. Pretty soon the jar got knocked out and broke because a BB shot went wild. Uncle Otis made the kids help him pick up the glass."

"He sure does like his tonic. Does he still brew it himself?" Angela asked.

"I'm not going to ask him, and I don't want to know," Loretta replied. "Treasury still busts up people's stills if they can find them in the woods. I don't want to draw anyone's attention to him."

"Well, he's no worse than Aunt Lootie with her sugar pills. She keeps them in her saccharine box and pulls them out when the conversation isn't going her way. By the end of lunch, she's nodding away in her chair. I had to find one of the bigger cousins to hold her up in her chair while I put her wig back on. I think this was after y'all had left," Angela said.

"Yeah, it was, but Mama made sure to call me and tell me about it."

Angela sat up. "I better get going. See you soon."

Loretta hugged her. "See you soon, baby sister."

Chapter Twenty-Two

Johnson had had it. Every damn pervert he'd talked to had come out of central casting: white, between forty and fifty, living with his mother. And none of them had helped on the O'Shea investigation. Plus, he was sick to death of reviewing the twisted images. Hell, he had kids. This stuff made him almost question God. What kind of sick mother fucker could do this to a child? Just when he thought he'd seen all the possible types of abuse, another worse image knocked him in the head.

He had trouble sleeping. He'd had to take a break during each suspect's interview to go smoke. Except, he didn't smoke. He went behind the dumpster behind the office and cried. He cried for each child who'd been a victim to unspeakable abuse, and he prayed for his own kids that they'd never come into contact with a monster that preyed on children. He returned to finish the interview trying to draw on his quickly depleting supply of compassion for all humanity.

Most suspects were cowed and barely verbal. One or two denied the possession of child pornography and insisted it was someone else's even though the images were on the guy's computer that was password protected, found in his locked bedroom.

Johnson wanted to jerk them out of their chairs and smash their heads into the brick wall of the interview room. Instead, in measured tones and through gritted teeth, he spelled out the evidence against each offender. For one particular suspect, it was pure agony to be in the same room so close to someone who excreted evil.

"Look, Felix, I'm gonna go over this with you one last time. This is your last chance to cooperate with law enforcement. After I leave here, you're going back to a cell. By yourself. Your lawyer's going to go home. I'm going home. You're going to get a bologna sandwich and jungle juice. That's it."

Felix looked up at him with dark emotionless eyes.

"Now, when the officers searched your home, they got consent from your mama to search the house. Then they asked if they could search your room down in the basement, right?"

Felix swallowed, barely getting the saliva past his large Adam's apple. "Yes."

"Okay. Now, they're in your room and it has a desk, bed, bedside table, a chest of drawers, and a closet, right?"

"Yes."

"And the room was locked, right?"

"Yes."

"And your mom didn't have a key to your room?"

"No."

"Okay. On the desk was a nice new laptop. In the drawer was a receipt for it from Walmart. Bought about two months earlier, right?"

"Yes."

"And the guys, the deputies, asked you for the password, didn't they?"

"Yes."

"And you gave it to them, right?"

"Yes."

"And this is some of what they found: a photo of you standing beside a scale with white powder with a recipe for crack cocaine; a photo of the tattoo on your neck for your first name, minus the "e," *Flix*; and ten videos of child porn and fifty photos of child porn."

"No."

"Okay, so which of these things is not correct?"

"None of it's mine."

Johnson stood up and stepped back from the rickety laminate table. His fists had been balled up for so long they were cramping. He really wanted to hit this guy. To hit him until he bled from every orifice.

Felix's lawyer, half cringing on the seat at the edge of the table, said to Felix, "Now, Felix, we've been over this. The detective will speak to the DA for you if you cooperate. I think that's in your best interest and a really good idea—cooperating. Now, we've been here an hour. Can you help out the detective or not?"

Felix swallowed audibly. "Yes."

Johnson wiped his forehead with an old handkerchief from his back pocket. And started again.

"Was the laptop yours?"

"Maybe."

"Was that your room?"

"Yes."

"Who else had a key to your room?"

Silence. Felix looked down at his hands.

"Jesus, Mary, and Joseph. Look, Mr. Crantz, I'm going to leave for five minutes to get some water. You or Felix want any?"

Each man shook his head no.

"Then I'm coming back in to either get his cooperation or to take him to his cell. Your choice."

Mr. Crantz looked at Felix. "You're in it now, boy. You better do some hard thinking and start talking."

When Johnson returned, Felix was wiping tears from his cheeks with the backs of his hands. "My computer, my pictures, my videos. But I didn't hurt anybody."

Johnson asked, "Did you email anyone the pictures or the videos?"

"A couple of people," Felix said.

"What about Patrick O'Shea?"

"Who?"

"Any communication with a Patrick O'Shea?"

"Never heard of him. Oh, wait, does his dad run Baby Joe's store on the way to Roxboro?"

"No. But let me tell you this, you asshole: every time you looked at or shared an image with your fellow perverts, you victimized that child. That child will never, and I mean never, be the same. I don't want to hear your sick reasons. I'll tell the DA you finally cooperated."

Felix left, and Johnson turned to Crantz. "You represent anyone else in the roundup?"

Crantz shook his head. "And Johnson. Please don't send me the images. I can't un-see that shit. I'll take the rest of the laptop and discovery when it's ready."

Johnson left him to pack up and headed downstairs to his office to call Katie.

Katie picked up her phone, "Yeah."

"Hey, LT, it's Johnson. I've finished up with my group. A lot of child porn, but nothing relating to O'Shea."

"That's what I'm hearing from everyone else. The FBI's been on me to send the reports. Yours about ready?"

"Will be in about fifteen minutes. Is Agent David harassing you?" Johnson asked.

"Not exactly," Katie replied. "He's just impatient. Looking for the smoking gun. I haven't heard from everyone that's involved, but so far no one's tied into O'Shea."

"I'm sure he was pretty careful about who he sent images to and who he received them from. Not hard to think it wouldn't be most of the group."

"Yeah," Katie agreed. "Unless they're in a chat room of some sort. These guys hardly left their basements. But the forensic people will start looking on each computer, and we may find something that way. They've supposedly started on a few hard drives."

"The guys who have cooperated, what kind of deal can they expect?" Johnson asked.

"They won't go federal and will stay stateside," Katie replied. "And if they've got clean records, maybe probation and register as a sex offender."

Johnson was surprised. "Not going federal is a pretty sweet deal on its own."

"Yeah. You can be on lifetime supervision there. Right now, we have only one more guy the feds want based on the number and type of images. The guy is trying to cooperate—he's even given information on dog fighting. He's ratting out his whole family, his neighbors, friends. He'll be glad to be in a jail cell once those folks find out he's talked to the feds."

"Damn, that's sweet. Okay, I'll get my report to you ASAP."

"No problem. See you tomorrow," Katie said, about to hang up, but then went on, "Oh, wait. Let's meet over at the SBI. Forensics will be well into the computers. I'd like to find out what connections there are to O'Shea or to the children living in our area, if any."

"I'll pick you up at seven," Johnson said.

"Good deal."

Chapter Twenty-Three

About an hour after a quick stop at Bojangles for biscuits and coffee, Katie and Johnson signed into the SBI visitor book and were escorted back to the crime lab by an assistant. The assistant told them none of the agents were in yet because they'd been up all night looking at the forensic copies of the hard drives of computers.

The assistant, "call me Steve," brought them to the room filled with long tables, wires, metal chairs, and computers. The small table behind the main door into the room was littered with coffee cups, filters, stirrers, and spilled cream.

Another SBI lab assistant slouched in a chair, his head against the back, and his eyes closed. Agent David sat beside him talking in low urgent whispers.

"Well, well. So glad you're here. I can't make sense of half the reports you sent in last night."

The lab assistants glanced at one another and quietly left the room.

"Good morning, Agent David. I'm glad to go over anything that you want me to, but no one stated he knew O'Shea or communicated with him. That's why we're here; to check for on-line chats or file-to-file transmissions from or to O'Shea."

"The damn forensic techs are late. Not sure how long they'll be."

At that minute, a troop of scientists filed in. The head of the group came over and shook law enforcement's hands.

"Sorry we're late. This is the second group assigned to the computers. We hope to make a good start today."

"I thought that's what you guys did last night," David whined.

"No. They logged the physical items into evidence and assigned a tech to copy evidence numbers down in a log. Then they copied the hard drives so only the copy would be examined and the original hard drive put into evidence. As you can see, there were a lot of devices seized."

Katie said, "What's a realistic time for forensic review and can we help narrow the initial search?"

"Absolutely. As far as the time, I'll check in with the other group and give you an overall estimate."

He moved over to the scientists, and they huddled up looking over periodically at David, Katie, and Johnson.

After more discussion, the head returned. "Yes, a narrow search option is welcome. All considered, thirty days from exam to reports."

David exploded. "What?! You're insane! We're not waiting thirty days for anything. Look, get your boss in here. Right now!"

"I think that's a good idea so we can talk about a narrow search and what we can expect," Katie said.

Twenty minutes later, the SBI head, Jason Roberts, entered the room.

"Ah, Agent David. Back again. I should have guessed where the seismic disturbance originated."

David bristled. "Look, you and your faux British accent. We can't be held up by your team or teams. We need to solve a murder, a *federal* judge's murder, and we need those machines examined now."

"We've taken resources off other cases and assigned them here. We're working 'round the clock starting when they came in yesterday. You've got to be reasonable about this," Roberts sputtered.

"Reasonable? This is just a ploy to get funds to support your unit. How much? How much to speed these guys up? I'll make a call," David threatened.

"You do that," Roberts shot back. "We'll wait right here for you. I'm afraid cell reception is almost nil in here."

With a huff, David followed the assistant down the hall to a better site.

Katie said, "Sorry about that. Can we give you the narrow query?"

He beamed at her. "Absolutely. Let's get everyone over here so we'll all be on the same page."

Fifteen minutes later, David returned, slamming the wooden double doors. "Here, I've got an additional $50,000 to pay more of your team to work on this project."

"Outstanding," Roberts smiled, then frowned. "But there's a problem."

"What?" David asked, exasperated.

Roberts announced, "We don't have any more personnel trained to evaluate the hard drives. There is no one else to pay."

Katie and Johnson chose that moment to shake hands with the head and make their exit. They did not want to perform CPR on the dangerously reddening David.

They fist bumped down the hall, still hearing David's voice, two octaves higher than normal, as he unloaded his frustration.

* * *

Elsewhere, federal agents took the two electronic devices associated with one of the suspects from the SBI scientists. The devices had the most numerous and most disturbing images. Later that afternoon, agents reported to David and Katie there was a link between O'Shea and the suspect, Sterling Silver Branch.

Sterling was well known to Katie and her deputies. He'd been involved in crime since he turned fourteen—about the time his daddy left for Central Prison for taking out a patron's eye with part of a beer bottle in a bar fight. First Sterling stuck to the misdemeanors of shoplifting, disorderly conduct, and trespass. He graduated to armed robbery and unauthorized use of a motor vehicle. He was doing life in prison on the installment plan. But, for the last six months, no one had really run into him. Now, they knew why.

When they arrested Sterling for child pornography, officers found a sophisticated set of cameras, laptops, and cell phones to manufacture child pornography. For some "clients," he took special orders of what they wanted filmed: specific types of victims or favored sexual poses. His nieces and nephews primarily starred in the twisted tapes—too young to fully understand the hell they were in and too astute not to believe Uncle Sterling when he threatened to kill them and their families if they told on him.

"O'Shea—or someone using O'Shea's computer—ordered some special tapes from Sterling. We found the chat but not the payment made or received. We're still looking."

Glancing over at David, the examiner said, "It will take a little time to corroborate, but the connection between the two is pretty solid. But I also don't see any bad blood between them, something that would make Sterling snap and kill the judge."

"But Sterling's definitely capable of taking out the judge," Katie said. "He's five-foot-eleven, 220 pounds, and an angry man. I think he's halfway in the Aryan Brotherhood. I say halfway because no way would they put up with the child porn."

Johnson nodded. "He's strong enough to do it. But, what's the motive unless the judge didn't pay him?"

David interrupted. "Forget motive. Let's go talk to him. Get him to confess. Now."

The examiner said, "Don't you want to establish the existence of the payment or nonpayment to O'Shea?"

"No. I don't care about that right now. Let's go talk to him."

Katie said, "He's already hired an attorney. We'll have to call him first. I'm not sure he'll give us the go ahead. Let me give the attorney a call."

She hit a number on speed dial. "Hey, Tommy," she said, "This is Lt. O'Connor. Yeah, doing fine. You've got a guy, Sterling, who we want to talk to." She paused. "Me and the feds. Oh. Okay, I understand. Will do. See you soon."

"Well?" David demanded,

"He'll talk to Sterling tonight and will call me if he wants to talk. He's not sure Sterling has anything to say to us."

"Goddamnit. Give me that yokel's phone number. Let me talk to him. What's his name?"

"Tommy Watkins."

"Oh."

"Yeah. No grass growing on Tommy. You want his number?"

"Yes."

* * *

David, Johnson, and O'Connor met Tommy Watkins outside the Wake County jail.

Katie said, "Hey, Tommy, good to see you. Thanks for setting this up. This is Agent David. You remember Detective Johnson?"

Watkins shook hands with Katie and both men.

"Katie, how are you? Thanks for meeting over here. Sterling knows this is his best chance to get help on his charges. I just don't know how much help he can give."

Waiting for the deputies to search them and box up their firearms, Katie said, "We get it. Thanks for meeting us so late in the day."

David balked at turning over his firearm.

The deputy said, "Look, sir. This is protocol. All law enforcement leave their weapons at the door. It's a safety measure."

"Be very careful with that," David sad.

The deputy studied him. "It will be here in the same condition when you get back. Haven't seen one of these since the Korean war."

The group laughed, and David bristled. "Just take good care of it."

David slapped his second weapon, an automatic, down on the conveyor belt. "Fine. There better not be a scratch on either one."

The deputy switched his toothpick over to the left side of his mouth. "Yes, sir, no, sir, there won't be."

The three were escorted to a small conference room on the third floor by another deputy. The third floor was the same one where Sterling was being housed. Various inmates stood at cell doors. Some avoided their eyes, some catcalled at Katie, and others acted like they'd not seen them.

A few minutes later, Sterling was brought to the tiny conference room in leg irons and cuffs. Katie directed the deputy to unshackle him. David and Johnson squeezed into metal chairs at a small metal table. Watkins, Katie, and Sterling took the metal bench bolted to the wall. The room smelled of stale cigarettes, weed, and a citrusy disinfectant.

Watkins said, "Sterling, these are the officers I told you about. Do you have any questions for me before we start?"

"Naw. Let's get this over with."

David leaned in, arms on his knees, "How do you know Judge O'Shea?"

"Who?"

"Judge O'Shea. One of the guys you traded files with."

"I don't know no Judge Oh-she."

"Patrick O'Shea. You traded several child porn files with him."

"Oh. Yeah. I guess I did if that's what you found."

"Yes. We found several recordings sent to him by you."

"Look, I can't keep up with who I sent what."

"Did you ever meet him?"

"No. Why would I do that?"

"To talk about money or the child porn?"

"Are you crazy? Why'd I want to show my face to someone who could finger me? This was business. You pay, and I email you the pictures or the art videos."

Johnson broke in. "Art videos?"

"Yeah. You know, children seeking love in this dangerous world. Having loving adults to guide them," Sterling said, crossing his arms.

Johnson slammed the metal chair against the back wall. "You mother fucking pervert. These were *children* for God's sake. And you ruined their lives."

Katie stood up and motioned Johnson over. She whispered, "Look, I get it. You've been at this stuff all day—talking to the suspects. Do you want to wait for us outside?"

"I'm sorry. It's just…yeah, I guess I better wait for you outside." He pounded on the cell door until one of the deputies opened it.

"I'm going. They're staying."

"Got it, boss. C'mon out. Got some coffee downstairs if you could use some."

Katie nodded at him. The door clanged shut.

"Damn," Sterling said. "Johnson's got a temper. He bent his chair." He pointed to the mashed leg.

"Look," Katie said. "We're here to listen to what you have to say. Don't give us bullshit about art films. We've seen the images."

David glared at him. "O'Shea. How did you find O'Shea? Or did he find you?"

In painstaking detail, Sterling described the chat rooms he and O'Shea frequented and other internet connections they used. Several weeks went by before Sterling felt like he could trust O'Shea and check he wasn't a cop. He began transferring files one at a time for money on his PayPal account. He only remembered O'Shea by his moniker, "peeshea." O'Shea came through with the money on the first film, so Sterling sent him more—one at a time—when he ordered them. Purchases and receipts were titled innocuously on the computer, but Sterling provided David with the file names. He had a massive "library" of images and videos in addition to his more recent manufacture of child porn.

Sterling had sharpened his computer skills and learned how to hide his digital footprints from his more recent incarcerations. He'd been housed in a pod made up primarily of sex offenders his last time in. The sex offenders loved to talk about their "collections." Less interested in the images, Sterling learned about the business end which was lucrative.

Sterling had always been gifted with all things mechanical and electronic. The computer was no exception. In shop at Webb, he'd taken the teacher's car apart over lunch, re-constructing part of it perfectly on the ground of the next parking space. He'd taken every computer class in prison he could and checked out books and periodicals from the library.

"So," Sterling said, "The last time I heard from peeshea was about a month ago. He ordered a film and paid for it. Since then, nada."

David looked closer at him. "Where were you staying then?"

Sterling leaned back. "Probably in the basement. I work part-time during the day at Auto Zone to make my p.o. happy—then spend most of my time off downstairs. Look, I couldn't pick peeshea out of a lineup. I don't know the man."

Watkins interjected. "Sterling, is there anything your friends know about him or his death? I know you guys talk sometimes. Anything you've heard from anyone?"

Sterling thought a minute. "If I had something, I'd give it to you. I know I fucked up, and its gonna cost me a lot of time. But you say peeshea was a judge? Seems like there was something out there. I think Junior was telling me something, and I just didn't listen to him. He talks nonstop. Usually about nothing. Give me some money on my phone, and I can call him tomorrow. All the calls are recorded so you can get a copy."

"Your mama gave me a twenty to put on your canteen. I'll give it to the deputies for your phone. Call me later this week," Watkins said.

"Hell no. I need to buy me some food from the canteen. The mess they serve you here tastes like shit. And some deodorant. Get this FBI guy to put a twenty on my phone. He's the one wants the info," Sterling sneered.

David winced. "Yeah, okay fine. I'll leave a twenty for your phone. You better produce though."

Sterling banged on the door and shuffled back down the hall after the leg irons went on. The linoleum was filthy, and a stray candy wrapper blew up as he walked by.

* * *

True to his word, Sterling called Junior the next day. Agent David picked up a copy of the disc of the recorded call from the jail. After a leisurely discussion of the various physical attributes of Junior's girlfriends, Sterling worked his way to O'Shea.

"Junior, what you hear about a dead judge?"

"Just this n'that, man."

"Yeah, okay. Anything to it?"

"Don't know."

"You hear if anyone's good for it there?"

"Good for what?"

"The judge."

"Oh. The judge. Why you want to know?"

"I don't. Just thought you'd said something last week."

"Last week?"

"Yeah."

Agent David looked at the disc player and thought about hitting it against the wall. Was Junior hard of hearing, dumb as a brick, or both?

"Dunno. How long are you in for?"

"Oh. I don't know. Probably a few weeks. I think they're gonna revoke me."

"Do what?"

"Revoke my probation."

"Oh. That sucks."

"Yeah, it does. Not much I can do about that."

"Yeah."

"So, you heard nothing on who capped the judge?"

"Oh yeah. It weren't no shooting."

"No?"

"No. Some mother fucker strung him up on the ceiling."

"Damn. Really?"

"Yeah. What I heard was somebody had a grudge against the ol' guy. Someone he fucked with."

"Yeah?"

"Yeah."

"Who'd do that?

"I dunno. Heard it was a revenge killing."

"Damn. That's fucked up. What'd he do to the mother fucker to get hisself killed?"

"No idea. I heard he a kiddy fiddler. Maybe one of them kids lit him up."

"No shit."

An automated voice interrupted: "You have sixty seconds to complete your call."

"Thanks for hollering at me."

"Yeah man. Stay strong."

In the FBI meeting room at the federal courthouse, David threw his ear buds down in disgust. "That gets us fucking nowhere. Your man Sterling is a dumb ass."

"I'm not sure he's dumb," Katie said. "He's trying to tweeze the information out without alerting Junior to what he really wants."

"What information? It's all just gibberish."

"No. It's not. We need to concentrate on those who think O'Shea wronged them. That is a long list. We can rule out Sterling and his child pornographers because it looks like O'Shea paid for his porn."

"Yes. We need to look at Mrs. O'Shea, Jennifer..."

"You've got to be kidding. Those two can barely carry their groceries much less string up the judge."

"It could be two people working together."

"Maybe."

Katie sighed. "I've called in a mechanical engineer from NC State to look at the courtroom and rope recovered to give us an opinion on how many it would take, and the strength needed to get O'Shea up there."

David snorted. "Thought that was an Ag school, you know pigs, horses, cows, sheep."

"Partly. It has a lot of other respected programs, including engineering. Let's head up. Buck's going to get him through security and up to the courtroom since he'd been to lunch with Judge Foster and wanted to catch a ride back."

Buck and Dr. Brady Pennell were waiting in the courtroom. Katie made the introductions.

David handed the rope to Dr. Pennell while the deputy marshal turned on all the overhead lights. He also opened the closet behind navy floor to ceiling curtains and dragged out a tall ladder.

Buck gave him a hand setting it up below the brass chandelier where O'Shea had dangled. The ladder swayed on the plush dark carpet.

Dr. Pennell cleared his throat. In a warbly voice he asked, "Now. What were the judge's height and weight, and where is the rope?"

David brought forward the rope, and Buck recited the judge's height of five-foot-eight and weight of 176 pounds.

Pennell said, "Umm. Hmm." He played the rope through his fingers. He headed toward the ladder. Buck rushed over to steady the bottom part. He ascended toward the ceiling and the rope snaked back down over Buck's shoulder. Dr. Pennell leaned precariously forward almost pitching off the ladder while trying to tie the rope onto the chandelier.

"Hey Doc, need some help up there?" Buck asked.

"No, no. I'm fine," he muttered. The ladder swayed as he inched forward to the closest arm of the chandelier.

The deputy looked in horror at Buck, who shrugged.

After tying the rope into a noose, Dr. Pennell jotted something down in a small notebook. He untied the rope and descended without incident. He produced a portable scale from his many-pocketed coat and weighed the rope. Then he had Buck and the marshal measure the courtroom.

Wordlessly, Dr. Pennell handed the rope back to Agent David and continued writing.

"Well?" David asked.

Startled, Pennell looked up. "Well, what?"

"What's the calculation for whether one or more people could have gotten the judge up there?"

"I need to sit down with the figures. I will need a little time."

David shoved a chair from the counsel table over to Pennell. "Have at it."

Pennell shoved his glasses up onto the bridge of his nose. He looked at the chair, then at David.

"Some more light would be appreciated."

David turned and glared at the deputy marshal who scurried away to find a lamp.

Buck and Katie sat in the jury box talking quietly while David paced up and down until a lamp was produced.

From somewhere in his jacket, Pennell produced a small calculator, a set of glasses, and his notebook. He aligned them on the table in a perfect row and then began tapping his fingers.

"Jesus God, what now?" David exploded.

Cowed, Dr. Pennell said, "Where is the men's room?"

The deputy marshal hustled him out of the courtroom and down the hall before David could say anything else.

David muttered to himself, "Not a goddamn thing has gone right in this investigation. I'm never getting out of here. I'll be here till the day *cows* come home."

Katie said, "Give him a few minutes. Pennell is supposed to be some kind of genius in his field. I had to call in a favor to get him to come over."

David sneered. "Did you promise to plow up the back forty or what?"

Katie said quietly, "I had to promise to go square dancing with him."

"What?"

"Square dancing. The man likes square dancing and needs a partner this Friday. So, I said I'd go if he'd help us out."

Dr. Pennell returned with his coat soaked at the sleeves. The deputy marshal shrugged but helped him pull out the heavy chair.

Silence filled the courtroom. The only noise was the periodic murmuring between Katie and Buck. Buck's shirt was rumpled and stained from moving the ladder.

Finally, Dr. Pennell stood up. "Okay, I've got it."

"What?" everyone said.

"It's possible but not probable that one person could hang him up there. The person would have to be very tall and very fit. It is much more likely that two people were involved. One on the ladder and one to hand up O'Shea. There are some things I want to check out on my computer, but that is my initial analysis."

CHAPTER TWENTY-FOUR

Katie could not sleep. She worried over Dr. Pennell's theory on who could have strung up O'Shea. Finally, about 4:00 a.m., she gave up and slipped out of Buck's bed. Charles came over for a pat, his nails clicking on the hardwood floor.

"Go back to sleep, Charles. I'm going to head home." She scribbled a note to Buck in the kitchen then let herself out. The air was crisp and dew soaked the grass. She pulled on her sweatshirt.

She pointed her car toward her small house about a mile away and turned on the car lights after she'd cleared Main Street. When she got home, she texted Johnson. Five minutes later, he replied. He'd told her he'd not been sleeping well since he'd rounded up the child pornography suspects.

At about 6:00 a.m., Katie and Johnson were headed down to Raleigh and to the courthouse. She'd gotten permission from the courthouse security and the U.S. Marshal to enter with the keypad at the back door. The night patrol agreed to unlock the courtroom for her.

Johnson, driving, was unusually quiet.

"What are you thinking?"

He yawned. "I'm thinking I should have ignored your text."

She laughed. "Probably should have. But I can't quit thinking about the distance from the floor to the chandelier in the courtroom and dragging his body over and up, especially if he was already dead. Also, there weren't any latent prints or fibers on it when the SBI first examined it and the FBI followed up."

"Yeah. I don't get it either. I think your science man's right though. Gotta be two people involved. Mrs. O'Shea is the size of a doll and Jennifer isn't much bigger. Could they have done it together?" Johnson asked.

"I don't see how. Mrs. O'Shea wouldn't want to spoil her manicure and besides, she's the one with the most money. What's the motive?"

"Exactly. Jennifer had motive, but I can't see her killing anyone or coming close to O'Shea since she started spiraling into depression."

"Is she depressed because she killed him?"

"Could be."

They rode on in silence. The sun was just coming up over downtown when they pulled up to the back parking lot. Orange rays reflected back off of the taller buildings nearby.

Shielding her eyes, Katie punched in the code for entry to the courthouse and held the door open for Johnson.

He grumbled. "Where's the light switch? Fumbling along the wall, he flipped on the overheads. Their eerie artificial light was weak and illuminated only half of the long hall. The other half was bathed in darkness. They heard a low moaning sound. Then silence. Then more moaning. The hair stood up on the backs of their necks.

Katie and Johnson drew their weapons and moved forward. Black fabric hit them both in the face and they almost fired.

"Gosh durn nabbit!" Clem yelled gripping his black raincoat in front of him.

"Jesus Christ, Clem, you scared the shit out of us."

"No more'n you did me! What in tarnation are you two doing sneaking up on me?"

Katie re-holstered her gun. "We have to go back into the courtroom to look at the crime scene. We thought security would've told you."

"No one's told me anything since George —God rest his soul—Bush was president. He took off his rain hat and bowed his head for a minute.

"I'm sorry we scared you. We heard moaning. Are you okay?"

Affronted, he shouted, "Moaning? I was practicing my opera. See, I got these fancy ear buds in, and I'm singing along and in Eye-talian." He burst into song so off key that Johnson coughed to hide his instinctive wincing.

When Clem was finished, both Katie and Johnson clapped and thanked him for the performance.

"Great. We'll leave you to it. Thanks for the recital."

He smiled. "I'll take you guys the back way up to the courtroom. Hey, when are those FBI boys leaving? I got somebody wants to rent the office. I'd like to get rid of them soon. Nasty business that Agent David."

Katie said, "We're trying to find the judge's killer, but it's taking some time."

Clem spat in his white Styrofoam cup. The contents sloshed alarmingly as he punched in a button for the service elevator. "Yeah, sad about O'Shea. It's gonna be hard to figure out who hated him the most, from what I read in the paper."

"Speaking of which, did the chandelier get replaced after?" Katie asked.

"Naw. No need to. That old brass beauty held up to his flying weight."

He shuddered. "Now seeing him without his underpinning first thing in the morning almost set me off my breakfast."

"You found him?"

"Naw, but I was right on the heels of the poor fella that did. I was coming in to polish up the woodwork before court.

Them chandeliers were triple-bolted in after hurricanes Floyd and Fran blew through here in the nineties."

Clem unlocked the double doors and held one open for Katie.

"Need anything else?

"Yes. Can we get into the closet for the ladder?"

"It's unlocked. You young people have a nice day." He turned and burst into an aria at full volume.

"Damn. That'd give me an aneurysm if I had to hear much more of that," Johnson said.

Katie laughed. "Come on. Help me drag this ladder over. You steady it, and I'll climb up."

"I'd be chivalrous and offer to, but you know I hate heights."

"I know. I wouldn't want to have to call your wife when you fell off."

"Ha. I got it. Go ahead and climb."

Katie examined the chandelier and the ceiling. "Hand up your flashlight."

Johnson tossed up the flashlight, and she squinted at the ceiling inside the round glow of light.

"Damn. These look like double holes near the chandelier. I can't tell what they're for."

"Courthouse is pretty old. Maybe another light fixture was up there before the chandelier?"

She gripped the ladder with her left hand and got her phone out. Taking a deep breath, she let go and leaned on it with her knees.

"Okay. I'm coming down now."

"Got ya."

On the ground, she showed him the photographs. Two distinct holes were in the ceiling.

"I see what you mean. That's not holes for a fixture. Wonder what they're for?"

"I'm going to send these to Dr. Pennell to see what he makes of them."

They dragged the ladder back toward the closet. Katie said, "Let's look around the closet before we put this back and see if we can find whatever made those holes."

They searched for several minutes. Johnson said, "Don't see anything…"

"I don't either. C'mon. Let's put the ladder up and find David to show him the photos."

"Guess we'd better."

She threw a look at him.

* * *

An hour later, Katie looked at her phone. She clicked on an email from Dr. Pennell. He was inviting her to come over to his office at State during his lunch break to talk about the photos. She glanced at her watch and then replied that she, Johnson, and David would be over within the hour.

Katie interrupted David's diatribe about their lack of success in solving the crime and specifically about his disgust of Sterling's interview.

"Agent David, Dr. Pennell has something for us and wants us to meet him. I told him we'd be over by noon. He is giving up his lunch break to talk to us."

He rolled his eyes. "What's he got that he can't tell you on the phone? This is a waste of time."

She shrugged. "Maybe. But I doubt he'd want to waste his time if he didn't have something to say."

She texted David the address. "Johnson and I will see you over there."

A few minutes later, she and Johnson pulled up in front of a nondescript store front in a strip mall near NC State.

Johnson peered out of the windshield and said, "Ooooh, Katie, you know the way to my heart." He shrugged off his seatbelt and practically ran into the store. Stew's had been

Raleigh's hot dog spot for years and Johnson's spot for about as long.

Johnson ate his three all-the-way dogs like a Kodiak bear. Katie enjoyed her hamburger and fries and looked away so she wouldn't laugh. After demolishing two orders of fries, he ordered a milkshake for dessert.

"Don't tell my wife you brought me here. She'll put me on a diet of kale and fish if she finds out." He shuddered. "There ain't nothing worse than a few thin slices of baked fish. My stomach growls all night when she does that to me."

"You won't need to eat anything for two days after shoveling all that down your throat."

She gathered up the remains and threw them in the trash. "Let's go see Pennell."

The drive through campus was maddeningly slow. Everyone was out in his pickup truck or car just cruising on a nice sunny afternoon.

Dr. Pennell had been allotted a big office by university standards, but that was not very big. It held a bookcase, desk, floor lamp, and one guest chair. Four people in it at a time had some awkwardly standing in the door. Unfazed, he said, "Those pictures you sent, I think I have an idea on the holes." He picked up some metal pieces from his desk and then a rope similar to the one found with O'Shea.

"See, it's a pulley system. I bet the murderer installed it to help pull the body up and then removed it when he was done," Pennell said.

"How long does it take to install it and then take it down?" Agent David asked.

"Depends, but not hours. In fact, it could have been installed prior to the murder and I doubt anyone would have seen it," Pennell replied.

"What about cameras? Would they have picked it up?" Johnson asked.

"Only if the camera angle was right, but I doubt any camera there is aimed at the ceiling."

Katie held up the pulley system, "Could this have held O'Shea's dead weight?"

"It could," Pennell said. "Now, it'd have to be installed correctly, but if so, it could."

David interrupted, "Could one person lift him up using just the pulley?"

"Possibly, but, it'd have to be someone strong and sure-footed to get up the ladder with no help. Two people makes more sense."

Katie said, "Thank you for your time, Dr. Pennell. This has been very helpful."

His smile softened the lines of his face. "Don't forget Friday at five.

"I won't, and thanks again."

Johnson, David, and Katie walked outside. The under-graduate students were hurrying to class with backpacks and earbuds.

When they were in the car, Johnson asked, "What's happening Friday?"

Katie blushed. "That darn Buck told Dr. Pennell at the courthouse I could square dance. So, I'm square dancing Friday as payment for his help."

Johnson started laughing.

"You'd better put a sock in it, Johnson. Don't you tell a living soul."

"Scout's honor."

"You weren't a scout."

"You're right."

On the way back to Oxford, they turned over every possible suspect and suspect combination. Neither had a good feeling about anyone on their current list.

"I don't see these child porn people strong enough to do it or coming out of their holes long enough to kill him.

They'd be more likely to lure him to their dark basements," Johnson said.

"I agree. But what about Mrs. O'Shea?"

"She's determined enough, and the courthouse wouldn't scare her. But she'd pay someone to do it. Margaret and the IRS haven't found any payment that looks like a hit."

"No, they haven't. So, Jennifer?"

"Puh-leez. She was sunk into depression, and she's tiny. How would she have the strength to strangle him or string him up?"

"Big boyfriend?"

"No boyfriend at all, at least not that we've found."

"What about Wilkerson?"

"He's definitely big enough and wouldn't need a helper, but he could probably have found someone. Or those lawyers from New York."

They burst out laughing. Johnson said, "Them New York lawyers may act big, but they'd have to arrange a hit. They couldn't lift much more than a heavy briefcase."

"Okay. Let's concentrate on Wilkerson and get financials for the New York lawyers. I'll call Agent David for the financials if you'll look into Wilkerson."

"Done," Johnson said.

After spending several hours in their respective offices, Katie walked down the steps to Johnson's basement office. His door was open, but piles of files spilled into the hallway.

"You're the reason the cleaner quit," she said.

Johnson raised his eyes above his half glasses and said, "No, she wanted somewhere nicer to work. It had nothing to do with me screaming at her to not touch my files, ever."

"Too sensitive," Katie said. "What are you doing?"

"I am organizing my files."

"Alright. What did you get on Wilkerson?"

"I'm still looking, but I talked to law enforcement near where he lives. He has a reputation of being a real hot head.

Back in the day, he had assaults and bar fights. Not a lot of anything in the last ten years though. The guys kinda like him. He's brash and mouthy but keeps his neighborhood nice and quiet with a neighborhood watch he organized a few years ago. Plus, he employs ex-military at his place. I've checked his criminal record and it all matches up."

"Hmm. Well, I've talked to Agent David, and after a few minutes of hemming and hawing, he said he'd put the IRS on Wilkerson and the New York attorneys' financials. Subpoenas are going out tonight to their financial institutions."

"How long until we get the paperwork?"

"It could be tomorrow or a few days depending on the bank and its legal staff. Most are more than willing to work with the feds."

"I don't envy Margaret having to look at more paper and more numbers."

"She loves it. Any puzzle, any nugget she can extract, she's overjoyed. And the IRS loves her. David will send over copies of what they get. I'm going to head out in a few, are you?"

"Yeah. I hardly recognize my kids, I've not been home to dinner in so long. I've got one more file to reshuffle. Then I'm gone," Johnson said.

"Hope you're not having hot dogs tonight."

"Damn, that'd be good." He groaned. "No, it's Brussels sprouts grilled with a hint of cheese, but only a hint, and baked fish. Maybe some corn on the cob. Glad I got some real food earlier today."

"See you tomorrow. Hug the kids for me."

Chapter Twenty-Five

She looked into his eyes. They shone with a love so pure she had to close hers. His body was pressed against her again. She gently held his shoulders and pushed back a little.

She said, for the millionth time, "You don't have to do this you know."

"I know."

"If we leave today, we can't come back."

"I know, but I don't need or want anyone but you. You make me so happy. Happier than I've ever been. Together, we're our own family."

She sighed. "Family. Mine's going to be angry and hurt."

He hugged her closer and whispered in her ear. "I know, baby, but you have to do what's right first. They love you. They'll understand. I hope mine will too."

"I just wish I'd been able to sit down with them. Explain."

"You know that wouldn't work."

She sighed. "I know it wouldn't. It's just…I'm gonna miss my folks."

"I get it, baby. I do. I'll try to make up for all of them. I'll try to be everything you'll need."

She kissed him. "You already are."

Reluctantly, he let her go. "I'll meet you?"

"I'll be there."
"No regrets?"
"No regrets."

* * *

Jeb met Katie and Buck at the Oak Room for lunch. It was open only on Fridays for lunch and featured one lunch cocktail billed as "exotic." Today's feature prominently displayed on an oversized board was "Mimosa Limposa," a green concoction. It was drawn in green chalk and looked suspiciously like a grasshopper. Jeb had to hold onto the board to squeeze by.

"Glad you two could take off for lunch. What's the special?"

Buck scanned the small page printout, and said, "Fried catfish and clam chowder."

"Red or white?"

"White."

Jeb shuddered. "Don't like the cream kind of chowder. Think I'll do the catfish. How 'bout y'all?"

"The Cobb salad for me," Katie said.

Buck looked at her for a minute. "Catfish. You know that's a risk on that salad. The last you one got, the lettuce was partly brown and the salad dressing was off."

Katie thought a minute. "Yeah, catfish it is."

After they'd ordered, Katie told them her deputies-—the ones she could spare—were still scanning images from O'Shea's computer for any clue or connection to the judge.

"That sucks. Guy was a pervert, and you have to spend all this time looking for his killer," Jeb said.

She shrugged. "I know. We've put a lot of work into this investigation. I'm about out of overtime pay for the officers. We're going to have to pull back on it soon."

"You can't have done any more than you're doing. You and the FBI have been at it night and day," Buck said.

Their lunches arrived on big plates overhung with crispy golden catfish. The slaw was fresh and the fries had some old

Bay on them. The first slice emitted a smell of white fish and steam. They made plans to meet at Johnson's for Memorial Day. Johnson always had a big spread and everyone brought a side dish or dessert. Mrs. Johnson did not condone hard spirits, so anything more than lemonade or light beer was left in the back of everyone's pickup for some surreptitious sipping. The kids ran around through a sprinkler or jumped on the trampoline or air castle Johnson rented. The adults gathered together under the shade of large poplars and maples.

"Where is Johnson today?" Jeb asked.

Katie picked up the last golden bite of catfish. "I told him to take the day off. He's been working a lot and into most nights. Plus, he hates these kiddie porn cases. It really gets to him—he's not afraid to say it."

"I bet. That's some mixed up shit. There was a girl where I was at in Wilmington who'd been a victim of one of those predators. Totally destroyed her. I thought she was brave just to get out of bed every day. The only thing she had going for her was her family, especially her brother. He came to visit all of the time. After a few weeks, she managed to sit in group without crying."

"That's terrible, what happened to her. To have family support is huge. She was lucky to have the brother there a lot."

"Yeah, I get that. Some of those victims didn't do so good. Most of them came in after suicide attempts. That and heavy drug use to forget what happened to them. I didn't know what to say to them. I felt so bad. I finally figured out they just wanted to be treated like everyone else, like a person."

"At least you saw a few good things happen there. Wasn't sure you liked anything," Buck said.

"I made some good friends, and the support group didn't suck. I just hated the staff."

Jeb dug into his catfish and slaw. "I missed this when I was picking fruit out-of-state. You can't beat it."

"Who were you closest to, or can you say?" Katie asked.

"Oh yeah. You know one of them, Angela, Loretta's sister. And a couple of guys I still run into."

"That's right, Angela."

"And the brother I talked about, he and Angela and me got close."

"Who's that?

"Phillip. He was going to law school or trying to get in while I was down there."

Buck's hand paused halfway to his mouth but he put it back down. "Your friend, Phillip, is a lawyer?"

Jeb smiled. "Yeah, not all lawyers are bad."

Katie laughed and patted Buck. "You're right. Some are pretty decent if you give them a chance."

"Anyway," Jeb continued. "I saw Angela and Phillip out the other night—when I was in Raleigh. I never thought they'd last—but they have. I think they'll even get married one day."

Buck looked at Katie. "That's law clerk, Phillip, I think."

Everyone chewed in silence for a minute. Then Jeb wiped his mouth. "Thanks y'all. I've gotta get over to Mom's. She wants the irrigation system fixed and asked me to come over before her bridge group. Here's my part of the lunch." He got out his wallet.

Buck waved him away. "No, I've got it. Go on to Mom's. I'll see you later."

When he'd gone, Buck looked at Katie, still seated beside him, and said, "Angela and Phillip?"

Katie was slowly shaking her head. "Angela and Phillip. But why? What possible motive?"

"I can't begin to guess. But it's no secret Angela hated O'Shea, and she loves Phillip."

"What does that even mean?"

"No idea. It's just—well strange—I don't remember anyone at the courthouse acknowledging them as a couple or talking about them. No pictures of her were in his office, I don't remember seeing any."

"Maybe they're very private."

"I guess."

Katie's cell phone rang. "Sorry, I have to get this." She said, "Yes. Okay. Yes. Umm hmm. You're sure? Thanks." She turned a serious face to Buck.

"That was Margaret. She and the IRS have tracked money from O'Shea's bank accounts and retirement accounts to off-shore accounts. They have found something that leads them to think O'Shea was being blackmailed— a deposit into an offshore account every two weeks. The amount was $20,000 each time. The account now has been open for about a year. They called in the FBI earlier this week, and one of their agents sent out bank subpoenas in the hope that some banks will answer it and produce the documents. They found an account name and number: 7445547.

"Do they know whose account that is? Is a person or a corporation?"

"They haven't said, but Buck—7445547 on the dial pad spells 'Phillip.' Plus, didn't he work for O'Shea slightly more than a year?"

"Jesus. Okay. What're you going to do?"

"I'm going to pick up Johnson and head to Raleigh to interview Phillip. Poor Johnson—but he needs to be in on this, especially if Angela is involved in anything. He's a friend of their family."

"I hope I'll see you tonight."

"Me too."

They quickly kissed, giving Reverend and Mrs. Clemmons at the corner booth something to talk about over their plates of catfish.

* * *

Buck ran into Jeb at home, changing into his old jeans and picking up his gardening gloves.

"Mom wants to see you, you know."

"Yeah, I know. I'll get over there this weekend, I promise."

"Okay. Hey, I texted Angela to see how she was because I was thinking about her, and she said she's moving."

"Oh. Where's she going?"

"She was in a rush, but I could hear sounds in the back. You know, like the speaker when you're at the airport."

"Is she going somewhere with Loretta?"

"No. She said she and Phillip are headed out. She'll let me know where she ends up or email me or something. Anyway, see you later—probably after six tonight."

Buck sat on the settee for a minute. Charles put his head on his knee nudging his hand to pat his head. "Hey Charles." Buck said. Charles whined a little until Buck concentrated on his silky ears.

"Katie," Buck said on his cell. "Phillip and Angela are at the Raleigh-Durham airport. Jeb just touched base with Angela on his own. No he doesn't know where they're headed. No idea which terminal. Want me to head to one while you all head to the other? Okay, call me back."

Buck walked out the front to his car in the driveway. Charles slid out before he got the front door closed.

"No Charles, you can't go this time. Charles! Charles! Oh, for the love of God, get in."

Charles hopped in the front passenger seat as Buck scrambled in and attached his and then Charles's seatbelt.

After fifty minutes of flat out flying down I-85 and then I-40, Buck swung into the multi- road ramp to the airport. He wedged himself between a Prius and a hotel shuttle trying to get to the short-term parking. A few minutes later, he pulled into a space and called Katie.

"I'm here at Terminal 2, the one with Delta and American. What can I do?"

"I'm in 2 with Agent David and most of the Cary field agents. Can you look for Judge Evans near the entrance? I called her about Angela. I feel bad but there was no easy way to ask questions over the phone. Call me if you see her."

"I will. Charles and I plan on finding a quiet spot."

Buck scanned the increasing crowds on the sidewalks in front of the terminal. He walked up and down in front of the busy drop off and pick up areas. The security guard flagged him down. "Whatcha doin' man?"

"I'm looking for a lady I'm supposed to meet. She should be here any minute."

"Huh. Well stand still, or better yet, sit still. You keep pacing up and down, that worries me. If I get worried, I'm gonna call in other folks to keep you company—you get it?"

Buck spread his hands out in front of him, still holding onto Charles's leash. Charles smiled his doggy smile. "I get it, I get it."

Judge Evans ran up to him. Breathlessly, she asked, "Have you seen Angela?" There were tears in her eyes. Charles whimpered.

"No, but Katie—Lt. O'Connor-—wanted me to meet you and stay with you until she can get away."

"Do you know why? No one would tell me." Pulling an envelope from her bag, she waved it at him and added, "This is from Angela. She asked me to open it but not until tonight."

"Let me call Katie and maybe she can tell you something." He guided Loretta over to a seat by the terminal entrance.

When she answered her cell, Buck said, "Katie, I've got the judge. She has a note from Angela. Uh huh. We'll sit here outside the entrance where the escalators are."

To Judge Evans, he said, "She's on her way."

"Loretta!"

Both turned to see Agent Thompson sprinting over and weaving between three lanes of cars. Most honked and some screeched on brakes to avoid hitting him.

"Sean. I tried you before I left. Do you know what's going on?"

Before he could respond, Katie and Agent David walked up. Katie tried to pull her to one side to update her, but David was having none of that. "Where's your sister, Judge Evans? We need to see her now!" David barked, six inches from her face.

Loretta looked from Katie to David totally confused. She handed over the note to Katie. "Angela left this for me on the mantle. She told me to open it after five o'clock. By happenstance, I just went by my townhouse at lunchtime. I'd forgotten to take in my dry cleaning."

David snatched it out of Katie's hands. "Gimme that." Thompson read it over his shoulders. Katie took Loretta back over to the bench to update her on their new information. Loretta began crying. "I don't understand what you're telling me. You think Angela killed O'Shea and is leaving the country with Phillip?"

Katie nodded. "It's just a theory. But we need to find them, if they're here."

"Oh my God. I can't believe this is happening.'

Katie allowed Thompson to take her place on the bench.

"We'll find them and sort this out. Don't worry."

"Thompson, now that you're here, let's go back in and keep looking," David said.

"With due respect sir, I am going to stay with the judge. I don't want to have her here by herself. I'll bring her in to the coffee shop in case you need her," Thompson said,

She looked gratefully at Sean. To David she said, "I'd really appreciate that. This has been a shock."

Buck, seeing the senior agent start to scream at Thompson, offered, "Hey, I'm glad to visit with Judge Evans while y'all do what you need to do. Okay with you, judge?"

She smiled at him. "That's great, thank you."

She turned to David without a smile and said, "You find my sister, you bring her to me. Don't question her. Her attorney is on his way."

David snarled, "Fine. Hope we find her."

After they all left, Loretta collapsed back on the bench. "Buck I am so worried about Angela."

He put his arm gently around her. "I know you are, but you need to be strong for her. Who'd you call to come out?"

She smiled weakly. "Tommy Watkins. He should be here in a few. The retainer is in my purse."

"That was quick thinking there."

"I wasn't always a judge. I used to scrap along with the best of them, including you."

Buck laughed. "That makes me doubly glad you're on the bench now."

Two minutes later, Tommy Watkins pulled up with a screech of tires in his Mercury Marquis. He ignored the security guard yelling at him to move it.

"Judge Evans, have they found her?"

"Not yet." She handed him an envelope, telling him it was his retainer for Angela and that she'd directed Agent David not to talk to her sister.

She pulled out a dollar bill from her wallet and handed it to Buck. "You're both hired."

Buck said to Watkins, "Agent David has the note Angela left."

Watkins asked Loretta, "Did you read the note?"

She smiled. "You know I did. And I made a copy for you. It's in your retainer envelope."

With relief, Tommy slumped back against the concrete post next to the bench. "Okay, here's what happens. If they find her, she says nothing. If they don't, well," he shrugged, "again nothing."

"We better head up to the coffee shop. They expect us up there," Buck said.

Charles shook himself so his tags clinked together and gave a great big yawn. Buck urged him forward with words like "water" and "ice cream."

The group walked in silence, lost in their own thoughts. The coffee shop was outside of the TSA preflight check-in. They sat in the corner so Charles would be out of the way. The waiter gestured to Buck once the drinks were ready.

"Tommy," Buck said, "I think my brother, Angela, and Phillip became friends some years back at the Wilmington rehab center. It may be that Angela and Phillip became more than friends."

Before he could respond, David rushed in with Katie and Thompson close behind him. He thrust a picture at Judge Evans, "Is this her?"

She took the photo from David and scrutinized it. "I don't know. She has some of the same features, but—"

David exploded. "For God's sakes woman!"

Judge Evans drew herself up. "I am a federal judge, and I will have your respect. I have answered you truthfully. That's all I can do."

David turned on his heel. Katie threw a look of apology back before following him.

The speakers continued to announce departures and arrivals. The boards continued to change with updates on flights domestic and international. They replenished their drinks several times. Charles lay at their feet snoring after the promised ice cream was devoured. Buck put money in the tip jar. And they waited.

Agent David hurried in holding onto a young Black woman who looked terrified. Three field agents trailed behind him trying to keep up. He shook the woman's arm at Judge Evans. "I've got her! I've got Angela. Now, what do you say?!"

Tears streaming down her face, the lady wailed, "I've told you a hundred times, I'm not Angela. My name is Brittany Walker and I'm headed home to Boston for the summer. I go to UNC during the year." This last ended in a sob.

Judge Evans looked horrified. "Agent David, let this woman go. This is not Angela. I know my own sister."

Reluctantly, David released his death grip on her arm. Judge Evans put her arm around Brittany and helped her get back over to TSA. After a murmured conversation with TSA, Brittany was rushed through the security checkpoint and to her plane.

A few minutes later, Katie came in and ordered a plain coffee. "We've found nothing on our end. Must have been a false tip. The bureau contacted TSA but no one matching their descriptions came through. We've scoured both terminals." She sat down and blew on her cup. "We're getting ready to call off the hunt. The FBI and TSA have run searches on both Angela's and Phillip's names and various combinations, but no luck. They have been reviewing tape, but no luck there either. But, they have entered a BOLO for the two at most of the travel destinations."

"A BOLO? You mean a be on the lookout for?" Loretta asked.

Katie looked down. "Yeah. I'm sorry. They just are convinced it was Angela and Phillip that killed O'Shea."

Loretta shook her head. "I won't believe it unless Angela stands here and tells me she did it."

"We're out of it now. The feds are fully staffed and committed to seeing it through. They've asked us to stand down. So, once I turn over any notes or interviews that are left, we're done. But I want you to call me if you need me. Any time."

Loretta smiled her thanks.

A few minutes later, Thompson, without David, dragged up a chair beside Loretta. He took her hand in his. "We didn't find her."

"I heard. Can I go now?" Loretta asked.

"No reason to hang around. Let me drive you home."

Katie looked over at Thompson and then Buck. "I'll follow you in your car, Judge, if Buck can give me a ride back. Johnson took the cruiser on back to Oxford a few minutes ago."

Tommy Watkins stood up. "I'll see y'all later."

To Loretta, he said, "Let me know if you need me."

"I will. Katie, here are the keys. My BMW is in section A ground floor. And thank you."

"Let's roll. C'mon Buck. Bet Charles is ready to go home too."

* * *

Loretta wiped her eyes with a crumpled Kleenex she'd found in her straw purse. She dreaded telling her parents Angela might be gone for good. They would be heartbroken. She called her aunt and uncle and asked them to meet her at her parents tonight. They'd comfort her folks when she went back to Raleigh.

Loretta had never done anything like this in her entire life. She'd always been a good girl, a rule follower. But two hours ago, she'd intentionally given Agent David only page one of Angela's letter. She knew this was wrong and felt like a liar. She'd given both pages to Tommy Watkins. That second page—it read almost like a confession to murder. She just couldn't hand her baby sister over to the FBI like that.

She looked over at Agent Thompson, at Sean. Sean was so worried about her and about Angela. This was going to come between them even if he didn't know about it. She couldn't believe she'd done it. She felt so guilty.

* * *

Several days later, from an unknown source, Loretta and Jeb each received a beautiful photograph of azure blue Caribbean waters. Infrequently, similar photos were posted and sent to either Loretta or Jeb, and sometimes to both. Dutifully, each time she received something, Loretta carried her phone into the FBI bureau in Cary and turned it over to forensics. Dutifully, the Bureau unsuccessfully searched for the source.

About a year after Angela and Phillip disappeared, one photo was posted with an identifiable building in the sunny photo. It was a photograph of a children's hospital sitting on a street in Havana, the capital of Cuba. An island paradise without a treaty of extradition to the United States.

Acknowledgments

Without the faith and generosity of my mother and father, and the love and support of my husband, children, and family, this book would not exist.

I am indebted to those who provided unwavering encouragement and helpful critiques during the writing process at the Queen's University of Charlotte MFA Creative Writing program. I am especially grateful to faculty members and novelists Naeem Murr, Fred Leebron, and David Payne, who continue to encourage me.

Thank you to my enthusiastic readers for reading the manuscript and providing excellent feedback: Teresa Blemings, Carole Griffin, Anne Lakusta, and Ellen Thompson.

Thank you to the extraordinary and dedicated team members at Authors Unite who worked tirelessly to make my publishing dream come true.

Thank you to Martin Clark, gifted author and supportive friend. To Lucy Jane, my tiny gray tabby rescue cat adopted during COVID and who slept on top of my drafts, thanks for providing the entertainment.

Thank you to the weekly writing group led by talented author David Payne: Kay Goldstein, Holly Hough, Allegra Jordan, Leslie Ketner, and Ame Sanders. I appreciate your thoughtful comments.

To friends and former colleagues who continue to believe in me (most *said* they'll buy a book): Larry Antill, Erin Blondel, Frank Bradsher, Felice Corpening, Margaret Davis, Dave Day, Julia Day, Robbie Dodson, Caroline Folger, Ed Gray, Eve Harris, Mack Harris, Amy Haddad, Jane Jackson, Tanisha Jeter, Courtney LeBlanc, Melissa Lemmond, Jenny Lewis, Katie Lyon, Kathy Maeglin, Michelle McAdams, Sita Payne-Romero, Jake Pugh, Thomas Manning, Joan Rashid, Susan Rector, Laura Russell, Sharon Still, Boyd Sturges, Cindy Lou Sturges, David Warren, Hope Williamson, Johnny Williamson, Lori Williford, Rob Williford and Sharon Wilson.

To the outstanding professors in the English Department at Wake Forest University: Dr. William Moss, Dr. Doyle Fosso, and Dr. Ed Wilson, and to those at the Wake Forest School of Law: Mr. David Logan (later Dean at Roger Williams School of Law), Mr. George Walker, Mr. Jimmy Sizemore, and Mr. Wilson Parker. I thank you all for a wonderful education.

To the exemplary judges for whom I was privileged to work, I give thanks: The Hon. A. Thomas Small, U.S. Bankruptcy Judge, Eastern District of North Carolina (retired) and the Hon. Eugene H. Phillips, N.C. Court of Appeals (deceased). To the North Carolina state court judges in Forsyth County, North Carolina, who took time to explain the legal process to me and with whom I volunteered: the Hon. William Z. Wood, N.C. Superior Court (deceased) and the Hon. Abner Alexander, N.C. District Court (deceased).